# Family Matters

# Family Matters

## Anthony Rolls

### With an Introduction by Martin Edwards

Poisoned Pen Press

Originally published in 1933 by Geoffrey Bles
Published by Poisoned Pen Press in association with the
British Library

First Edition 2017
First US Trade Paperback Edition

10 9 8 7 6 5 4 3 2 1

Library of Congress Catalog Card Number: 2016954041

ISBN: 9781464207426    Trade Paperback
     9781464207433    Ebook

Poisoned Pen Press
4014 N. Goldwater Blvd., #201
Scottsdale, AZ 85251
www.poisonedpenpress.com
info@poisonedpenpress.com

Printed in the United States of America

# Contents

To
O. G. S. Crawford

# Introduction

*Family Matters* is a long-forgotten novel of domestic crime that richly deserves republication. Witty and original, it was very well received on its original appearance in 1933. Reviewing the book in the *Sunday Times*, Dorothy L. Sayers—as stringent a critic as you might wish to find—heaped praise on it: "The characters are quite extraordinarily living, and the atmosphere of the horrid household creeps over one like a miasma."

As Sayers said, the story "concerns the efforts of various members and friends of the Kewdingham family to get rid by poison of one of the most futile and exasperating men who ever, by his character and habits, asked to be murdered. Oddly enough, the poisons they select counteract one another, and this leads to a most original and grimly farcical situation, and an ironic surprise-ending, pregnant with poetical injustice."

The intended victim is Robert Kewdingham. In his late forties, Robert has been out of work since losing his job in the Slump. Increasingly, he dwells in a world of make-believe, and his behaviour becomes a source of deep frustration to his young and lovely wife Bertha. She is admired by a doctor and by a novelist, both of whom would prefer Robert to be out of the way. But the plot soon begins to thicken. Sayers commented that she had no idea whether the medical details about poisoning that play such an pivotal role in the narrative were technically correct (and nor do I, come to that), but although she was normally a stickler for accuracy, she concluded: "I am quite ready to accept anything that is told me by so convincing an author". Praise indeed.

Colwyn Edward Vulliamy (1886–1971) was a man of many accomplishments. A Welshman, he was born in Radnorshire (now part of Powys) and educated privately before studying art under the guidance of the Irish painter Stanhope Forbes, founder of the Newlyn Art School. During the First World War, he served in the King's Shropshire Light Infantry and the Royal Welch Fusiliers, and when peace came, he set about establishing himself as a writer. The Fabian Society had published his *Charles Kingsley and Christian Socialism* in 1914, and later books reflecting his wide interests include *Voltaire, The Archaeology of Middlesex and London, English Letter Writers* and a book about the Crimean campaign of 1854–6.

He turned to crime fiction in 1932, with *The Vicar's Experiments*, published under the pseudonym Anthony Rolls, and known in the United States as *Clerical Error*. He was no doubt inspired by the success of *Malice Aforethought*, an ironic study of the psychology of a middle-class murderer by Francis Iles (a pen-name of Anthony Berkeley Cox, who also wrote as Anthony Berkeley.) *The Vicar's Experiments* was highlighted by Julian Symons, in his pioneering study of the genre, *Bloody Murder,* as one of the most notable books written under Iles' influence. As Symons said, it concerns: "a clergyman who suddenly begins to suffer from homicidal delusions…a good deal of what follows is very amusing, although the story falters sadly once suspicion of the clergy-man has been aroused".

Vulliamy's fondness for satire is evident in much of his work, including his crime fiction. *The Vicar's Experiments* was well received, and he was encouraged to continue in the same vein. *Lobelia Grove*, *Family Matters*, and *Scarweather* appeared under the Rolls name in quick succession; each book displayed Vulliamy's inventive turn of mind, as well as his wit. Yet after producing four crime novels in three years, he abandoned the genre until the fifties.

*Don Among the Dead Men* (1952) was the first of six crime novels which Vulliamy published under his own name. The storyline resembled that of *The Vicar's Experiments*, but this time the deranged killer was an Oxford academic. The sto-ryline was developed for the cinema by Robert Hamer, who no doubt hoped to repeat his triumph with *Kind Hearts and Coronets*. After Hamer died, Don Chaffey took over, and the film was released in 1964 as *A Jolly Bad Fellow*. This black comedy, also known as *They All Died Laughing*, boasted a superb cast including Leo McKern, Leonard Rossiter, Dennis Price, and Miles Malleson, and a soundtrack written by the young John Barry, but the whole did not quite add up to the sum of its impressive parts. Vulliamy's later work received less attention, but it remained interesting and unorthodox. His last book, *Floral Tribute* (1963), was rather ahead of its time, and is possibly the first crime novel to address in some depth the subject of dementia.

Vulliamy was a more ambitious novelist than most writ-ers who display comparable versatility. His satire was sharp, but he also made serious points about human behaviour and the nature of society. As Symons noted, he found it easier to come up with intriguing and unusual narrative premises than to sustain and resolve a complicated plot over the full length of a novel, and this is why the renown of his books never quite matched that of Francis Iles's work. But such is the flair and wit of his crime fiction that it does not deserve the neglect into which it has fallen. It is a pleasure to welcome this fascinating writer back into print.

Martin Edwards
www.martinedwardsbooks.com

# Chapter I

## 1

If you fly over the town of Shufflecester at an altitude of ten thousand feet you see the town below you like a dirty grey splash on the variegated patterns of brown, purple and green which mark the level landscape of the great Shuffleshire plateau. Through the middle of the town run the gentle sinuosities of the River Shuff like a white ribbon. Seen from a lower altitude Shufflecester has a most fantastic and irregular appearance, reminding you of a lot of grey and yellow bricks thrown at random upon a carpet by some heedless child. The builders of the town seem to have been sobered or restrained by the wide levels of the country; their houses are flat, uniform, depressed, with hardly a tall building among them. Only the towers of the cathedral suggest a vertical idea, and even these are square and heavy. Outside the town are purple masses of timber, green or dun streaks of arable land, flowing towards the misty line of the Wyveldon Hills, above the sea.

Even this aeroplane view gives the impression of a placid, agricultural place, resisting innovation, unmoved by the hustling spirit of the age. On the outskirts of the town, it is true, smudges of amber smoke hang above the brickyards;

but these brickyards are few and isolated, nor do they indicate a prosperous industry. As for the breweries of Malworth,
they hardly come within the Shufflecester scene.

It may be said, without much fear of denial, that Shufflecester is one of the most English of English towns. If
the archaeologist is not mistaken, it was a fortified place in
Roman times—the Tasciodunum of the Antonine Itinerary.
Its fine alms-house is one of the oldest in the kingdom. All
the inconvenience, though not the charm of antiquity, is pre-
served in its narrow streets, where even the moderate crowd
of a market-day wanders perilously in the main thoroughfare
because there is no room on the pavement. There is no plan
or regularity. The market has an open space, and there is a
little green square near the cathedral which is called (heaven
knows why) the Queen's Bower. No single street runs for
any distance without reaching a curve or corner. Even the
main road, which comes level and straight over the plateau,
a Roman military way, has to bend and wriggle in a series
of bewildering contortions before it gets out of the town.

The same absence of intelligent planning gives a perverse and unhappy appearance to those parts of the town
which are termed "residential". Blocks, curves and angles of
grey and yellow brick, with roofs of lilac slate, produce an
effect of morose, impregnable respectability. Here you have
streets no longer; you have roads, avenues and crescents.
The more pretentious houses arrogantly stand in twos, or
even singly, with handsome gardens; the humbler dwellings
cling together, distinguishable only by numbers. It may be
doubted whether you can see in any other town so many
perfect, unaltered examples of 1860 design, or so many
areas which faithfully preserve the high Victorian standard.

We are particularly concerned in this drama with a house
in one of the less fashionable quarters—Number Six, Wellington Avenue. It is like all the other houses in the Avenue,

small, with a slate roof, a grim bit of grass between the front and the pavement, and a scrubby garden at the back. In this house lived Mr. Robert Arthur Kewdingham, his wife, his young son, and his venerable father.

## 2

Poor Mr. Kewdingham had not been lucky. He came of a good middle-class family, of the sort which is capable of producing anything from a bishop to a broker—his father had been estate agent to the Duke of Tiddleswade. Mr. Kewdingham was (or had been) an engineer, employed by the great firm of Hayle, Trevors and Ockersley. He had served in the firm for twenty-one years without reaching a very high position. Yet he was competent in his way, and was considered reliable. The firm came down heavily in the post-war slump, and in 1925 two hundred members of the engineering staff were reluctantly dismissed. Mr. Kewding-ham was among the two hundred. He was then forty-five years of age, a man who believed himself to be afflicted by a series of subtle though deadly disorders, which caused him to administer to himself a series of subtle though deadly drugs.

Mr. Kewdingham was tall and solid. His face had an expression of baffled, vague tenacity, such as you may often see on the face of the Nordic man who feels that he ought to have done better—feels, rather, that he would have done very well if it had not been for the unaccountable hostility of circumstances. It is like the face of a bulldog who wants to bite something, but has nothing to bite. He could be extremely amiable, he could be extremely rude. When people asked him what he intended to do (in view of his obvious poverty), he said that something would be sure to turn up. But he had not, so far, gone to the length of looking for a job.

And yet it must not be supposed that Mr. Kewdingham was idle. To begin with, he was a famous collector. "I am a born collector," he said with a touch of pride.

He did not limit himself, as a man of narrow vision might have done, to any particular class of objects. Other collections might be more valuable, but few were so comprehensive. Since his father had occupied the spare rooms, this collection overflowed in the most undesirable and unlikely places. Great cabinets thrust out their angles from the corners of the drawing-room. On the tops of these cabinets wobbled immense, precarious piles of cardboard boxes. More boxes, tins, trays and paper parcels were standing on each side of the fire-place and on various parts of the floor. Inside these receptacles there was an astounding medley of junk: bits of coral, broken pots, beetles and butterflies impaled on pieces of cork or stuck on cards, odd fossils, bones, brasses, dried flowers, birds' eggs, little figures in soapstone and ivory, ushabtis from the tombs of Egypt, fragments of uncertain things, weird scraps of metal, badges, buttons, mouldy coins and innumerable varieties of suchlike trash. But everything was arranged with meticulous care, and indeed with a certain dexterity. Even the most unrecognisable rusty bit of iron was mounted on a card, with the date and place of discovery—"Field H. Probably Roman." Mr. Kewdingham also had a vast library of occult books and magazines, which he was constantly reading.

In a huge cupboard in the bathroom there was a collection of a less harmless kind—Mr. Kewdingham's medical department. On the shelves of this cupboard were hundreds of bottles, lotions, washes, drugs, tabloids, mixtures, glasses, tubes, bulbs of india-rubber, jars, tins, brushes; and again bottles, bottles, whole companies of bottles—plain or fluted, big and little, green, blue, white, amber, flat, round, polyhedral, full, empty; with creams, liquids, powders, crystals, juices, distillations and goodness knows what.

In these collections there was enough to keep Mr. Kewdingham busy, or at least to occupy his leisure. He prided himself, not unjustly, upon his knowledge as a collector and upon his wide experience of medicine. But there were other things which took up a good deal of his time.

Like many engineers, Mr. Kewdingham was a mystic. He knew the occult meaning of the Pyramids, he had a private revelation of things long concealed, through a long series of transmigrations he was aware of life—his own life, presumably—in the lovely regions of Atlantis.

Then again, he was political. He was a local leader in that interesting though reviled organisation, the Rule Britannia League. He believed in the divine mission of arms, the rights of the conqueror, dominion of the azure main. To him, pacifism was a poor wishy-washy stuff, the shirking of ordained responsibility. After all, he had been concerned in the production of guns and high explosives, he had taken his part in the shaping of those monsters which fought (we are told) for the noble ideals of civilisation. His views, if archaic, were perfectly sincere.

Unemployed as he was, in the vulgar sense, Mr. Kewdingham had a lot to think about: science, politics, mysticism. Perhaps it was for this reason that he thought so little about his wife and his family.

## 3

Mrs. Bertha Kewdingham was a plump though very handsome woman with reddish hair and large languorous eyes. She was the daughter of a village schoolmaster. Her father, Josiah Stiles, the son of a Wesleyan minister in Quebec, had come to England when a young man in the eighteen-sixties and set up a school for farmers' children at Pen Dillyn in North Wales. Here, in middle life, he fell in love with, and married, a young French governess, employed to teach the daughters of Sir Walter Wilkins of Dillyn Castle.

Stiles was a gentle, dim creature. He was intensely serious, loved Ruskin and had a complete set of the Waverley Novels. His young wife, a gay, alert and very intelligent woman, helped him to make the school a success. But she was unpopular in the village, not so much on account of her smartness and vivacity but because she was a foreigner. They had two daughters, Rachel, the elder by seven years, and then Bertha. In 1912 Stiles's wife died, and he, sorrowfully giving up the school, bought a little house in the village and settled down to end his days in peace.

Bertha and Rachel had shared their mother's unpopularity. They had learnt French in their childhood, and they had the misfortune of speaking with a definite foreign accent. There was no place for them in the society of Pen Dillyn. They were too good for the farmers' families and not good enough for the gentlefolk. Of the two girls, Bertha was the more attractive. The neighbours thought her absurdly proud; and while the women were jealous of her beauty, the men were afraid of her wit, for she had cruelly snubbed not a few of them.

Richard Kewdingham, Robert's uncle, had bought a small property at Pen Dillyn. In the spring of 1914 Robert Kewdingham came to spend a fortnight's holiday with his uncle. On the day after his arrival, as he was tramping over the moors with a gun, he met Bertha Stiles. He met her again, and yet again, and before he left Pen Dillyn he announced his engagement.

The Kewdingham family did not welcome the news. The daughter of a Wesleyan schoolmaster was not good enough for Robert Arthur Kewdingham—or for any Kewdingham, if it came to that. But Uncle Richard, who knew and liked old Stiles, and who had often talked to his daughters, observed in his bluff way that his nephew might have done a damned sight worse for himself. Bertha, said Uncle Richard, was a devilish fine girl; and what was more, she had brains and knew how to use 'em.

Old Stiles died in the winter of 1915, and Rachel went to live with her father's people in Quebec.

The situation of Mrs. Kewdingham in Shufflecester was not by any means a pleasant one. After losing his job, her husband had chosen Shufflecester for his residence, because it was a stronghold of the family: there had been Kewdinghams in Shufflecester for nearly forty years.

To Kewdingham, therefore, Shufflecester was a thoroughly congenial place. In times of trouble he could shelter himself in the family as in a warm and comfortable recess, an impregnable refuge. He could shelter in tranquil obscurity, avoiding unpleasant encounters or unfair criticism. Whatever the world might say, the family knew his worth. The family patted him on the back, telling him that he was a brave, good man. If he was unlucky in some ways, if he found it extremely hard to live on his reduced income, that was due to no fault of his own; it was all in the wonderful and merciful design of Providence. But Providence only plagues the Kewdinghams—that chosen family—in a playful sort of way, and it would be all right in the end.

So in moments of perplexity Mr. Kewdingham gladly turned for reassurance to his aunt and cousin, Mrs. and Miss Poundle-Quainton. To them he brought his doubts and grievances, and those doubts and grievances were quickly dissolved in the warm flow of their affection, quickly dispelled by the gentle murmur of their friendly voices.

Perhaps he was not quite so sure of his other aunt, Mrs. Pyke, a sturdy old widow; or of his venerable uncle, Richard Kewdingham, who had now been established in the town for several years. But of course he was strongly supported in his own house by his even more venerable father.

Robert Henry Kewdingham, the ancient father, was neat, springy and vigorous for his age, which was about eighty-one at the time of our story. His lean, clean-shaven face was raw, cruel and rather stupid, the face of a man who had always been a bully. And yet there was something unguarded and credulous about it: you could baffle the bully easily enough, if you knew the trick. He had two rooms on the top floor of his son's house. He did not thrust himself upon the others. If it was fine he pottered about in the tiny garden; and if it was cold or wet he sat upstairs reading the innumerable volumes of Victorian magazines which he had brought with him. When he retired from the employment of the Duke of Tiddleswade in 1907 he had a respectable income, but as he was misled by an imaginary knowledge of the stock market his capital was quickly frittered away. For some years he had lived in comfort upon his wife's money; and then his wife had died, revengefully leaving the greater part of her fortune to her young daughter, Phoebe Kewdingham. The ancient father had still the meagre residue of an income, and he made a reasonable contribution towards his maintenance, as, indeed, was only proper.

Phoebe Kewdingham, who was unmarried, lived in London, where she had a spacious flat in Dodsley Park Avenue.

The family was also represented in London by a young man of whom we shall see a good deal presently—John Harrigall, the son of old Kewdingham's sister, and so the cousin of Robert Arthur.

It will be time enough to speak of these interesting people when they make their first appearance on our scene. Let us only observe here that Mr. Harrigall, a literary young man, was a welcome visitor at Mr. Kewdingham's house. Mr. Kewdingham and his wife both liked him, though for very different reasons. John was one of the few people who really did seem to appreciate the collection, and he was also one of the few people who went out of their way to be agreeable to poor Mrs. Kewdingham.

Shufflecester is only seventy miles from London, and London visitors can easily run over for the day.

Michael, the only child of Robert Arthur, had been sent away to school at Barford. Michael was a problem.

And thus the situation of Bertha Kewdingham was in every way unfortunate. Robert Arthur had not been a success. He was now in middle age, without a profession, impecunious, full of absurd notions, a wretched hypochondriac, irritable, silly and resourceless. So, at least, he appeared to his wife. There were horrible quarrels and reproaches, futile arguments, incessant bickering. Poor Bertha, with her French impetuosity, her intolerance, her snappy wit, did not know how to manage this dreadful man, this lamentable situation. There was not enough money, there were no hopes of inheritance—though it was understood that Uncle Richard intended to help them in the education of Michael. Everything was wrong, everything was going from bad to worse.

Bertha knew well how much the family disliked her; she knew they considered her partly responsible for Robert Arthur's collapse. A woman who understood her job as a wife, a woman who could sympathise and make allowances, they said, would soon have got him on his feet again: never mind how—she would have done it. But of course Bertha was a failure. She was of no use at all. Instead of gently raising the prostrate Robert Arthur, instead of guarding his dignity and warming his diminished hopes, she had added to his vexations—poor fellow!—by wickedly indulging a spiteful and rebellious temper.

The family as a whole disapproved of Bertha. Mrs. Pyke detested her; the Poundle-Quaintons were grudgingly tolerant; the venerable Kewdingham was openly hostile; only Uncle Richard was really amiable, and she seldom saw him. She had no relations in England. She was half foreign—and she looked it. People thought her rude, farouche and melancholy, and so she had few friends.

Nor did Kewdingham encourage visitors. The family was enough. His collection, his Britannia League, kept him busy. The shortage of money, the difficulty of providing for Michael's future, did not seem to worry him at all. Providence would never desert the Kewdinghams. They had only to wait, and something would be sure to turn up—it always did. As for his wife—well! He would say, sighing noisily, women are funny creatures, they never understand the problems of life.

It needed no subtle observer to perceive at Number Six Wellington Avenue a state of affairs bordering upon tragedy. No one cared for the Robert Kewdinghams. No one cares for a failure; and then Robert was such an odd man, such a peculiarly irritating bore, with his innumerable disorders, his mysticism, his red-hot politics. And few people can tolerate the angry jangling of husband and wife or the tart allusions to family matters which are so provocative.

Apart from the members of the family in Shufflecester the only visitors at Number Six were Dr. Wilson Bagge, a frequent caller; John Harrigall, who occasionally ran over from London to see the family; and Mr. and Mrs. Chaddlewick, two kindly people who lived at Sykeham-le-Barrow, about five miles outside the town.

<h1 style="text-align:center">4</h1>

The Kewdingham drama may be said to have begun with a conversation which took place on a September afternoon in 19—. It was market-day. The Chaddlewicks had come to the town in order that Mr. Chaddlewick might see the famous Tiddleswade bull, and they had looked in at Wellington

Avenue on the way home. Mr. Kewdingham was feeling unwell, and when he was unwell he had a distressing way of talking about occult experience. He felt that such experience was a ready channel for sympathy. Now he was talking of his Atlantis visions, a very dangerous theme.

Mrs. Pamela Chaddlewick flipped her fat little hand up and down, expressing her astonishment. Her soft, luminous face was gently animated, but even gentle animation meant a good deal in a face usually as blank as the painted wooden mask in a milliner's window. Mrs. Chaddlewick was a pretty, fluffy woman, very expensively dressed.

"But how marvellous!" she piped. "I'm rather like that myself, you know. Rather an odd little person. Doctor Mackworth said he'd never met anyone so curious as me, didn't he, George? Only, of course, I've never—"

Mr. Kewdingham had a monocle, and he now adroitly screwed it over his left eye, at the same time puckering up in deep creases the whole of his long yellow countenance. He stared at the amiable vacancy of Mrs. Chaddlewick with a flicker of unmistakable admiration.

"It is a very strange thing, very strange indeed." Mr. Kewdingham spoke in a slow, melancholy voice. "To feel in touch with these Atlantis people who lived so many thousands of years ago—"

"Thousands of years ago!" repeated the shrill piccolo of Mrs. Chaddlewick.

Mrs. Kewdingham jerked up her shoulders nervously. She was talking to Mr. Chaddlewick about gardens, but the fatal sound of Atlantis caught her attention at once.

"Oh, Lord!" she said, with muffled exasperation, "Bobby's off again. He's got Atlantis on the brain at present."

"Eh?" replied Mr. Chaddlewick politely. "Atlantis? Very exciting, but rather beyond me, I'm afraid." And he paused to listen.

"I have been having these experiences for a very considerable time," said Robert Arthur in his most impressive manner, though still mournfully. "At first I was rather disturbed. Now I may say, in a sense, that I am getting used to it. Psychic people tell me it is quite remarkable."

"It must mean something," said Mrs. Chaddlewick.

"Is it a dream? I don't clearly understand the nature of this experience." Mr. Chaddlewick spoke with an exaggerated seriousness, as though he was talking to a child.

Mrs. Kewdingham bit her lip and sharply tapped her toe on the hearthrug. There are few things more dreadful than a husband who will persist in making a fool of himself in public. She looked out of the window at a grey line of cloud above the housetops.

"Do you think it will rain?" she said to Mr. Chaddlewick.

Robert Arthur sighed heavily, tilting his face sideways and fixing his eye on a corner of the ceiling. These people are really interested, he thought, and of course Bertha has made up her mind to spoil everything, as she always does. He could not help thinking how different life would have been with a lovely sympathetic lady like Mrs. Chaddlewick.

"In a way, it is a kind of dream. I am aware of my own identity as a—a high priest or something of that sort. I feel that I have mysterious knowledge and power."

"How lahvly!" cried Mrs. Chaddlewick. "Do go on. I'm simply mad to hear the rest of it."

Bertha looked at the other woman darkly—a quick level glance full of new suspicion. Damn her! she thought; is she trying to humiliate me? or is she flirting with Bobby? or is she merely an astounding idiot?

"I am always in the same place, standing in the temple. There's an enormous crowd. In front of me are a lot of girls in white dresses, and I can see a white bull with a garland of blue flowers on his neck. There are a great many pillars and that sort of thing. Tall men with golden axes on the end of silver poles—"

He paused, as though endeavouring to recall some detail.

"How simply exquisite!" Mrs. Chaddlewick twittered. "It's like a play. Go on! Oh, do go on! It's too fearfully thrilling for words."

"Then I seem to raise my hand and I make a sort of speech. I proclaim my title as the High Priest of Atlantis, Keeper of Wisdom. All the people fall on their faces in front of me—all except the men with the axes. Then I say, ' Bring me the Belt of Stars!' An old man comes along on his knees, and he says, 'Oh, my Lord! Must I indeed bring thee the Belt of Stars?' And I say, 'Verily; for it is my will, the will of Athu-na-Shulah.'"

"That is very curious," said Mr. Chaddlewick, with a shadow of a smile on his good-humoured face. "And what language are you speaking?"

"The Atlantis language, of course," Mr. Kewdingham replied. "No living person knows it, and that is what makes my dream so remarkable. I have the knowledge of this tongue in my astral brain, you see. I cannot remember it when I am using my mental brain, my physical brain, as I am now." He saw the shadowy smile on Mr. Chaddlewick's face, and he looked rather hurt.

"The High Priest of Atlantis—"

Mrs. Kewdingham groaned. Her husband stared at her for a moment with a flash of nasty malice. Only a flash, however, and he turned back to Mrs. Chaddlewick with a delightful sense of being understood—and perhaps admired.

"You see," he said, "I can remember my name, and that is the most amazing part of it all. Athu-na-Shulah."

"Oh, do write it down for me!" cooed Mrs. Chaddlewick. "I should like to have it in my address-book. The High Priest of Atlantis!" She beamed in her soapy, enveloping way at

Bertha. "Don't you think it's too gorgeous, Mrs. Kewding-ham?—don't you think it ought to be written down?"

"I am not thinking about it at all," said Bertha rudely. "I am looking at those lovely amber beads of yours."

"Oh, they don't suit me one little tiny bit! I only wear them because an astrologer told me I ought to wear yellow things. Professor Motoyoshi—a Japanese. Have you heard of him? My dear, he's marvellous. Told me all about George—didn't he, George? He seemed to know George even better than I do; told me a lot of things that would never have come into *my* head, I can assure you."

"Be quiet, Pam!" said Mr. Chaddlewick, but he said it in a playful manner.

"And he told me all about sex and marriage—yes, really, everything. It was just too wonderful. And I asked him, What does it mean when you have a funny feeling in both ears? Because I often have it, you know. And he said it was the influence of a star that is only *just* visible to the naked eye. I forget the name of it, but I wrote it down in my address-book. I have to write everything down; there are such a lot of things in my head. And then he looked at my hand, and said he'd never seen such a happy little hand in all his life. Wasn't that sweet of him? So he gave me the dearest little horoscope on blue-and-pink paper. He did it in a few minutes. He's a most frightfully intriguing person. Of course, he doesn't advertise. You have to get an introduction, and then he sees you as a sort of favour."

"Does he do it for nothing?" said Mr. Kewdingham, rather peevishly. He wanted to come back to Atlantis.

"Practically nothing. Only five guineas."

Mr. Kewdingham started again:

"There's a connection between the Atlantis mystery and the inch-year-circle system of the Pyramid builders—"

"I don't quite see what you mean," said Mr. Chaddlewick.

"Nor does anyone else," said Mrs. Kewdingham, with a wry, irritating smile. "It's all nonsense."

Feeling trouble in the air, Mrs. Chaddlewick was pleasurably excited. She opened her tantalising vermilion mouth:

"Oh!" she said, "the Pyramid—"

Bertha lost control of herself. A sudden hatred of Mrs. Chaddlewick flamed up within her. The woman had got all she wanted—lovely clothes, money, an amiable husband; why need she come along making fun of Robert Arthur, or making love to him? Anyone could see, now, that Robert Arthur was fascinated by Mrs. Chaddlewick. Bertha had woes and grievances enough, accumulating until their pressure was almost intolerable, and now she was to be humiliated by a little fluffy puppet. It was a sense of this cruel humiliation, rather than a sense of jealousy, which caused her to flash out:

"Can't we talk sensibly for a change?"

Again her husband glanced at her venomously. A black sparkle of anger came into his eyes. His monocle fell, rattling faintly over the buttons of his waistcoat. Deprived of that piece of glass, his face looked suddenly naked and evil. Mr. Chaddlewick was evidently pained; he coughed a little, and shuffled his feet on the carpet.

"You've no need to be so abominably rude," said Mr. Kewdingham in a hard, exasperating tone, "even if you don't understand what we are talking about. I'm sorry my wife sees fit to be so outrageous, Mrs. Chaddlewick. She is probably out of sorts—"

"Out of sorts!" Bertha rose from her chair, trembling. "Out of patience, if you like. That's nearer the truth, anyway."

"Oh, I *am* so sorry, my dear Mrs. Kewdingham," piped Mrs. Chaddlewick. "It's all my fault, I'm sure. It was the Pyramid, you know—"

Realising her awful mistake, poor Bertha subsided weakly.

"No, no," she said. "The fault is mine; it always is. I am sorry if you think me rude. I apologise."

"It's the least you can do," said Mr. Kewdingham acidly. "You might have the decency to let us choose our own conversation. If we are interested—as we all appear to be, except you—"

Bertha remained standing by her chair, but she said nothing. Once more she gave Mrs. Chaddlewick a searching, level glance, full in the eyes.

Mrs. Chaddlewick flushed. "Oh, *please*!" she said, on a tremulous, fluty note, almost the note of appeal.

"Quite right, quite right!" observed Mr. Chaddlewick without much relevance. "Nothing at all. Slight misunderstanding. Absolutely, of course." And he smiled amiably, for he hated a scene.

"Well—" Mr. Kewdingham began; but here the situation was mercifully changed by the arrival of his father.

The old man knew the visitors. He shook hands with them pleasantly enough.

"We've been hearing all about Mr. Kewdingham's wonderful dream," said Mrs. Chaddlewick in a patronising coo. (Old men are such ghastly bores, my dear!—but you have to be polite. And she was not going to let Bertha have her way, not if she knew it.)

"Ah, yeh!" replied the ancient fellow, rapidly moving his chops and clicking his firm white teeth. Secretly he thought it was all nonsense, but his opposition to Bertha prevented him from saying so. "Tell me not in mournful numbers— And how are you, Mrs. Chaddlewick?"

"Now that daddy has come," said Bertha, "I'll go and see about tea. Will you have it with us, daddy?"

Old Kewdingham looked at his daughter-in-law with a grim, unaccountable flicker of dislike. He felt the tension in the room, he knew that something was wrong, and he guessed the cause. For a moment there was a curious resemblance between his expression and that of Robert Arthur. But it was only momentary. "Thank you, my dear; I think I'll go upstairs again," he said in the sweetest of senile voices.

Mrs. Chaddlewick rose.

"We simply must be going, I'm afraid," she said. "I have just remembered that I want to get some mackerel in the town. I adore mackerel. And then George has promised to see the rector at five o'clock—such a nuisance! Thank you most awfully, but we shall have to wrench ourselves away. Your Atlantis dream is quite the most wonderful thing I've ever heard, Mr. Kewdingham. I should like you to tell me more about it; I'm simply crazy to know how it goes on. It makes me feel all shivery down my back—like I feel when the Archdeacon is preaching, you know. Do let us hear the rest of it. If you could spare the time…And I know George would like you to see his dahlias."

Mrs. Chaddlewick's intention was perfectly clear to Bertha. The terms of the invitation might have made it clear to the others, but men are slow to perceive such things. Mr. Chaddlewick smiled in his most amiable way. "Yes," he said, "we've got a fine show this year."

Robert Arthur looked positively cheerful. "Thank you very much. I should be delighted." He replaced the monocle in his eye as he beamed at Mrs. Chaddlewick. "Your interest in my—my Atlantis experience is very gratifying—very. Some people think I just make it up."

"Oh, but you couldn't possibly, could you?" cried the lady. "I'm frightfully like that myself—spooky, I mean. So I really *do* understand. And I'm tremendously interested." Her placidly sensual eyes were turned full upon the face of Mr. Kewdingham.

"She takes these things very seriously," said Mr. Chaddlewick, moving towards the door.

"So do I," said Robert Arthur, gently releasing the soft hand of Pamela Chaddlewick, and thinking that she must have married George for his money.

He walked down to the gate with them, while the old man shuffled upstairs again, and Bertha stood alone in the drawing-room.

Bertha stood alone in the drawing-room, wondering how long it would be before she reached the limit of her capacity for endurance.

## 5

After Mr. and Mrs. Kewdingham had finished their tea—in silence—there was another visitor. The maid was out, so Mrs. Kewdingham opened the door to Dr. Wilson Bagge.

The doctor was a trim, slick little man with a ruddy face, a brushy auburn moustache, and rather wild, roving blue eyes. But the wildness was all in the eyes, perceptible only to the observant. In manner he was tight, punctilious and extremely careful. He spoke with a studied modulation, picking his words in a delicate though snappy fashion, like a smart little bird picking up grains on the tin floor of a cage. Indeed, he was not unlike a well-behaved little bird, a twinkling fellow, always fresh and always dainty, hopping away unruffled through the garden of life. So he seemed at first; but when you saw the quick dancing flash in his eyes, the sudden electric flicker of something wild and incalculable, something active though controlled, you wondered if he was altogether trustworthy.

The sullen, humiliated face of Mrs. Kewdingham sparkled up warmly as soon as she saw the doctor on the doorstep. He was a family friend, the constant, though not too expensive, attendant of Robert Arthur. In fact, a number of his visits were purely social.

"Ah, doctor! How nice of you to look in. Come along upstairs."

She was looking pale and rather nervous, but it suited her. A momentary flash came into the blue eyes of the doctor, a little snippet of blue fire like a spark out of a flint, but he spoke with deliberate formality.

"I was calling at Number Eight, and so I thought I would just pop in for a minute. How's your husband?"

"Oh, he's—"

But Robert Arthur, recognising the chirrupy voice, had come out on the landing.

"Hullo, Bagge! You're the very man I wanted to see. I've got something for you to look at, my boy!"

The doctor put his hat and coat in the hall and ascended the stairs with Mrs. Kewdingham. When they entered the drawing-room Robert Arthur was fumbling among his tottering boxes. He was glad of this timely relief, and he smiled in his most engaging manner. Doctor Bagge astutely noted the smile, he noted the strange excitement of Robert Arthur, and he knew there had been a row.

"Now look here, Bagge." Robert Arthur produced a little glass-topped box with a beetle inside it. "What about this one? It's the rare type mentioned by Sylvester. I got it on the churchyard wall at Easton-under-Frogg the other day."

Bertha moodily took up a basket full of socks and began to busy herself with the interminable task of darning.

The cabinets rattled, the boxes flopped, the tins clattered, the wretched collection began to disgorge its dilapidated treasures.

From time to time the doctor glanced at Mrs. Kewdingham. Her head was bent over her work, but he could see that she was angry and sorrowful. Then the door-bell tinkled faintly. Robert Arthur looked at his watch.

"That will be Smith," he said. "You know Smith? The Secretary of our League. He wants to see me about some business. Don't go. I shall have a word with him in the dining-room. I'll come back in a minute." And he ran down the stairs.

The doctor felt embarrassed. He pushed some corks and cards on the table, took up a swallow-tailed butterfly and stared at it with a critical frown. As he did so he knew that Bertha raised her head, looked at him for a moment and then bent over her work again. The door below had opened and shut, and they could hear Kewdingham talking to another man in the hall. The doctor wanted to speak. He wanted to show that he was sympathetic, friendly; that he understood the situation. Bertha was a quick, intelligent woman; no fool. Like other unhappy people, she had a reputation for sarcasm. The only words that came into the doctor's mind were "damned nonsense", and they were hardly appropriate. So he said in a hollow, dry and purely conversational tone:

"Is Michael quite well?"

"Oh, yes, thank you," said Bertha, knowing that he was not interested in her answer. "What do you really think of all that rubbish?" She jerked her head towards one of the cabinets.

The doctor shut himself up in a shell of impenetrable decorum.

"Come, come! You mustn't call it rubbish," he said. "Why, there's remarkable industry in all this, and a very considerable degree of skill in arrangement."

Bertha frowned; then she plunged her hand roughly into her work-basket, drawing out of it a tattered grey sock which she appeared to study with close attention. And then she looked up with an abrupt, uncanny smile.

"You need not be a humbug," she said. "Not with me."

Again there was a sound of voices in the hall, the front door was opened and shut, and Robert Arthur could be heard coming up the stairs.

"Very well," said the doctor quietly, and he nodded his head in a perky, bird-like way. He understood.

"Ah!" said Robert Arthur, coming back into the room, "we shall be very busy in the League before long. This election, and one thing and another…Are you in sympathy with our work?"

"Well," replied the doctor, with an almost demure quality of reticence in his voice, "I can only speak as an outsider."

"But you mustn't be an outsider!" Kewdingham was obviously excited. "Only just now I was saying to Smith how extremely useful you would be in the League—a man of your influence, and all that sort of thing. He agreed with me. Why—do you know? Shufflecester is full of Bolsheviks. We have a secret list of them, and I can assure you that you would be astonished if you saw it."

"That is very probable," said Bertha grimly.

Robert Arthur ignored the interruption. "My dear fellow, I wish you could see your way to joining the League."

The doctor became even more impenetrable, more discreet. "Well, Kewdingham, I could hardly give you a promise. Of course I am entirely in favour of those who seek to maintain order by legitimate and rational means; but I can hardly believe that we are threatened by anything very sudden or very violent."

"Rational means—yes, I agree. But you don't know as much as we do, if you'll allow me to say so. When the band was playing 'God save the King' in the Town Hall the other night, Cliffe saw a fellow standing with his hat on. So he got behind the fellow quietly and knocked the hat off his head. It then appeared that he was a chemist. Well—I mean to say—"

"No, Kewdingham; I still don't believe that anything dreadful is going to happen. We are a slow-going, easy people, we are constitutional, we are homely; and our police are remarkably efficient."

"True. But when these agitators try to persuade people that wages might be higher, and that war is wrong, and nonsense of that sort—what are we to do? After all, if they let the cat out of the bag, we can't sit down under it."

And again the great Kewdingham collection opened its dismal jaws, disgorging its innumerable and indescribable bits and pieces, its meaningless odds and ends. For a while the doctor endured it with prim patience, cocking his little head to one side in the gravest manner. Then he had to go. And before he went he smiled in a particularly subtle way at Mrs. Kewdingham. Poor lady! he thought, poor lady!—I know what's the trouble, and I really am most terribly sorry for her. Perhaps I may be able to help in some way—who knows?

# 6

Mrs. Kewdingham invariably retired to bed long before her husband came upstairs. While he was reading, or fiddling about with his collection, she just got up and walked out of the room, and as soon as she was in bed she pretended to be asleep. It was a recognised convention, a dreary convention, by means of which they avoided the necessity for saying "good night" to each other…

On the night which followed the scene with the Chaddlewicks, Bertha was in her room soon after ten o'clock. Something on Robert Arthur's dressing-table drew her attention. It was a photograph of herself, taken at the time of her engagement. The photograph was in a silver frame, and the glass had cracked across from one corner to the other.

"That's unlucky," she said.

Then she slipped off her dress and saw herself, white in the tall mirror.

"It's unlucky," she repeated. "My God!—it's terribly unlucky."

# Chapter II

## 1

Doctor Wilson Bagge plays a very strange part in the Kewdingham drama, and we must know something more about him before we proceed.

The doctor was a widower. His wife, an exasperating invalid, had died rather suddenly—indeed, suddenly enough to cause a certain amount of whispered suspicion. And yet he had been a most patient, attentive and apparently devoted husband. An old aunt, who left him £15,000, had also died suddenly, after he had been called in by her regular doctor.

When his wife died he was badly upset, and went away to Italy for six weeks. After his return, the postman delivered quite a number of letters addressed to the doctor in a sprawling feminine hand, and with *Firenze* on the post-mark. When he received these letters the little man was curiously disturbed. On one occasion, after getting a letter with a Firenze post-mark, he had rushed up to London in his car.

Now you are to observe that Doctor Wilson Bagge was extremely correct. So trim, meticulous and polite, he was almost inhuman. He had a miniature pomposity, but he quickly checked any sign of disrespect by a sudden glare of his electric blue eyes—for one alarming moment all the primness faded and he looked positively dangerous. But he was never angry. No fierce or bitter word ever came out of that small, pursy mouth. No one could charge him with indiscretion.

And yet, in spite of the curious rumours about his wife, and in spite of his odd little ways, he was popular. It is true that he had no intimate friends, but then he had no professed enemies. He was very gentle and very kind. He was never hard on people, and he did a lot of good, careful work for nothing. Whenever he was able to do so, he read the morning lessons in the Church of St. Egwulf.

To women he was unquestionably attractive; perhaps because they were piqued or puzzled by the little blue demon who flickered up so quickly, even when the doctor was saying the most ordinary things. There were no scandals about Dr. Wilson Bagge; at any rate, no definite scandals—and that is as much as you can expect in a country town, where even vicars have to be careful. The two elderly women who kept house for him had nothing to say, except that he was a kind and a generous master.

His few amusements were extremely simple. If he had an hour to spare, he would go off to Pluck's Gutter for a little fishing, or he would go for a walk on Dewlash Downs. Always by himself. He did not seem to avoid people, but he was a solitary man, with all the sleek independence of a cat. He was not considered unmanly, and he occasionally drank a glass of sherry (never more than one) at the Conservative Club. After all, he was busy. He had a very fair practice; and a more than fair share, according to the other doctors, of the profitable old women. In the sick-room he was at his best, never flippant, never depressing, never foolishly confident.

Among the peculiarities of the doctor was the singular, old-fashioned practice of running a small dispensary. He did this, so he said, in order that poor people could get what they needed without having to pay the wickedly exorbitant rates charged by the chemist, and in many cases without paying anything at all. He also said that he liked to have a free hand with his medicines—whatever he meant by that. And he often declared that nothing was more grateful to him than a quiet hour in his dispensary, nothing so truly sedative as the complicated smell of his drugs, the subtle prevalence of medical odours. Looking round him at the lucid whiteness of his bowls and basins, the sparkle of his chromium taps, the beautifully trim order of his jars and bottles, he would say to some privileged visitor: "Ah, my boy! No man is fit to be called a doctor unless he really is a medicine-man. Those bottles are full of mystery and experience—magic, power, death or healing—but more of mystery than anything else. We ought not to pretend to know so much, when we really know so little. The secret of all practice is experiment. Yes, my boy! Healing is an art, it's intuitive, experimental, perhaps inspired!" Then he would suddenly whisk round again, shutting himself up in his impenetrable shell of mere politeness.

A man with an extensive knowledge of criminal types (such men are unfortunately rare) might have suspected that Doctor Bagge had the makings of a poisoner.

So often the poisoner is the last man who would be suspected by the ordinary person. His exquisite respectability and his almost invariable refinement throw dust in the eyes even of those who are not incapable of observation. He is kind, he is plausible. You are told of his deeds of unobtrusive generosity. His outlines, moral and physical, are as clean as if he was cut out of a piece of stiff cardboard. Precise, dainty, there is a kind of mechanical restraint about him.

What has become of his emotions? Are they smothered? Are they subdued by heavy doses of moral atropine? He has got to express himself in some way, and how will he do it?

You feel there is something unnatural and ominous in this even composure.

Wilson Bagge was a good physician. He loved what he truly described as his art. New theories, new discoveries excited him. He read eagerly the latest monographs, he took the medical journals, and he often visited the laboratories of his old hospital in London. Sir James Macwithian, the eminent gynaecologist, used to enjoy a talk with Doctor Wilson Bagge, and greatly admired his acuteness in portraying the action of glucosides in the body. And it may be doubted if Doctor Bagge was ever happier than when he stood in a white coat by the side of Sir James Macwithian's microscope.

For some years Bagge had been studying the medical uses of aluminium. He considered, rightly, that we ought to increase our knowledge, whether in medicine or in toxicology, of the pharmacological action of this very interesting metal. People had been poisoned, it was alleged, by the mere use of aluminium vessels in the kitchen, and yet hardly anything was known of these cases. They were hushed up. There was a disappointing lack of postmortem opportunities. But here was a grisly problem which really ought to be investigated. And that was not all. The value of aluminium in practical therapy was only beginning to dawn upon the medical imagination. Professor Kolhaus, in his remarkable experiments with colloidal hydroxide of alum, was leading the way; but that was only a start.

Bagge, as we have seen, loved his dispensary. It might be said that his dispensary was a hobby, a recreation. It was more than this, however; for mere dispensing is no fun without experiment. And you have no idea what delightful experiments may be carried out with various preparations of alum.

The doctor had a small but well-chosen laboratory equipment, so he was able to test all manner of ingenious theories.

His methods were purely scientific. First of all there was the phase of cogitation, the mental phase. Then came the mixing and measuring in the dispensary. After that, of course, the launch of a new discovery into the living body of a patient. Once, it is true, he had been a little too venturesome: an elderly woman had died. But then she would have died soon in any case—and her death was remarkably instructive.

At the time of our story, Wilson Bagge was contemplating a grand experiment. He had succeeded in producing an alum compound, and he was now anxious to watch the effect of this compound on the human organism. There might be a certain danger; if he increased the proportion of chlorate there would be a very definite danger. He would have to make a careful choice. And he did not hesitate: he chose Robert Arthur Kewdingham.

## 2

Mrs. Bella Poundle-Quainton and her spinster daughter Ethel lived in a large Victorian house on the edge of the town. The old lady was genial in character and ample in proportion, living cheerfully and charitably in the simplified world of the aged. If she had a weakness it was an undiscerning belief in the honour, virtue and ability of those who were related to her by ties of blood. Ethel was very tall and angular; she exposed a good deal of her cartilaginous bosom, but she was a woman of stern morality, devoted to her mother and perpetually occupied in works of unobtrusive kindness. On the day after the Chaddlewick episode, Kewdingham was having tea with these excellent women.

"Yes," Aunt Bella said, "we are not sorry the Pardishes have gone. They were not very nice people, I'm afraid."

"They hung up their washing," Ethel explained, "on a high line right above our wall."

"Such colours!" Aunt Bella continued. "It was like a—what is it they call them?—like a flag day. So we had to write a very serious letter, telling them it was quite impossible for us to ask a gentleman to have tea in our garden. The new people are very pleasant, I believe. Mr. and Mrs. Fadshaw and their grown-up daughter. Mr. Fadshaw is interested in fossil fishes, or something like that: he is a gentleman, of course."

"And how is Bertha?" said Ethel, with a vague, fugitive smile.

Robert Arthur looked exceedingly grave. His mouth opened, emitting a sound between a groan and a sigh.

"I have been rather worried about her lately," he said. "Ever since they laid the new drains by the cathedral she has been decidedly off colour. So irritable, you know. Only yesterday she was frightfully rude to—to the Chaddlewicks." He was on the point of saying "to Mrs. Chaddlewick", but somehow or other he felt the inhibition of a guilty mind.

Aunt Bella was evidently distressed. These occurrences were becoming too frequent, and people were talking about them.

"Of course, Bobby, she does seem a little odd at times. I can say this to you because you know how much we love and admire her. Don't you think she may find it rather dull? I mean…well, after all, she's young—"

"Dull!" Kewdingham was dismally jocular. "How can she be dull when you are all so kind to her, asking her out and all that sort of thing? You've no idea how she looks forward to her evenings here."

"But you said she was not well?"

Robert Arthur was uneasy. He had no wish to talk about his wife, unless he could air his grievances at the same time. It vexed him when people showed a tendency to sympathise with Bertha, instead of realising the tragedy of his own position.

"Well," he said, "she's not as easy to understand as she used to be. Flares up with no rhyme or reason, you know. At one time I knew her very well, but now, frankly, I am often puzzled by her behaviour."

Mrs. Poundle-Quainton, although merely tolerant of Bertha, did not like the idea of anyone being unhappy. Leaning forward and tapping Robert Arthur on the knee, she spoke with a genuine desire to improve matters:

"Bobby, I've known you since the days when you were crawling about on the carpet, and you mustn't think me interfering if I tell you what's in my mind. We have noticed that Bertha is not always very cheerful. Of course, we know how fond you are of each other, but we can't help wondering if you are as—as friendly with her as she would like you to be. Perhaps friendly isn't the right word, but you know what I mean. We have been talking about this, and we wanted to say—Eh, well! Companionship means so much to a woman, and perhaps she is rather lonely at times, especially with Michael away at school."

Kewdingham, although he knew that he could not make a mistake, had a great respect for his aunt's opinions, which usually resembled his own. Moreover, the remarks of Aunt Bella had implied suggestion rather than criticism, and he smiled amiably as he answered:

"I am glad to hear you say that, Aunt Bella, for I have been thinking about it myself. I've been very busy, for some time, with my League work and my collection and one thing and another. You are quite right."

And as he walked homeward he reflected upon the advantages of domestic harmony. If only Bertha would make things easy for him, how much better it would be! They had got on well enough—years ago. Why couldn't they patch things up again? It would be much pleasanter for both of them; it would save him from the strain of perpetual annoyances, always a source of danger to a man with delicate health. Yes; he would make a final effort.

Poor Robert looked up at the gable of his little house with a sentimental softening of the heart, a creeping, titillating warmth at the pit of the stomach. It was not his fault that he was so busy and had so many interests, but there was no reason why he should not give his wife an extra half-hour every now and then.

So after supper, when the old man had retired to his room and Bertha had settled down in silence (as she usually did) with her work-basket, Robert Arthur, instead of playing with his collection or reading his occult authors, pulled his chair towards her and said pleasantly:

"Look here, Bertha! You and I don't seem to hit it off as well as we might, somehow. That's a pity, isn't it?"

Bertha pulled herself back in her chair, bolt upright, staring at Robert in sheer amazement. What on earth was the man getting at? She let her work fall in her lap, and a wriggle of grey wool came away from one of the needles. Robert's tie, she observed, was dirty and crumpled, and this annoyed her.

"Oh, it's all right, Bobby—at least, I suppose so."

"No, it's all wrong, Bertha."

The doomed, uncouth fellow awkwardly bent forward and took her hand in his. It was a terrible moment. She smiled wryly and drew her hand away.

Kewdingham leaned back in his chair, frowning, but quickly recovered himself. Incomprehensible woman!—Perhaps she was not worth the trouble, after all; but he would see what could be done with a little patience.

"I have many occupations, and they are by no means unimportant. My work in the League takes up a good deal of my time; and then I have my collection to arrange. We can't afford a gardener, as you know, and that means an hour or two…But I naturally wish to study your happiness—eh—before anything else in the world. And—eh—Michael—" It was a sort of dull compunction, a sense of the hollowness of the entire performance, which brought him to a stop. He glanced uneasily at Bertha. He felt himself crumbling before her steady though astonished eyes.

Bertha understood, or guessed, the reason for this disconcerting, unprecedented behaviour. Those damned old women, she thought, had been interfering again.

"Why do you talk like this, Bobby? I don't want to take you away from the things that really interest you. Why should I? After all, I think I carry out my duties moderately well. Let us go on as we are."

"Yes, of course." Robert Arthur did not want her to think that he was going to suggest a radical change in their relations. Good Lord, no!

"But I may have been thoughtless," he said, gently rubbing his waistcoat, and getting his voice on a high, plaintive edge that was peculiarly irritating. "All I meant to say was that we might have a bit of a talk in the evenings, and go about occasionally, and so forth." His magnanimity pleased him; a residue of honest emotion began to warm his residue of a heart.

"My dear Bobby, I have not reproached you—"

She was trying so hard to be patient. But her affection for Robert had perished long ago, and there could be no miraculous revival. A compromise there might be, but it was not in her nature to accept a compromise.

"Reproached me? Why, of course not. What should you reproach me about? I never thought of such a thing."

He was aware of her resistance, he felt the imminence of collision. Still, he would not retire. He was piqued. His expression was not that of a happy man or a confident man, and Bertha was almost sorry for him. Yet she looked at him with an involuntary frown. If only he would face reality!

"No, Bobby. There is no need to—to rake it all up, is there? It's rather painful."

"Painful? I am not quite sure what you mean, my dear. I will admit that I devote a good deal of time to the arrangement of my specimens—"

"And why shouldn't you?"

"True. I am adding to knowledge. Professor Jennings was decidedly complimentary…After all, we know each other pretty well, don't we?"

"We ought to by this time, Bobby."

"If I seem—what shall I say?—preoccupied?" The wretched woman was becoming desperate. She told herself that she must not on any account lose her temper. Bobby was trying to compromise with his muddled conscience, and it would be just as well to leave him alone. A muddled conscience is presumably better than no conscience at all.

"I dare say that I too am often preoccupied, if it comes to that," she said. "And I expect I am terribly annoying."

"You need more companionship." What was it Aunt Bella had said? "Companionship means so much to a woman, and perhaps you are lonely at times, when Michael is away at school. We might, for example, read a book together." It sounded perfectly ridiculous, but he lumbered on doggedly, turning a rather wild eye on the bookcase. "Eh? There's *The Voyage of the Beagle.* Darwin, I believe—yes, Darwin. I remember trying to read it some years ago, and thinking how remarkable it was. One of our great English explorers, you know. Good book for Michael as well."

"That's very nice of you, Bobby. Only I would much rather you didn't worry about me. I would rather we went on just as we are—indeed I would." Robert Arthur was getting uneasy and cross, and feeling that he had been ill-advised after all. Things were not coming out according to plan. Bertha was being very difficult. She did not seem to recognise the magnificence of his gesture, nor did she respond suitably to the deep affection which alone could make such a gesture possible. Seeking for a timely reinforcement he blundered fatally:

"I may as well tell you that Aunt Bella concurs entirely in this opinion. She was talking about you in the kindest way, dear old thing—"

Robert Arthur pulled himself up abruptly, as a man pulls himself up when he sees danger on the road. All Bertha's good and wise resolutions were carried away by a hot blast of uncontrollable anger.

"Good God! Why haven't you got the sense to leave me and my affairs alone? Things are bad enough as they are, and now you go making them a hundred times worse. Tittle-tattle—you are like an old woman yourself. Damn your precious aunt! What does she know about life? And what do *you* know, if it comes to that? Can't you leave me alone? You will drive me mad, I tell you, with your paltry tea-table confabulations, your family conferences and all the rest of it. Do you understand? I have not interfered with you, have I? I have not talked to you about your laziness, and your silly make-believe of a collection, and your asinine League which everyone is laughing at, your Atlantis twaddle, and your deplorable rudeness. Then why can't you leave me to myself? Must I be spied upon and criticised by—by a lot of old mummies? I won't endure it. I tell you I won't endure it. Oh, leave me alone, can't you? Run off to Pamela Chaddle-wick and ask her to console you. But leave me alone. What do you want me to do, anyhow? In what way have I failed in my duty? Oh!—if I had not been such a fool—"

She ended with a jerk in her voice, almost a sob. She had risen from her chair and was looking down on him like a white cloud of wrath, but already she was beginning to tremble, she was twining her fingers nervously together, waiting for the usual counter-attack, the attack which beat her down into silence or brooding desperation.

Kewdingham was not angry. He knew that he was greatly superior to an hysterical woman, and he possessed the grim and proud advantage of having been repulsed in the performance of his duty.

"Very well, my dear; very well. I shall not say the hard things which I might say in the circumstances. Fortunately for you, I have a conciliatory disposition. Any other man would have kicked you out of the house long ago—and I wouldn't have blamed him. Is father in? I hope he didn't hear you. Really, you were making an awful noise. Of course I understand you. I know! You have to be treated like a child."

Meaning to crush her with mournful dignity and with an overwhelming display of patience—the patience of a sadly injured man—he brayed through his nose in the most exasperating manner. His wife, bitterly regretting her lack of control, sat down again.

For some minutes they were silent.

Robert Arthur was profoundly shaken; he felt as though a cold fluid was running through his entrails. He was confused. For some inexplicable reason he could not find the energy for a quarrel.

"I feel rather unwell, my dear. Will you bring me the bottle of old Bagge's mixture—the yellow one—and a wineglass and some water."

Without looking at her husband, and with the indifferent air of a servant obeying orders, Bertha went out of the room. She presently returned with a medicine-bottle, a wineglass and a jug of water on a small tray.

Kewdingham poured out a dose, and then, with a tightening of the lips and a wrinkling of the brow, he sniffed at the bottle. It could be seen that he was now angry. He put the bottle roughly on the tray, making a sharp tinkle of glass and metal, and looked up at his wife. She stared back at him placidly, perhaps with too much indifference.

"Well, Bobby—what's wrong?"

"What's wrong? Yes; that's just what I want to know."

"I don't understand. Is it the medicine?"

"This is not the medicine. Do you mean to say you don't know the difference between one bottle and another? This is the stuff I made up for mosquito-bites. It is highly poisonous. What the devil are you thinking about? Do you want to poison me—eh? It's not quite as easy as you seem to think, if that's the idea. Of course, I could see at once by the smell—"

Very quietly, very steadily, she took the bottle off the tray and read the label.

"Evidently I was mistaken," she said.

"And is that all you have to say?" He was furious.

"My dear Bobby, why are you working yourself up in this ridiculous fashion? The two bottles are very much alike. It was dark in the cupboard. I am sorry."

Why did she look so tired, so dull, so indifferent? Robert Arthur was trembling. He took up the jug and poured some water into the wineglass. The lip of the jug clicked unsteadily on the rim of the glass, and he splashed the knee of his trousers. Let me be sensible, he thought; and he drank a little of the water. He was appalled by the dreadful notion which he himself had invoked. A monstrous absurdity!

"I don't say that you really wanted to poison me. It hasn't come to that, has it?" He grinned unpleasantly. "But you are so infernally careless. One thing is as good as another. It's all one to you, I suppose, whether it's the right bottle or the wrong bottle. Some day you will get a shock. You are making me feel positively ill."

And, indeed, he looked ill; the flush on his face was fading to a chalky whiteness.

"I am very sorry, Bobby. Truly I am."

"Take this away and bring me the mixture, will you?"

Still with an air of dull subservience, Bertha took the bottle and went out of the room.

Kewdingham sank in the chair with his arms dangling over the sides of it. He appeared to be staring at the toe of his boot, and with his toe he traced the outline of an acanthus, worked in pink wool on the hearthrug.

## 3

The episode of the wrong bottle, in whatever way it might be explained, made a very curious impression upon the mind of Bertha Kewdingham. Something new—something harsh and formidable—was controlling her. It was not a pleasant discovery; it never is a pleasant discovery when you find in yourself a contest between your ordinary, familiar thoughts and a sudden rush of invaders.

Suppose that she had really given him a dose of poison?

It was hardly possible, was it? He would have noticed the bottle.

Yes; but suppose, for the sake of argument or speculation—suppose that he had not noticed the bottle. How very awkward it would have been if he had died. If he had died...There would have been a dreadful enquiry, and people would have said—what would they have said? He would have been dead, anyhow. Could anyone have proved that she wanted to kill him? Kill him? Murder him? What an appalling thought!—it could not be admitted, not for a moment! Still, it was there.

The wrong bottle, the wrong dose. Poison. What a sinister word it is! There is hardly another word which gives you such a feeling of unqualified horror. Poison is unequivocally bad,

in whatever sense you choose to think of it. The stealthy
coiling of a serpent; the hidden cause of agony; the smell
of death; or the cowardly shadow of a crime. The wrong
bottle—poison——death.

Then she thought of her marriage.

At the start it all appeared so happy and promising. But
the later voyage of the matrimonial ship had been nearly
disastrous: either in flat Sargasso calm, or in the black tumult
of hurricanes; either at large on a vast unfriendly deep, or
driving, ungovernable, towards the leeward rock. Then the
old man had settled upon them, strengthening the hostile
family group, and keeping up within the house itself an
atmosphere of harsh disapproval.

Kewdingham, disappointed, uncomprehending, had
become stupid or careless. And yet he believed himself to be
incontrovertibly superior. He clung to the uncertain privi-
leges of his uncertain position. He tried to keep himself in
countenance by mystery and invention, by what he would
have called scientific and political activities. In given circumstances he could be perfectly amiable, and even entertaining.

But Athu-na-Shulah, in his Kewdingham incarnation,
had a darker side. The fatal downwash of adversity had worn
away his earlier charm, denuded him of original candour, and
left exposed a core of hard, impenetrable egoism. Perhaps
he did nothing wrong—indeed, that is very probable, for in
one sense he did nothing at all. There was really no provision
for the child, unless the benevolent Uncle Richard would
help them. The situation was becoming desperate. And in
recent years there had been some dreadful scenes of brawling
and bullying. There were times when the whole domestic
menagerie was completely disordered. Bertha did not often
lose her temper, but when she did lose her temper—poor
woman!—she was loud and horrible.

Well!—She had taken the wrong bottle from the cupboard, and had nearly given Robert a dose of mosquito-bite lotion. It was a mistake; it must have been a mistake, of course.

Looked at from one point of view, it was a funny mistake. She could not help thinking of Robert's face when he sniffed the bottle. It would have served him right if he had drunk some of the stuff. It would have served him right if—well, if he had been just a little bit sick. Running away and talking about her with those old women!

After all, was the lotion poisonous? How could she tell what it was made of? And the bottle was one which had originally contained Dr. Bagge's mixture. No one could say it was not an excusable mistake. Robert ought to have marked the bottle in some conspicuous way. His tiny addition to the label—"Mosquito"—could hardly be seen. He himself could not possibly have read it without his glasses, He had been warned—and immediately warned—by the smell alone. He had "seen at once". Nothing like having a keen eye for a smell. But he ought to be more careful; he was far too fond of playing about with drugs. It was a dangerous pastime, and one that might lead to a shocking disaster. A man with so many ailments, real or imaginary…

Poison—poison—poison. The word kept on drumming deeply in her mind, like the beat of the bass in a fugue; or like the pulse, the rhythm of some infernal engine. Poison—poison—poison.

# Chapter III

## 1

John Harrigall, the young cousin of Robert Kewdingham, was a most fortunate man. Without being sentimentally or conventionally handsome he was picturesque and attractive, with a fresh, wholesome and candid appearance not usual among the intelligentsia. John could certainly rank with the intelligentsia, for he was a man of letters with quite a respectable reputation, besides being considered no mean authority on astronomical matters. He had written three successful novels and a monograph on the Einstein Theory.

Whether it is fortunate to be intelligent is perhaps doubtful; but there can be no doubt of the blessings of a comfortable income. John had inherited a comfortable income from his mother and we are, therefore, justified in calling him fortunate. His father, a venerable squire with a weak heart, lived on a small family property in Northumberland.

John himself lived in Chelsea. His rooms were elegant, his library was of enviable proportions, his occupations were delightfully varied. Chelsea parties knew him well. He was acquainted with a whole crowd of painters, authors, critics, and even publishers. He had been intimately acquainted at different times with different women; many of his little affairs would have been severely condemned by the puritanical, to say the least of it. But he was not what you would call, nowadays, a bad young man; that is to say, he had no criminal or depraved or vicious tendencies, though it is true that he never had a cold bath. In his loves, he was not indiscriminate. He chose nice, intelligent women who knew how to manage him. So he came to no great harm, he was the cause of no offensive scandal; though more than once he had been saved from disaster, or marriage, by mere fickleness, mobility or impatience. At the time of this drama he was a little over thirty.

For some time John Harrigall had been thinking a good deal about his cousin's wife, Bertha Kewdingham. She was older than he was, but not by many years. Undoubtedly she was fond of him.

Poor woman! he thought, she is unhappy, and yet she dares not hoist a signal of distress. He did not see any moral objection to an intrigue with Bertha, because he knew that she had "finished" with his cousin Robert. He saw a geographical objection, of course; for Shufflecester is seventy miles from London.

Well! He was no brutal pursuer. How about a sort of emotional friendship? It might be rather amusing; an agreeable interlude when he was visiting the family at Shufflecester, as he did fairly often. But there was a lurking cynic in John, a dirty elf who occasionally broke up through the undergrowth of his mind. The minor components of a character frequently determine its line of action, and it was the lurking cynical elf who now persuaded John that a friendship, however emotional, was not what he wanted. After all, if she was really fond of him…well—why not?

## 2

Late in October, John came to spend a few days with Uncle Richard in Shufflecester. It was rather grey and cold. On the first evening, after dinner, he said:

"If we're going to look at the Tadsley plantations to-morrow, and the Holtons are coming in for bridge in the evening, we shall have rather a long day of it. Do you mind if I just run over now and have a look at the Bobby family?"

"Yes, do," said the cheery old man, "but come back in time for a drink before we turn in. And, I say—don't let him bore you with that awful rubbish-heap of his!" He rolled his tongue out of the corner of his mouth and winked at John.

So ten minutes later John stood inside the porch of Number Six Wellington Avenue. Through the blue-glass panels of the door he could see, in wavering gaslight, the black horns and the bare white frontal bones of a sambur, trophies of a sporting uncle who had died in Bombay. He prepared himself for a jovial encounter with his cousin. He might even say, "Hullo, old boy!" or something like that. Good nature, far more than a sense of strategic design, made John particularly anxious to seem cordial to those who bored him; to hurt wantonly the feelings of others appeared to him the most inexcusable outrage.

But on this occasion it was Bertha who came down the staircase. He could see her through the blue glass, looking rather ghostly.

"Why, John!" she said, as they shook hands, "I didn't know you were here. How jolly of you to come round. I'm all alone. The old man has gone to stay with a friend at Eastbourne. Bobby's out at a smoking concert; but he'll be back soon after ten, so I hope you can stay."

Then, heaven knows for what reason, they laughed—as if they were children making up their minds to be naughty.

John followed Bertha up the stairs and into the little drawing-room.

"I have been stitching away, making things for Michael," she said, folding up her sewing and putting it in the basket, "but your arrival gives me an excuse for idleness. It is very pleasant to see you here."

John could not have said why he felt so curiously excited. In spite of his calculations, his prepared attitude, he felt that something had taken him unawares. This encounter—a very ordinary social encounter on the face of it—was new, adventurous and puzzling. It was the first time he had been alone with Bertha. He looked at her without speaking. She, too, was excited. It seemed as if a screen had fallen and left them facing each other. In a subtle yet decisive way they felt the imminence of complete familiarity, of intimate association. What was happening? John was uneasy. He was not accustomed to any sensation that he could not explain. Besides, he was really conventional; he believed in approaches, preludes and preparations, advance in accordance with plan, all the nicely considered moves of a gambit. Women are less mental in these affairs, less concerned with mere matters of procedure; they do not try to manipulate affection, as men do. Bertha was quite content to know that she was feeling unusually happy.

She began to talk to John about his work, about plays and books and the joy (as it seemed to her) of living in London.

"Ah, John! You are a lucky man."

"Am I?" said John. "Why?"

"Because you know people who can talk intelligently, people whose minds are alive, people who can do things worth doing."

"Is anything worth doing?" he daftly answered.

"Don't be silly!—And then, do you know how nice it is for me to meet someone who does not discuss me to my face, and correct me, as though I was a child or an imbecile? But there was a time when I used to be horribly afraid of you—yes; really afraid!"

She leant forward, pressing the end of her cigarette on the ash-tray.

"That was very unreasonable," said John.

"Perhaps it was. At any rate I seem to know you better— better in the last ten minutes than I have since I first met you, twelve years ago. Is it really as much as twelve years? Good heavens! Of course, you were very young then. So was I. Probably you didn't think about me at all. We are dull people, Bobby and I. But, you see, I was afraid of you because—"

"Because?"

"Well, you are one of the family—"

"And is the family as hopeless as all that?"

"Stupid!" She tapped the fender-rail petulantly with her foot. "You know what I mean. Naturally they did not want me. Why should they?"

"Bobby wanted you, I suppose."

"He thought he did. Perhaps he has repented."

"My dear Bertha—"

"Oh, yes, I know. A really nice woman could not say a thing like that, could she? A really nice woman is always blind and speechless, isn't she?—No matter what she may see or what she may suffer. Do you think me ungrateful—treacherous?"

She looked at him squarely.

"I think—" John began. "Well, of course—"

He sounded forbiddingly formal. He was conscious of a moral vertigo, the ordinary predicament of a man who is afraid of being too sincere. He knew that he would have to choose and pronounce his words very carefully, as though he was drunk. There was a tinkling in his ears and a drumming in his breast.

"I think it is always possible—"

But she interrupted him with a little cry, and yet a cry so reverberant that he started, like a man who is called to simple action by an appeal for help.

"Oh, John! I am not a very happy woman. I feel all alone in this confounded place. Will you be my friend?"

"Why, yes; of course," said John, swinging back to his balance, and telling himself that he must take care not to go too far all at once. After all, Bobby might return.

Bertha had rested her elbows on the table, and the clenched fingers of one hand were pressed into her cheek. He could not say if she was miserable or angry. Her head was turned away from him and she was looking in the fire.

"Yes, Bertha. Haven't I always been your friend?"

Without changing her position, and speaking very quietly, she said:

"It's all pretence here. That's what makes it so awful, John. Nothing is real. He and I—we pretend that nothing is wrong. Daddy pretends that his son is the best man in the world. Those old women shut their eyes if there is a chance of seeing anything ugly. Is it my fault? Sometimes I am sorry for him. And then again I am angry, and we have frightful scenes. No doubt I am exceedingly unpleasant. But he is such a difficult man, such a difficult man; he does not give me a chance. I have tried, but I cannot give him what he wants. It's no good. We don't understand each other. The worst of it is, we don't care."

John could not help wishing that she did not take things quite so seriously. But then, he reflected, she is half French, and therefore highly emotional.

She looked at him with a curious, whimsical tilt of the eyebrows, as if she understood his bewilderment.

"Now I have said to you what I have never said to anyone else, and perhaps I ought to be ashamed of myself. Do you think so? Do you grudge me the luxury of confession? But I want your friendship, if you can give it to such a poor, discontented creature. I want to get away from all this damnable pretence. It is choking me. I do want something real."

"Well," said John, "I had been hoping, ever since our last meeting, that—that we might get to know each other somehow. But it didn't seem so easy. You say you were afraid of me: God knows why. Now, I always thought you rather a formidable woman. I did, really. I think I do still."

"Formidable!" She laughed. She was beginning to feel happy again. "Formidable!—Well, what an idea!"

"It was a positive conviction."

"Oh, nonsense, John!—Don't be such an idiot. How can you expect me to believe you, if you talk like that? Let's have another cigarette, shall we? I want you to tell me about all sorts of things, if you really think it worth while to talk to me. As for these commonplace grievances of mine, please forget them. Most women have to make the best of a bad job in one way or another. It's a bad job being a woman, anyhow. I tell you again, you're a lucky man, and lucky to be a man. Now I want to hear about this new book of yours. What did you say the title was?"

"*Brave Old Earthquake.*"

"Is it a satire? Do tell me…"

And so, without reflecting upon the strangeness of their sudden intimacy, or upon the greater strangeness of the fact that they were now taking that intimacy for granted, they began one of those delightful conversations which can only occur in the early stages of a real friendship. John was enjoying himself thoroughly, but he did not feel at all wicked. Perhaps the deep springs of our thoughts and actions bubble on muddy levels for ever unknown to the conscious mind.

Robert Arthur had not returned by a quarter past ten. John, who had no wish to meet Robert Arthur, even if he was not positively anxious to avoid him, decided that it was time to go.

"I must go now," he said. "Uncle Richard expects me to have a drink with him before turning in."

"I mustn't keep you," said Bertha. She, too, felt that the arrival of her husband before John had left would be awkward, inappropriate; it would destroy the unity of a pleasant episode.

"Bobby will be so vexed—"

"But I can run round in the morning before we start for Tadsley."

"Yes, do. He is sure to be here."

To-morrow would be all right. She was hoping, now, that John would manage to leave without meeting Robert; as though he was a venturesome lover, stealing away from the house at dawn. It may be that she was already thinking of him as a lover, for women are terribly definite in their conclusions, terribly honest in facing every sort of possibility.

"And shall I see you?"

"I hope so. I don't go out before twelve. Let me come down and open the door for you."

"No, no. I can let myself out, thanks."

He glanced at the ugly cabinets, the drawers and tins and boxes, all the various containers of the great collection. In that confusion of rubbish it seemed as if Kewdingham himself was present in a piecemeal sort of way. Boxes, bags, packages, lumber, confusion of lumber, methodical yet mad accumulation of trifles, dreadfully symbolic.

"Hullo!" he said, "What's this?"

Three bottles, two containing fluid and one containing a greenish powder, were standing on the top of a cabinet near the door. By the side of them was a medicine-glass.

"Some of Bobby's awful decoctions, waiting for him. I do wish he didn't dabble about with drugs like this, you know. Some day he'll poison himself, and then I shall get the blame—as I do for everything."

"He was always fond of doping himself. But he can't get hold of real poisons, can he?"

"I'm not so sure. He gets mysterious little packets from Vienna and New York, and, I think, from London, too. Doctor Bagge has been talking to him very seriously, but Bobby doesn't give himself away. I'm sure I don't know what he's got in that cupboard of his."

"Ah! He ought to be careful. He may be doing himself a lot of harm. I wonder what's in those bottles—they are not labelled."

"It's no use talking to him. Anyhow, don't let us think of unpleasant things. We have had such a delightful evening. And we are friends now, aren't we? Good night."

He took her hand and held it in his own. Then, bending suddenly, he pressed his lips for one moment on her wrist. She did not oppose his movement, and as their hands unclasped gently with a lingering touch of the fingers, she said:

"I am so glad."

Then she stood by the fire, watching him as he left the room.

John Harrigall, already trying to account for his uncalculated and romantic gesture, let himself out of the house and walked rapidly up Wellington Avenue.

An easterly wind was blustering sharply, embittered by showers of sleet. As John reached the end of the Avenue he turned and looked back at Number Six. He could perceive dimly, in the scattered radiance of the street lamp, a strenuous lanky figure, with a long waterproof clip-clapping against his legs. It was Kewdingham returning. John laughed, rubbing his chin from side to side on the upturned collar of his coat. Then he strode quickly round the corner.

## 3

Mr. Kewdingham was delighted to find out how well Mrs. Chaddlewick understood him. Far from laughing at his Atlantis fantasy, as most people did, she treated it in the most serious and enthusiastic manner. He went in the bus to Sykeham-le-Barrow and called on the Chaddlewicks, at a time when it so happened that Mr. Chaddlewick had gone to see the new herd of Jerseys at Tiddleswade Castle. No doubt his call had the appearance of eccentricity, for Robert Arthur was generally considered a formal and retiring person, but Pamela had received him with entrancing flutters of coyness. The truth is that Pamela (who had no children and did not care for dogs) was rather bored.

Then, on the very day after John's interview with Bertha, Mrs. Chaddlewick's elegant car pulled up in Wellington Avenue and Mrs. Chaddlewick rang the bell at Number Six. She was not surprised to hear that Bertha was out, for she had caught a glimpse of her in town. But Robert Arthur, lured by the cooing voice, came tripping down the stairs.

"Ah, Mr. Kewdingham! What a lahvly day it's turned out, after all, hasn't it? I was wondering if you could both… George was so frightfully sorry to miss you the other afternoon; he was quite jealous!—No; I simply can't stay. I promised George to be back to tea. Why not come to Sykeham with me? Or would Mrs.—would Bertha think me too horribly rude?" She giggled invitingly.

"I should be delighted," said Robert Arthur, "if you are quite sure—"

"Of course! George is dying to show you that wonderful lawn of his. Oh, *do* come, Mr. Kewdingham." And she lightly touched him on the arm with her little grey glove. She could not foresee—poor flighty lady!—the part she would be called on to play in the Kewdingham drama. She did not think of such a thing as drama. All she wanted was a bit of amusement.

"Really, that's very kind of you. I'll get my hat and coat." Middle-aged men are peculiarly susceptible to these advances.

So in less than two minutes Mr. Kewdingham was sitting beside Mrs. Chaddlewick in the car. She proposed to drive round by the Tadsley plantations, where, so she said, there was a simply too heavenly view. Mrs. Chaddlewick drove her own car—an Upton-Ryder saloon—and she drove it as well as the average woman does drive a car; that is to say, she made it go from one place to another.

At the edge of the plantation Mrs. Chaddlewick swung off the road and pulled up on a soft grassy stretch below the trees.

"Now just look at it!" she said. "I always think it's the most gorgeous view I know anywhere."

She made a silky, sidling movement towards Mr. Kewdingham.

"Yes; those tints are very beautiful," said Robert Arthur, to whom a landscape was merely an expanse of earth. Instead of looking at the hills and the woods he looked at the melting fluffiness of Mrs. Chaddlewick.

"It makes me *think*," Mrs. Chaddlewick fluted. "I simply can't think of nothing, you know. George always knows when I'm sort of thinking. I look at the trees and I think of all the dear little birds, and then I look at the farms down there and think of the dear old wise doggies, and then I look at the hills—and oh, they are so *lahvly*! Don't you *lahve* Nature?"

"There is nothing like it," said Mr. Kewdingham.

He was flustered. With an awkward fumbling movement he fished up his monocle, fixed it over his eye, and glared at the slim trees. He looked as though he was trying to find fault with something—like an English traveller in a foreign land.

"Life is so wonderful!" Mrs. Chaddlewick nearly closed her eyes in a silent ecstasy of sentiment.

"Sometimes it is," replied Mr. Kewdingham. And then he made a really astonishing remark: "If only we could get over the tendency to die."

The lady threw back her head with a little yelp of laughter. "Oh, but how thrilling! What do you mean?"

"It is not easy to explain. Death has become a habit—"

He began to flounder about in a mess of mystical nonsense, talking of the Tribe of Reuben, the Pyramid, the Seven Rules of the New Life, the Sealed People, the Panacea, and heaven knows what. He wanted to show Pamela that he was a man out of the ordinary, a man of strange powers, occult, fascinating. Pamela was duly impressed, though she had anticipated something rather different. She looked at him with adorable vacancy. At times her big, luscious eyes beamed with a sort of rapture.

"Now, this Panacea. It is, in one sense, only a matter of chemistry. I have been guided—mystically guided—to certain experiments. I would not speak of this to anyone else. But I know that you understand."

"It's all right: go on." Mrs. Chaddlewick gave these simple words a most unexpected richness of meaning, a newly created world of meaning. She could see daylight again.

"I don't say that I've been entirely successful. But I have found out that, by combining certain drugs—well, you do get a really astonishing result."

He said this with a look of monumental emptiness, a nullity so massive that you might have wondered if he was not inspired. There was a dree, enervating quality in his voice, like the sound of a distant saw-mill.

"Of course, I have some difficulty in getting my drugs. Many of them are poisons."

"Then you must be very, very careful!"

"I am guided."

"You're a terribly strange man, indeed you are!" Pamela swooned upon him; a mass of enveloping charm. Her large luminous eyes were full of tenderness. "And now—now I suppose we must be going." But even while she said it she gave him the glad signal. She looked right through him, right through his monocle into the very soul of him, the hidden soul of Athu-na-Shulah.

Kewdingham took a lot of moving, but he read the signal. He put his hand on the soft fur of Mrs. Chaddlewick's collar, and he said huskily:

"You are a wonderful woman!"

Now it will be remembered that John Harrigall and Uncle Richard were going to visit the Tadsley plantations. And, as luck would have it, they were coming along the grassy path to the road while this peculiar conversation was going on in Mrs. Chaddlewick's car. Uncle Richard was going across to the plantation on the other side of the hill, where his own car would be waiting for him, and now he was rather puffed by the walk up the hill and they were trudging along in silence. Just as Mrs. Chaddlewick had reached the hidden soul of Athu-na-Shulah, Uncle Richard and his nephew came in sight of the road.

"Look at those two blasted spooners!" rumbled Uncle Richard, always Victorian.

"A most immoral vehicle, the big saloon," John observed. Then he looked more closely.

"Why—hul-lo!"

Mrs. Chaddlewick saw them. In the twinkling of an eye she flopped out of the car and ran prettily towards the wood. She was not the woman to lose her head in a contingency.

"Mr. Kewdingham!" she twittered. "How charm-ing, charm-ing! Oh, yes, I have met Mr. Harrigall! I have read one of your naughty little books, Mr. Harrigall. We are just running back to have tea with George. Isn't it a lahvly afternoon? So warm for the time of year."

She saw John's elfish grin.

All right, my lad! she thought, I'll be even with you. I know you think me a fool; but I've got eyes in my head.

As for Uncle Richard, he was admirably discreet, though he looked rather whimsically at the car. Indeed, they all began to look at the car. Mrs. Chaddlewick had slammed the door behind her, and now Robert Arthur was tugging frantically at the door on his own side, but he didn't know how to open it, so he could only bang and rattle, and the whole saloon was quivering and shaking with his agitation. John let him out: he could not refrain from a detestable snigger, which filled Robert Arthur with rage.

"Never mind," said Mrs. Chaddlewick, when the others had gone and she had started the engine. "Never mind. It doesn't matter one little teeny tiny bit, does it?"

She spoke with all the grand indifference, all the confidence of a pretty woman who makes her own world.

"Certainly not," said Robert. "Why should it? But I must say it's very odd I didn't see them sooner. I had no idea—"

"Ah!" said Pamela, with a melting smile of comprehension. "I know! I'm terribly like that myself; I can only think of one thing at a time."

## 4

Mrs. Robert Kewdingham had been up in London for the day. She had been taken there by Doctor Wilson Bagge in his car, and she had lunched with the doctor.

There really was something very attractive about the little man, with his neat birdy movements and his quick discerning eye. He made you feel that he knew things without being told, and yet he was never obtrusively sympathetic. Mrs. Kewdingham liked him very much. She enjoyed her drive to London and she enjoyed her lunch with the doctor. It was the first occasion on which she had been alone with him for any length of time.

Their conversation, though discreet, had been subtly intimate. Doctor Bagge had confessed that he was a lonely man; he had spoken in the most touching manner about his late wife; it was obvious that he looked upon Mrs. Kewdingham as a friend in whom he was free to confide. Such confidence is, in itself, the most delicate avowal of intimacy.

Then, while they were having coffee after lunch, the conversation had turned upon Robert Arthur.

"Your husband is a very singular man, Mrs. Kewdingham—a very interesting man."

"Is he?" Bertha appeared to be watching a garrulous party of young men, busy ordering cocktails.

"Yes. But he's not an easy patient."

"He's not an easy husband."

Doctor Bagge did not reply for a moment. He blew softly from his little rounded mouth a jet of blue smoke.

"When I say that he is not an easy patient I mean that he is far too fond of playing about with drugs—and what's more, with drugs that ought not to be in his possession. He doesn't tell me very much about it, naturally; but I have seen enough to make me feel distinctly uncomfortable. You know I have warned him."

"It's no use warning him."

"Patients who will persist in giving themselves drugs are difficult in any case. It is not so bad when they stick to harmless preparations, patent remedies, and things of that sort. But when it comes to the handling of dangerous poisons—"

The doctor, prim and immovable, suddenly looked full in the face of Mrs. Kewdingham. No one could possibly have guessed what he was thinking about, but he was evidently thinking hard. A flush of warm colour spread over Bertha's generally pale cheeks, and she raised her voice involuntarily as she said:

"Well, I can't help it, can I?"

Do what she might, this awful thought of poison was being continually presented to her.

Doctor Bagge did not answer the question. "Such cases are very difficult," he repeated.

"Do you think Bobby is likely to do himself any real harm?"

"Unless he is careful—yes."

Why did she not look more alarmed? Why did she take it so quietly? Bertha herself knew that her attitude was terribly compromising, and yet she could not even simulate the concern of a really affectionate wife. She was giving herself away to Doctor Bagge. Indeed, the cunning little man had carefully prepared this experiment. He watched her closely.

"Unless he is careful, he may poison himself."

Still she could say nothing.

"Well, well!" The prim little man was brisk and cheerful again. "Let us talk of something else. Perhaps there is not much cause for apprehension after all. So your friend Mr. Harrigall is bringing out a new book very shortly?"

The doctor was not returning until the following day. He was dining with some old friends from the hospital, and he had an appointment with Sir James Macwithian in the morning. So after lunch Bertha did some shopping, and then she had tea with her charming sister-in-law, Miss Phoebe Kewdingham.

## 5

Now she was in the train on her way back to Shufflecester.

In one corner of the compartment was a heavy, pallid commercial gentleman, falling into a beery sleep. In another corner were a young man and a young woman holding each other's hands.

As the train jogged thunderously along over the black, hidden country, past the winking lights of Cranford and then the more distant lights of elegant Filton, Mrs. Kewdingham languidly turned over the pages of a fashion magazine she had bought at Victoria.

She always felt rather languid when she was on her way home after the excitement of London. Back to Bobby and the cage again. Back to the old women and their hateful sham-Christian tolerance. Back to the snapping and the snarling and the infernal tugging strain of daily humiliation—all the muddy, clinging mess of a miscalculated marriage, a fool's marriage. Back to the ugly, disheartening little house, the boxes and cabinets and all the rest of it. Not even Michael now. Oh, Lord!—It was not a happy prospect.

She looked at the magazine, frowning abstractedly, as if she was reading with some difficulty in a foreign language:

> "At a very trifling expense you can make enough of this excellent hair-wash to last you for years. I took three large bottles with me to India in the spring of 1925, and have still enough for another month's use. There is no difficulty in procuring the ingredients. Here is the formula: Lead acetate…precipitated sulphur… glycerin…lavender water…rum. Of course, it is just as well to remember that the lead acetate is poisonous, and as it has a sweet sugary taste and the appearance of a soft white powder, it should not be left lying about, especially if there are children in the house. Any chemist will sell you as much as you require, however, for it is not one of the scheduled poisons."

She read no more, but sat with the paper in her lap, looking out of the window at the flying night. The train was clattering through Hedgerley, the lighted platform slid in a long yellow blur past the window. In a few seconds they had flung away the tiny sparkles of the little town, and again they were chuffing and booming along in the hollow, rushing night. The heavy commercial gentleman, waking with a groan, lowered the window in order that he might spit out of it, and then settled himself for another doze. The young man and the young woman giggled happily together: Bertha glanced at them with a mingling of jealousy and pleasure. The scurrying drum-drum-drum of the train beat into her mind with a persistent rhythm. Presently the rhythm was associated with definite words, endlessly repeated, sometimes at one pitch and sometimes at another, in solo, in unison, in deafening chorus, like a fugue.

Acetate, acetate, acetate of lead…

But remember, it is a poison. A poison with a pleasing, sugary taste. Invaluable in a hair-wash—one of the ordinary ingredients. Any chemist will give you as much as you want. Only you must be careful, especially if there are children in the house. Lead acetate is a poison, and there might be deplorable accidents. Oh, yes! It's cheap enough to buy.

Acetate, acetate, acetate…The train was rattling and lurching over a mesh of points.

Cheap to buy, and a little goes a long way, you know. It is quite reasonable to buy it if you are making a hair-wash. Perhaps Bobby was using it already for some of his medical decoctions. He ought to be careful, or he might poison himself.

Mrs. Kewdingham looked out of the window at the rushing, noisy stream of the night.

Acetate—poison.

The inception of the idea of calculated murder is not immediately recognised. Such an idea enters the mind in disguise—a new arrival in a sinister mask, not willingly entertained and yet by no means to be expelled. Or, in more scientific terms, it is introduced by a sort of auto-hypnosis, the mere repetition of thoughts or words not immediately connected with personal action. Between the highly civilised individual and the act of murder there are so many barriers, so many conventions and teachings—or so many illusions.

# Chapter IV

## 1

Miss Phoebe Kewdingham lived, as we have said, in a spacious flat in Dodsley Park Avenue. And she managed to live in a very comfortable style.

Now, the Kewdingham family was not one of your grubby, grabbing middle-class families; it could produce a bit of everything. Phoebe was a poetess. Her verses were printed in the elegant Bodoni type and were bound in black and gold with a yellow top: uniform edition, two volumes, three and sixpence each. In order to match these pretty, slim little books, Phoebe (who was herself slim and pretty) dressed in black and gold. She acknowledged the sovereignty of the passions, and for that reason had abstained from marriage. At the time of which we are writing, she was about thirty-eight—nearly ten years younger than her brother Robert.

Like many families of indeterminate race, the Kewding-hams described themselves as Irish. Those Kewdinghams who were intelligent enough to recognise their own haziness of thought declared that such a failing was peculiar to the Gael, and indicated an hereditary mental twilight. During the disturbances which preceded the establishment of what is called a Free State in Ireland, Phoebe had learnt the Gaelic tongue, and in that tongue she had written a number of exciting poems about the heroes of liberty and the blood of the gods. She had received important letters from someone in Dublin to be delivered to someone in London—and she had lost the letters. Ministers of State had stealthy suppers in her kitchen, and told her what a joke it was trying to govern the Irish.

Family sentiment was aggressively developed in Phoebe. Her brother Robert appeared to her as an unlucky man, kicked by fate for no fault of his own. After all, he had "fine qualities"—you could no more imagine a Kewdingham without fine qualities than you could imagine a fish without fins. He was the right sort of man to deal with a leaking tap or a troublesome dog or a squeaking window. He was one of the family, this poor Robert Arthur; and "we Kewding-hams"…well, heaven knows what we Kewdinghams would have done, if it had not been for one thing and another, and things in general.

Phoebe often met her cousin John, but it cannot be said that she liked him. John was a gossip, a purveyor of literary small-talk, and he had a way of being unforgivably spiteful. You could not tell when he was in earnest.

Phoebe herself was in earnest about everything. Even the shadow of hypocrisy was hateful to a nature so candid, so intense. She was an artist; and the purpose of all art is the discovery of truth.

## 2

A cloudy assemblage of ideas induced Robert Arthur Kewd-ingham, early in November, to pay a visit to Dodsley Park Avenue. Robert hated London and he seldom went there; it made his head ache. But now, although forty-seven, he was thinking about getting a job again. He still knew some of his former engineer friends, and they might give him a tip or two, at any rate. A residue of normal self-esteem made him feel that he ought to seek employment. Besides, he really had a special knowledge of the Heinz-Beckford heavy-oil engine. He would make a final effort; and then who could say that he had not done his duty?

He reached London by a late train, and it was half-past eight when he struggled out of a crowded bus in Hammersmith. The street lights were shining dimly under the dull copper spread of a thick fog. A winter slush gleamed on the slippery pavements. The life of the town was moving between two layers of dirty moisture, one overhead and one underfoot. He anticipated with satisfaction the greeting of the dear girl, the homely comfort of the flat.

It was not his custom to write letters to the family. His rare visits were made without announcement. He took his chance. Even if the spare bed was occupied, Phoebe could give him a shake-down somewhere. The dear girl was always glad to see her brother. He was feeling tired, and he did hope that he would find her alone.

But a little party was in full swing at the flat when Robert arrived. He quietly opened the door of the drawing-room, and there he stood, somewhat abashed, with a shabby raincoat folded over one arm and a bulging, amorphous bag in his hand. He tried to look amiable, but he was confused by the clamour of jolly voices, the presence of several strangers, and the sense of an atmosphere which (to him) was intensely uncongenial. What a damned nuisance! he said to himself.

There were some very distinguished people at the party. There was Mr. Fordyce Youghall, the Great Man of Fleet Street; Mr. Jacob Dobsley, the sculptor, whose distorted nudes gave such offence to Parliament; Mr. John Harrigall, an author of rising fame; Mr. Petrick Sundale, the financier; and Miss Dodie Doodar, whose cabaret turns were the best in London—she married Sir Bertie Parkes-Boundle not long afterwards.

John looked up with annoyance as he saw Kewdingham; and so did Mr. Fordyce Youghall, who was holding the attention of Mr. Dobsley—or thought he was—by a discourse on the revival of realism. But Phoebe gracefully rose with her smooth Donatello smile.

"Ah, Bobby! How unexpected, but how delightful! Staying the night with us, of course?"

Quickly grasping the situation, she ran up to her brother and kissed him.

"Come along and put your bag in your room. It will be ready for you in two shakes."

Robert retired for a time. When he came back there was a clatter of lively talk in the room.

John was saying to Phoebe:

"Peabright has a frightfully high opinion of your poems—a justly high opinion. I was having lunch with him the other day, and he said it was only a matter of time before you took your place among the modern masters—yes, really, my dear!"

At the same time Mr. Dobsley, keeping within reach of the bottles and siphons on a table in the corner, was earnestly refuting Mr. Youghall's views on realism:

"It's li' this, ol' man—y' must rec'nise thrubbly romazzic inkerlation of gerral tenzies. Gerral tenzies *always* romazzic."

Robert Arthur, with his glinting monocle in his eye, his face corrugated with bewilderment and the effort to appear at ease, looked very unhappy. He regarded most of the company (and with some reason) as "queer", and he believed that most of them led immoral lives. It was a great pity that dear Phoebe would insist on knowing such people. Phoebe, who was trying to make the best of her mixed company, again rose to the occasion. She led her brother to a secluded corner of the room.

"You've got some strange people here," said Robert, looking at Phoebe with gratitude and affection.

"Not much in your line, I'm afraid, Bobby. You see, one *has* to know these people, because they help one. But there's John—you know him."

Yes; Robert knew John, but somehow or other he did not feel that he wanted to talk to him. John was a curious fellow, vaguely dangerous. This was a new idea, but Robert did not examine it closely.

"And how are the Shufflecester people?" said Phoebe. "Why didn't you tell me you were coming?"

Robert replied that he didn't want to make a nuisance of himself. Just for one night—or maybe two, if she could manage. He explained that he was looking for work. After all, they were terribly hard up. He would see Jackson and Arkwright and one or two others who had promised to help him if they could. True, he was getting on in age; but then he had experience. He was ready for anything—anything with a bit of money in it.

And here John came up to them, and Robert told him about his plans. John, who had had a whisky or two, rubbed his chin and looked rather queerly at Robert, and Robert gave him an ugly, sharp glance and went on talking to Phoebe.

Now this good girl, so anxious to forget herself and to help other people, had a sudden inspiration.

"I say, Bobby!—There's a man over there who would interest you very much, and who would like to meet you, I think. Probably he's quite as much bored as you are by all this jargon. Mr. Sundale, the great financier. He was telling me about some new scheme of his—sharks, I believe—in the Pacific—"

"In the Pacific! That sounds interesting."

Robert, smarting a little from his encounter with John, felt at once that he was on the track of a job. He had a nimble fancy, he was mentally adventurous. The mere word Pacific stimulated him. John would see—they would all see—that he was a man who could pick up a first-rate job, a job calling for real enterprise. And he would escape; he would fly away from his troubles, fly away to the blue seas and the waving palms and the pearly-white beaches of a southern archipelago. Certainly an inspiration.

Soon he was talking, gravely, confidentially, to Mr. Sundale.

Mr. Sundale had a kind of oily black brilliance, he shone like a bit of polished coal. His beautiful Assyrian locks were discreetly pomaded, his black eyebrows were always twitching about—archly, derisively, invitingly, fiercely, always moving up and down. A black moustache curled in a pair of fine little horns over his luscious red mouth. He spoke in a rich drawling bass, harmonious and virile.

Furtively glancing with his black eyes, Mr. Sundale quickly formed his opinion of Robert Arthur. It may or may not have been a correct opinion, for Mr. Sundale thought that Robert might be of some use to him. When he learnt that Robert had been for many years with Hayle, Trevors and Ockersley he was obviously impressed.

Mr. Kewdingham implored Mr. Sundale to give him more precise information—in confidence.

"Certainly," said Mr. Sundale, allowing his eyebrows to drop level for a moment. "You see, Mr. Kewdingham, it will be an Anglo-Batavian company. The Van Kloopens, the sugar people, are willing to provide a dozen trawlers for a start. These vessels are at present in the Scheldt—under repairs. The fish will be caught in nets of steel wire, made flexible by a new process. The cost of each net is about a hundred pounds. As for the shark, I don't suppose that you realise his commercial possibilities. His liver resembles that of the cod, only it is much larger, and its oil has the same valuable properties as real cod-liver oil. Hum, hum!" Mr. Sundale looked extremely knowing, his eyebrows tilted to a most cunning angle. "The fins of the shark are eaten by the Chinese, who regard them as a great delicacy and pay ridiculous prices for them. The bones are ground into a chemical manure of the finest quality. The skin, treated in a certain way, can be made into a sort of leather. It is better than leather, and more quickly and easily prepared."

"Then, of course, you will install a fair amount of plant at your factories?"

"Yes. Our main power units will consist of Heinz-Beckford heavy-oil engines."

"What!" cried Robert, "the good old H.B.! That's my own particular line. I put in a dozen of 'em at Seaforth harbour."

"Now look here, Mr. Kewdingham—" The conversation became highly technical.

Presently Robert said: "And how about the men who will take charge of the stations—the factory managers?"

"Ah, hum! I will admit a slight difficulty." The black eyebrows made a whimsical arabesque. "You see, we need rather exceptional men. We need men with organising experience, intelligence, courage, a sense of responsibility, initiative, loyal devotion to the interests of the shareholders, and the ability to control native labour." Mr. Sundale had said that before—at a directors' meeting. "An engineer, if he possessed the necessary qualities, would be ideal; he could probably act in a double capacity, and so draw the pay of two appointments."

"Frankly, Mr. Sundale, I think I might be of some use to you."

Mr. Sundale appeared to cogitate. He dreamily took a golden case from his pocket and offered Robert a cigarette. Then he flicked up his brows into an arch of pure candour and frankness.

"I should not think of asking you seriously to join us until I was in a position to say something more about the prospects of the company. You see, I am interested in scores of concerns; and this is quite a new one—attractive to me because it is highly speculative, one might almost say romantic. Dierick Van Kloopen is a personal friend of mine, and I know he's a sound man; but I should like to wait a little—just a little. I know your sister very well, Mr. Kewdingham, and so you must allow me to treat this, if I may, as a family matter. I don't want to propose anything that would not be entirely to your advantage. In the meantime, I'm very grateful to you for your interest. Here is my card: it has my City telephone number. If you would care to see me again, I should be delighted—"

Mr. Sundale's rich, thick voice drawled out a number of commonplace amenities.

Here was a possibility, a shadowy scheme, which appealed strongly to Robert's imagination. A pleasing fantasy of coral islands, of dusky natives, of busy trawlers industriously sharking, of a life in which periods of delicious ease alternated with shorter periods of vigorous command. A symphony of Heinz-Beckford oil engines rumbled an accompaniment.

John looked up and saw Robert as he was drifting away from Mr. Sundale. Robert's beaming countenance irritated him profoundly. He thought of Bertha. So he decided to be extremely polite. He went up to Robert and asked him to have a drink.

Giddy with his new vision, Robert eagerly told John all about the steel nets and the sharks and the coral islands. The more John was bored and exasperated, the more amiable his expression.

And Robert Arthur, regretting his momentary impatience with John, became amiable in his turn. He accepted with pleasure John's invitation to tea on the following afternoon.

## 3

Kewdingham, when he arrived at John's quarters in Margaretta Terrace, was not quite at his ease. Although he had every wish to make allowances, he was feeling rather defiant. Yet he would have found some difficulty in explaining his attitude. He could not admit that he was jealous.

He wished that John was not such a good-looking young man, and so well dressed. Without asking himself why he should have resented these advantages, he knew that he did resent them, and he also resented the comfort and the elegance of John's rooms. The man had too much money. What did he want with all these kickshaws and rotten pictures—and a divan. A divan, of all things! No decent fellow, said Robert to himself, would have any use for such an immoral piece of furniture.

But John was so pleasant, so assiduously attentive and subtly deferential, that he melted the weakening hostility of the other man.

Robert Arthur was readily convinced both of the friendship and of the intelligence of those who agreed with him. Soon he had almost forgiven John for the disquieting divan, the silly pictures. He smiled indulgently. The artistic temperament!

"And how's Bertha?" John enquired.

Robert sighed, letting the air flow noisily between his teeth. A dim uneasiness moved in his mind, like a shadow in shallow water.

John perceived the shadow. He knew what it meant, even if Robert himself was unaware. It was the shadow of jealousy.

"Oh, she's all right," said Robert. "I say, what a fine lot of books you've got over there."

"Review copies, most of 'em. That reminds me—I've got a book here for Bertha. Could you manage to put it in your suitcase? It's quite a small one."

"Why, you sent her one only the other day! You are much too good to her, my dear fellow—much too good to her."

"Oh, nonsense, Bobby! I'm always giving books away— and it's not so easy to get new ones in Shufflecester. This one was only published yesterday. But if you haven't got room for it—"

"No, no. Quite all right. Very good of you." He looked at the mottled cover of the book which John handed to him; he opened it and saw the uneven lines of Mr. Peabright's verse. For a second time he sighed heavily, slipping the book into his pocket, and then giving it a tap as if he was afraid it would bite him.

The landlady, Mrs. Appleton, brought in a very nicely prepared tea, with cherry cake. By degrees, Kewdingham felt more at home. The conversation veered back to family matters.

"By the way, John, what do you think about this affair of Sundale's? You know—the shark business. We were talking about it at Phoebe's last night. I have seen Jackson, and he thinks there may be something in it; at any rate he knows of nothing better."

"Well—there's not much to go on at present, is there?"

"No, but it does look rather promising. These Van Kloopens, according to Jackson, are very big people. They are understood to be approaching the French Government with a view to concessions in the Marquesas."

"Would you really care to take up a job so far away from home?"

"Why not? If they make a good offer—"

"And what do you suppose Bertha would think of it?"

"Oh—Bertha!—"

He produced from his pocket, and unfolded with a wide stretching of arms, a fine map of the South Pacific which he had purchased that very afternoon. Certain red pencil marks indicated places mentioned in the course of Mr. Sundale's conversation. How could Bertha stand in the way of this great enterprise?

Kewdingham's finger wandered over the blue ocean, the purple deeps, the pale shallows, the rushing arrows of the equatorial stream. "There you are!—right away out here—the Marquesas; that's as far as we go. The Manihiki—Tuamotu—"

He rambled gravely away, talking of sharks and of trawlers, the boiling-house, the drying-rooms, the oil-refinery, the stores, the dynamos, the huts for the workmen, the manager's house and all the rest of it. And he spoke with such authority that you might have wondered if the Van Kloopens would have anything to say in the matter, once Robert Arthur was in the Pacific. A bit of crumpled paper was produced; the red pencil was busy.

"I should put a veranda here, facing the works, so that I could see the men coming up from the tannery. Here—the main engine-house. Here—the quay. No doubt it will be necessary to inspect the nets every morning. The coal store—under my immediate supervision. They will have to get my written order before they draw for the bunkers. Fuelling is a very tricky business."

John himself was almost carried away by this measured enthusiasm, this convincing knowledge of detail.

"Well, Bobby—I wonder—"

"You see? Now tell me what you think of it."

"Really, it's not easy to say." A vague, irrational hope came into his mind. There might be something in it, after all. It might be the salvation of Bertha. It might be the means of preventing some dreadful catastrophe. "I think you are the right man for a job of that kind. Your present life—it's quite all right, I know—but it's not good enough. A man with your technical knowledge and your experience..."

"Yes, I agree with you. Only, of course, as you were saying just now, there's Bertha and Michael." He was unconsciously preparing the line of retreat.

"Probably you could take them with you."

"H'm, well—I don't know—" There was a cloud somewhere.

"Not at first, perhaps; but later on, when you were settled."

"That's not quite the point. Bertha loves the old home, you know. She might not care to leave it. She's very happy there."

"She might be quite as happy in the Marquesas. No doubt she would like to meet some French people. In fact, she would be extremely useful to you in such a position."

"Do you think so?" He was relieved (for more than one reason) though undecided.

"Of course."

"But she—she's rather a funny girl, you know."

"Ah!"

"Quite happy; but she takes a bit of managing, I can tell you. They all do. You may give them all they want, and they still go on crying for the moon."

John put the lid on the bubbling broth of his indignation. He said cheerily:

"Well, I think it ought to be most carefully considered. I know some people in the City, and if I can be of any use to you, do let me know at once. I should be very glad to help, if I can."

And that night, in Robert Arthur's Pacific dreams, John played the part of a gentle islander, dusky but recognisable, pointing with a faithful forefinger to the sharks in the offing, and loyally devoted to the Kloopen interest.

# 4

Two days after this conversation, John was lying awake in bed, thinking about the Kewdinghams. It was half an hour before getting-up time.

He thought about his memorable talk with Bertha. A woman's words, he said to himself, have to be translated, not from one language to another, but from one sense to another. You must form your opinion of a woman (if you think an opinion is necessary) by observing what she does, not by listening to what she says. Obviously Bertha was very fond of him. Suppose that Bobby really did go to the Marquesas? No!—it was impossible. Anyone could see the shark business was only a piece of bluff. And yet—was it only bluff? The Van Kloopens were solid people with a big reputation. He would see Jack Wainwright and find out if he knew anything about Mr. Sundale and his Pacific fishery.

Again he thought of Bertha. He was no professional Don Juan, in spite of his lurking cynicism, and he was really fond of this poor woman, really falling in love. She had a lot of intelligence and she was quick and responsive. Thirteen years of virtuous married life—and with a husband like Bobby Kewdingham! It was positively tragic. The best years of her life miserably wasted. Who would blame her if she contemplated a little diversion?

John tumbled luxuriously in his warm bedclothes. The landlady knocked at the door.

After breakfast he rang up the garage and told them to get his car ready and bring it round. Soon after twelve o'clock he was in Shufflecester.

That was on a Friday. On the following Tuesday he was in Shufflecester again.

God bless the family! It's a fine institution; you ought to keep in touch with it. Mrs. Poundle-Quainton was delighted with John. So nice of him, she said, to take Bertha out in his car; it wasn't often that she got a treat. Which was perfectly true.

And where had they been? Oh, such a long way!—all over the South Downs. That was a slight exaggeration, for the car had been standing for three hours in a disused gravel-pit.

Then Bertha went up to stay in London for a day or two with her sister-in-law, and of course she had lunch with John in Margaretta Terrace. Was there a mild suspicion, faintly discernible, in the attitude of the Shufflecester family? "Rather eccentric, my dear," Aunt Bella said with a glint of disapproval, "but things are so different nowadays."

Robert Arthur was clearly disturbed, and yet he could not admit the nature of his disturbance. He was jealous in a perverted, peppery way, a dog-in-the-manger way.

He did not know what to make of John. After all, John had been as good as his word; he had made enquiries about Mr. Sundale and the Van Kloopens, and the result of those enquiries had been moderately reassuring. Indeed, he had been far more active than Robert in this matter; he had procured books from the steamship companies and had found out all about the Marquesas. But then, John had a Dutch grandmother. When a man has a Dutch grandmother, you cannot very well be too careful.

Instead of returning to Shufflecester after her two days' visit, Bertha was persuaded by Phoebe to stay in London for another night. Phoebe had three tickets for the first performance of Sulzer Bollard's new comedy, *The Apricot Uncle*, and so she took John and Bertha to see the play, and they had supper at the Gilded Lily afterwards, and everything was delightful.

Nothing is unimportant in a reasoned theory of causation. A mere hint, the shadow of a thought, is enough to start a blaze of jealousy, enough to change or subvert the whole course of a life. This innocent extension of Bertha's visit, a thing of no visible consequence, flung a fatal spark into the mind of Robert Arthur.

# Chapter V

## 1

Mr. Kewdingham had received a telegram from his wife informing him that she would not return until Friday afternoon. That was all very well, but when he came down to breakfast on Friday morning he was decidedly annoyed. His father had breakfast in his own room, but it was only a few days before Christmas and his son Michael was home for the holidays. The table was, therefore, laid for two.

Mr. Kewdingham gloomily opened his *Daily Post*, and what should he see in it but a long article by John, with a portrait of the author. The article was called "A One-Way Universe", and it was a popular version of John's theory of cosmic expansion. As he looked at this article, at the portrait, at the big headlines, Mr. Kewdingham felt suddenly angry.

All this talk of cavity-radiation, of spectroscopic velocities, of orbital planes and so forth—what infernal nonsense! Any man versed in the wisdom of Atlantis would reject these ideas without hesitating for a moment. Those who built the Pyramids, they were the men who knew the secret of the stars; and pray, what did they care for cavity-radiation? It was not by such a vain effusion of words that a man could penetrate the mysteries of the Universe. A "One-Way

Universe", indeed! What a shoddy, debased conception of the supreme realities!

Mr. Kewdingham, disciple of Paracelsus and of Swedenborg, read the article with many snorts of rage. What could be in more execrable taste than John's libellous picture of the Universe? And what could be more offensive than his style, at once condescending and arrogant? Look at this, for example:

"I must ask my readers to consider for a moment the nature of atomic nuclei. It is not easy to get a mental image of a thing so infinitely minute, yet so inconceivably energetic. Think of the Haymarket Theatre, and imagine, inside the auditorium, a swarm of a dozen lively bees…"

How could a man write such twaddle? The whole thing was an outrage, a bit of cheap advertisement. "Mr. John Harrigall, who is well known as the author of *The Marble Onion*…"

The idea of John advertising himself by means of the Universe was too much for Mr. Kewdingham. A dark stream of accumulated hostility began to filter through all the crevices of his mind, a whole mob of nasty thoughts began to jostle about in the obscurity of subliminal slush.

Michael came clumping down the stairs.

With a gesture of crazy spite, Robert crumpled up the paper and flung it away.

"What are you staring at, you silly oaf?" he said to Michael. "To look at you, nobody would think your father was a gentleman."

## 2

When he came back to his own house, Bertha had returned. He could hear her talking to Michael in the drawing-room.

Kewdingham stood for a moment outside the drawing-room door. That ridiculous article had disturbed him unreasonably. He slipped on the mat, and when he recovered his balance he was trembling most uncomfortably. He went to the bedroom. There was an open suitcase on the floor, and he savagely pulled away a mass of crumpled paper that lay in the bottom of it. What was he looking for? Heaven knows. He felt ashamed of his own crazy impulse. He told himself that he was being a fool again. What he needed, clearly, was a sedative.

So he went to his medicine-cupboard, and presently there was a tinkling among glasses and bottles and a swish of water running through the basin. Robert Arthur swallowed his potion, looked at himself in the mirror, tugged his neck-tie straight, coughed harshly, and walked across the landing to the drawing-room.

Not liking the appearance of his father, Michael scuttled away.

But Robert Arthur said nothing. He went to the window and stared out of it, standing with his back to the room. He had not even glanced at Bertha.

For soldiers at night, sailors in a fog, and women at all times, nothing is more terrible than silence. Bertha had not yet taken off her hat and coat; she stood by the fire, clasping and unclasping her fingers nervously. She wanted to run away. She did not know how to begin the conversation. Robert was in a strange new mood, and one that she was incapable of explaining. He appeared to be angry. Well!—They had better have it out, whatever it was. She braced herself for a scene.

"Anything wrong, Bobby?"

"Ha!" cried Robert Arthur, jerking himself round with a snap, as though discovering with surprise that he was not alone. "What? I forgot to ask you—did the man bring the coal the other day?"

"Yes: half a ton, I think."

"Good."

"Phoebe is anxious to know if you have heard from Mr. Sundale."

Robert Arthur did not reply. He walked fiercely to one of his cabinets, opened a drawer and thrust it back, jarring and rattling. He took the lids off three of his cardboard boxes. With glum curiosity he poked his nose into a tinful of expiring beetles, and then he dropped them on the carpet. It was amazing how finely he kept himself under control.

Old father Kewdingham, awake somewhat earlier than usual after his nap, came into the room. Robert Arthur, hunched up on his knees, was recovering the beetles. Bertha stood by the fire-place. The old man, with his lean, red face, his withered arrogance, was yet real and alive and human. Bertha smiled at him pleasantly. At least he was more of a man than the other, fumbling and fiddling over his tin box.

"The traveller has returned—yeh? Home is home, be it never so homely."

Father Kewdingham clicked his teeth as if he was chewing sand.

"A charm from the skies seems to hallow us there—yeh? Well, my dear, I hope you enjoyed yourself in London."

"Very much indeed, thank you," said Bertha. And for the first time in her life she felt really grateful to the old man. There he was, tall and vital in spite of his age, disliking her with a real human sincerity; and this real dislike was a hundred times more desirable than Bobby's horrible evasions and pretences.

As for the other, he was still hunched up on the carpet, looking small and mean and futile as he fumbled about with his tinful of expiring beetles.

## 3

It was curious, how often Doctor Wilson Bagge met Mrs. Kewdingham. He came now and then to see Robert professionally, for Robert's inside often gave him trouble. But he kept on meeting Bertha in the town, and he had more than once taken her out in his car. Indeed, people were beginning to talk.

Then the doctor went a step farther. He asked Mrs. Kewdingham to help him in the choice of new carpets and curtains, new papers, new chair-covers, a new scheme of interior decoration. She came to his house and spent a long time with him, looking at the rooms. Her taste was excellent and her suggestions were of immense value.

They measured the walls and the floors, each holding an end of the tape. They stood together, absorbed in considering the arrangement of chairs and tables, of pictures or piano. The dapper little man twittered and fluttered in shy sparkles of delight; he perched on a rickety step-ladder like a sparrow on a twig; he cocked up his neat little head and waved a two-foot rule in his hand, briskly running here and there as though he was a fairy carpenter with a magic wand, a fairy carpenter at work on Titania's palace.

Somehow or other, Mrs. Kewdingham was frequently seen going in and out of the doctor's house. Patterns had to be examined. Papers were held up on the walls. Bits of chintz were pinned on the backs of chairs. Demure draperies were flung over the nakedness of the piano. Even the kitchen was explored, greatly to the annoyance of the elderly females, Doctor Bagge's cook and housekeeper. "And she a married woman and all!" they said. "Did you ever see the like of it? Ah! little he knows what folk do be saying."

But the doctor was always correct, seldom quitting the tone of unbending formality. He never said anything that he would not have said in the hearing of all Shufflecester. Only sometimes, as when his fingers lightly touched by accident those of Mrs. Kewdingham, that curious blue electric fire quivered for a moment in his eyes.

What was he thinking about? Was he amorous? Or was he only behaving with a lack of discretion? People talked about him, but they could not say that he was being immoral. He was just as neat, kind, formal and reliable as ever. Good old Mrs. Poundle-Quainton shook her venerable head, but she did it in a whimsical way, with little smirks of gentle amusement. It was good for dear Bertha, she said, to have an interest outside her own home; she could see no harm in it, as long as Bertha was careful.

Robert Arthur, of course, saw nothing. He had unlimited confidence in Doctor Bagge, and his jealousy pointed in another direction. But the old man, guided by the vigilant hostility of the aged, saw a good deal, and suspected more than he could see.

He fired off a number of venomous quotations at Bertha, including a spicy bit from *Othello*, and made a senile joke about "An apple a day". It was thus, by proverb or quotation, that he showed his disapproval; he did not like Doctor Bagge, he preferred his own doctor, young Matthews.

One day, as Bertha was busy with her needlework in the drawing-room, the old man came in. He looked at her sternly. Evidently he had prepared a quotation and was about to fire it off. She knew the look: he was assembling his words before he launched them, for the effect of a quotation is lost if it does not flow steadily from the lips. Bertha was partly amused and partly irritated.

"'Tis beauty that doth oft make women proud; 'Tis virtue that doth make them most admir'd." The old gentleman snapped his jaws together and gave her a penetrating glance.

Bertha laughed. She could not help enjoying these attacks. After all, he had the sense never to say anything that was directly offensive.

"Yes, daddy," she said, "but the first line doesn't apply to me, because I'm not beautiful."

## 4

Early in the New Year there was a dreadful scene, catastrophic and decisive, between Robert Arthur and his wife.

It was the day of Michael's party. Some little boys and their mothers were coming to tea.

On the previous evening Robert Arthur had been sadly rattled. He had gaily unfurled the Pacific Ocean upon the hearthrug, and then he had begun to chatter, with unwonted confidence, about Mr. Sundale and the shark business. It was the happy chance of a lifetime. Pamela Chaddlewick had assured him that he was the very man for this adventure, and he was fool enough to say so. Perhaps he wanted to show his wife that he talked about everyday things with Pamela in a spirit of candour and of innocence.

"You see, my dear, I should go out and get everything ready, and then I would send for you and Michael."

"Thank you!" said Bertha.

"Well—I mean—naturally you would have to go where I went. I am sure that you would find the life extremely congenial. There's a French colony at Nukahiva—charming people, so I am told."

"So we have to obey orders, do we?" Unhappy woman!— She could not listen with patience, could not humour the fantasy.

"But how on earth do you expect—"

"How on earth do you expect Michael is going to be educated?"

"Educated? Educated for what? He can go into the business. What's the use of turning him into a bookworm? He will have no need to be ashamed of business if his own father isn't. Life out there will make a man of him."

"And where is all the money coming from?"

"Money! That's how you women always look at things. No enthusiasm; no encouragement. You ought to back me loyally in this—not leave me to fight my way alone. I want my wife by my side, ready to—to—"

"To mend your clothes and cook your dinner."

"Do you think it's clever, to sneer like that? You were talking about money. Well, I am assured that the factory managers will draw anything up to two thousand a year."

"And suppose I would rather stay at home?"

"But you can't. It's impossible." He flicked an inquisitive spider off the edge of his blue Pacific. "A woman can't stay away from her husband."

"Indeed! And may I ask why you should want me?"

"Good Lord!" cried Robert angrily. "Why do you talk like this? You and I have got to stick to each other, through thick and thin, to the bitter end. Can't we give way to each other now and then, if it's necessary?"

He spoke with some reason, for Bertha had never understood the meaning and use of compromise, she had never learnt how to manage her husband instead of fighting him.

"Well, it's a cheerful prospect, isn't it? But I can't see that it matters very much, anyhow. You know quite well that you won't get much nearer to the Pacific Ocean than you are at present—so why need we argue? It's foolish to lose our tempers over a mere fantasy. There are quite enough real things to worry about."

She was brutal, and she knew it. Her nerves and her patience were giving way. So when Robert got up the next morning he was already cross and ruffled.

## 5

After lunch on that fatal day Robert Arthur went for a walk. It was about half-past three when he returned. His walk had not been enjoyable. He had been driven off a potato-patch, after some altercation with a rude lout; and he had fallen into a muddy ditch. He was therefore charged with high explosive, approaching the climax of a mental disturbance which had been going on for several days.

Bertha was in the dining-room, preparing the table for the party. Michael was in his room, tidying himself. Martha was changing her dress. The old man had gone out to have tea with a neighbour.

Robert Arthur walked into the dining-room, and the awful scene began abruptly, without a sound or a signal of warning. No casual observer could possibly have said how or why it started.

Kewdingham looked at his wife. She was arranging a little pile of crackers, brightly-coloured flimsy things, in the middle of the table. Her head was bent, and the light from the window fell on her mass of coppery hair, making it look almost crimson. Robert Arthur stood by the door. He said nothing, but all at once he began to tremble with insane anger. She looked up at him.

"Why, Bobby—"

A flush of hot blood came into her cheeks and then faded out again. She held a yellow cracker in her hand, gay with frills of silver tinsel, and having, in the middle, the grotesque image of a policeman.

"Bobby, what's the matter with you?"

Robert Arthur was dithering. Had it not been for a nasty animal quality in his rage he would have been ridiculous. He looked as though he would shake to pieces, and he was grinning with anger. In a high keckling voice he spluttered out:

"What right had you to throw away money on all that frippery?"

He pointed unsteadily to a number of little toys and a few pretty decorations at the corners of the table.

She stared at him blankly. For the first time, he was making her feel afraid.

"Well! Answer me, can't you?"

"I don't understand. Why are you so unreasonable, Bobby? It's Michael's party, and we have all these people coming in. You knew all about it, didn't you?"

"You—pff!—you whippety-snippety little nothing! Who the devil gave you leave to throw all that money away? Who are you, to play the grand lady with your presents and your kickshaws? I won't have it, I tell you! Pff!—" The words blew out of him in a kind of puthering spray.

Bertha's incipient fears were overcome by a rush of anger.

"Surely, when I am entertaining people in my own house—"

"Your own house! Your own house!" He raised a jerking arm and swung it vaguely in the air. "Your house, did you say? Let me assure you, my lady, this house isn't yours; it's mine; and so is all the money you have been flinging about. If you want money to spend, you had better get it some other way. You had better go to your dear John Harrigall and ask him—"

"How dare you, Bobby!" She was glowing with a swift, uncontrollable hatred. "How dare you speak to me in such a way! Your insult is foolish, if it is not unforgivable. I cannot say, but I feel now that I shall never forgive you. And so you tell me that I am nothing! At any rate, I am the mistress of the house—not a position to be proud of, God knows! But one that does give me definite rights. We are supposed to be a civilised people. I tell you frankly, when I am entertaining my friends—"

"Entertaining! What the devil have you to do with entertaining? I suppose it's John who puts all these fine ideas into your head. Why don't you go—"

"I shall not stay any longer in this house, at any rate, if you persist in behaving like a lunatic."

"Very well, then—go! Get out of it! Get out of it, you little devil! Do you suppose I care?"

He came towards her with his fist raised to the level of his shoulder, and then for a moment they stared at each other without moving or speaking.

A door was gently closed in the upper part of the house, and there came a sound of shuffling feet on the staircase. Martha had come down to the landing, afraid to come any lower, but listening with intense excitement. Her sympathies, up to this point, had been sometimes on one side and sometimes on the other.

Suddenly, with a downward fling of his arm, Kewdingham struck heavily the edge of the table. In that action the psychologist may discern a compromise, and perhaps a lucky one. Two of the little toys, a tin motor-car and a clockwork rabbit, fell on to the floor and were broken.

He laughed gruesomely.

"I'll teach you who's master here. You f-f-fool. You can go and tell him all about it, if you like. You—pff!—"

Bertha moved back towards the table. Her face, though white as chalk, was totally without expression, her movement had the mechanical precision of one acting under hypnosis. She kept her eyes on Kewdingham; but there was a sudden flick of her right hand, and she was holding a knife.

She did not raise the knife; she merely held it, as though she was guarding herself.

And then they sprang together, and he was twisting her arm, so that she screamed with pain and the knife dropped with a rattle on the polished boards. No one could have explained that hideous encounter, no one could have said whether it was caused by mutual hatred or by mutual fear.

In three-quarters of an hour, Bertha, pale and a little strained, though very charming, was receiving her visitors.

"My dear," said Mrs. Henderson, a motherly soul, "how cold your hand is! Are you feeling quite well?"

"Perfectly, thank you," Bertha replied. "I've been icing those cakes in the back kitchen—a most horribly draughty place."

# 6

Bertha went up to her room early, complaining of a head-ache. At first she tried to calm herself by a purely mechanical exercise of thought. But that was no good: a knowledge of something fatal thrust into the centre of her mind and would not be denied.

When she sat alone with Robert after supper there had been no apology, no explanation. They were past all that. Now there could be no recovery, no compromise or truce. She had been driven beyond the limits of her endurance. Something in the crazy face of Robert Arthur, when he stood glaring at her, had swept away every trace of affection, every thought of mercy, every hope of settlement. A primitive hatred fixed her in a cold, unswerving purpose. She faced the stark reality of her design with calmness. Her mind was made up. Thoughts formerly repelled were now admitted, a vague desire gave place to a desperate plan of action. She could bear it no longer. She would kill him.

Perhaps she had really been meaning to do this for some time. Perhaps that was why she had been thinking, with such an odd, automatic persistence, about poison. Perhaps that was why the unaccountable affair of the wrong bottle had made such a curious impression on her mind.

Anyhow, she knew, at last, what she was going to do. And this knowledge, appalling as it was, gave her a grateful sense of tranquillity.

If it had not been for this new fear of the man, she might have gone on, even without hope; she might have repressed the lurking impulse. Fear, as it so often does, drove a desperate mind to a fatal decision. It was not the resolution of a criminal; it was the unavoidable rebound of a nature overloaded with wrongs and finally governed by the necessity not so much for revenge as for mere preservation.

# Chapter VI

## 1

At the very time when Mrs. Kewdingham had reached her fatal decision, Doctor Bagge was carrying out the most memorable of all his experiments.

It will be remembered that he had been investigating the properties of aluminium. His researches had been eminently successful. Now he was testing in the laboratory a marvellous compound of alum. The nature of this compound is not to be disclosed to the public, nor would it be comprehended by the general reader. If the medical profession are interested, they will find an analysis of a rather similar compound in the great work of Professor Wolfgang Druffelheim (vol. VI, p. 642 ff.). At the same time, it is only fair to state that many of our own experts (Brill, Chesterton and Rawlings, for example) do not agree with Druffelheim in his account of the chloric hydrate.

The medical use of Bagge's alum compound, as the doctor knew very well, might be dangerous; it might also lead to the most important discoveries.

When he got past the laboratory stage he would give it a trial. He would choose a suitable patient, and he would give him suitable doses. As a matter of fact, he had chosen the patient almost before he had evolved the mixture.

The compound, suitably prepared, would be administered to Robert Arthur Kewdingham.

There would be no difficulty in giving the new aluminium solution, or anything else, to Robert Arthur. He was a gastric subject with a groggy heart and a chronic disease of the kidneys, and he had a passion for swallowing drugs and medicines, whether of his own mixing and prescribing or otherwise. What is more, he believed in Bagge and frequently consulted him, in spite of the doctor's warnings about the highly dangerous and immoral use of prohibited chemicals. He found in Bagge an infallible source of relief.

If Bagge was in many ways the ideal poisoner, Kewding-ham appeared to be in every way the ideal victim.

And as he meditated upon his forthcoming experiment, the doctor grew more and more precise, more perkily formal, more quaintly restrained. Only when he was alone in his dispensary, watching a lovely blue liquor foam and whirl in a glass burette—only then would he allow himself to whistle a gay, catchy little improvisation.

## 2

In the meantime, the situation of Mrs. Kewdingham became more and more intolerable. Her insufferable husband would have driven her crazy, had it not been for her resolution. Her father-in-law glared at her in his red, beaky way, like a bloody old vulture. Old Mrs. Poundle-Quainton sparkled with glassy eyes of affected indulgence. Mrs. Pyke wrapped herself in a cloak of stuffy disapproval. Of all the family in Shufflecester, only Uncle Richard was really amiable, but as he disliked his brother and his nephew he seldom came to see them.

By the middle of January, Bertha decided to employ lead acetate. She knew already that she could buy it in any quantity from any chemist without having to make a record of her purchases. She knew that it was a soft white powder with a sugary taste, a powder which could be readily added to food or beverage. Reference to an encyclopaedia in the Shufflecester Free Library taught her that she would need patience, small doses would have to be administered over a long period. The symptoms of lead poisoning are distinctive—but then, was there any reason why Bobby should not dose himself with acetate? In the event of any question, there would be no difficulty in making this appear highly probable. Moreover, the symptoms are frequently modified. Once a woman has made up her mind, she thinks clearly enough.

She felt no scruples whatsoever. It was necessary to take many precautions, to be prepared for many emergencies. Her designs were regulated by intelligence; she did not go rushing ahead, nor did she make any conspicuous blunder. Everything was foreseen—everything except what actually happened...

Had it not been for the choice of *Plumbi Acetas*—and it was purely accidental—we should probably have known nothing of the Kewdingham drama, or the drama would have been comparatively simple and unexciting. After all, women do occasionally kill their husbands—and, less often, their lovers. What is peculiar in this case of Robert Kewdingham is not the mere fact of murder, but the extraordinary conflict of design which is presently to be revealed.

### 3

On the 21st of January Bertha went up to London for the day.

She went to no fewer than seventeen pharmaceutical stores, and at each of these she bought two ounces of lead acetate. "I want it for a hair-wash," she said. It was quite easy. Sugar of lead is frequently, indeed usually, sold in these small quantities. She dropped the little packages into a suitcase, neat little white packages with dabs of red sealing-wax on the flaps.

Then she went, by appointment, to have tea with John Harrigall. He had got a new cover of blue Indian silk for the divan.

John was very charming. He had the dangerous appeal of apparent simplicity, audaciously gentle and respectfully enterprising. Love, with him, was a question of mutual discovery, mutual inductance.

He insisted on Bertha staying in London until the time of departure of the last available train, and he took her to have supper with him at the Gilded Lily.

Whom should they see at the Gilded Lily but Mrs. Chaddlewick, who was staying with her mother in London. She was sitting at a secluded table with a grey-haired, fox-faced man, and she rose with a yelp of surprise and came over to have a word with John and Bertha.

"Oh, my dears!" cried Mrs. Chaddlewick in a trill of excitement (she was drinking champagne). "How perfectly marvellous! Fancy seeing you here! How nice you look! Where's Mr. Kewdingham? I've been to see my dear little Motoyoshi, and he has told me the most *incredible* things about my life—he's too frightfully weird for anything. Supper in London is gorgeous, isn't it? I'm going back to Shufflecester to-morrow; George is meeting me with the car. So I do hope we shall see you soon?"

Her piccolo notes came tinkling out with painful audibility.

"That's poor Colonel Billit having supper with me. So sad, my dears. He's got an inferiority complex. You know—quite a lot of nice people have them now. George met a man who told him that anyone who had been at the relief of Kut would have an inferiority complex. I'm trying to cheer him up a little: he's the dearest old boy, when you get to know him.

George likes him tremendously. His wife died just before Christmas. He lost his hat in a taxi, and we had to simply roar with laughter."

So she went on chirruping away for a dreadful minute, while John stood up looking rather grim and peevish.

"I don't like that woman," he said, when she had gone back to her colonel.

"Bobby's very fond of her," said Bertha. "She pretends to understand all that Atlantis nonsense of his. I think they are flirting in a silly sort of way. I don't know, and I can't say that I care."

"Bobby flirting? Oh, surely not!"

"Well, it doesn't matter, does it?" She looked at him in her strange, whimsical way—intimate, though still inscrutable.

John, with a broad smile of amusement, looked across at Mrs. Chaddlewick.

And as he did so, Mrs. Chaddlewick, who was obviously explaining all about John and Bertha to the colonel, looked up and met his glance. To Mrs. Chaddlewick, that glance was unmistakable and unforgivable. For the second time she made up her mind that she would get even with him—and with Bertha too. After all, what business had they to make fun of her? They were not in a very good position for throwing stones. Mrs. Chaddlewick was not such a fool as she appeared to be; at least she had the ordinary feminine perceptions.

## 4

Two days later, at about half-past eleven in the morning, Mrs. Chaddlewick met Mr. Kewdingham in Shufflecester High Street. Within a few minutes of this happy encounter (which may or may not have been accidental) they were drinking coffee in the Omar Khayyám Restaurant.

"Oh, do you know?" piped Mrs. Chaddlewick, "I met your wife and Mr. Harrigall in London on Tuesday. I expect she has told you all about it. Having supper at the Gilded Lily. They seemed to be having a frightfully good time. I was there with a very dear old friend of ours, Colonel Billit. Have you ever been to the Gilded Lily? It's one of those terribly chic places."

Robert Arthur frowned.

"John Harrigall?" he said. "Oh, yes!—he's always been like a young brother—"

Pamela noted the frown with secret pleasure; obviously she had scored a hit. She guessed, quite correctly, that Robert knew nothing about the supper at the Gilded Lily.

"Young brother?" said Pamela with a giggle. "He wasn't behaving like a young brother exactly. I say, you know—you're rather confiding, aren't you?"

It has to be assumed that such impudence was warranted by the degree of intimacy established between Robert Arthur and Mrs. Chaddlewick. From any other person, these words might very well have thrown Robert into one of his tantrums. As it was, he looked gloomy and bitter as he replied:

"I've always treated him like a brother, anyhow. His mother was awfully decent to me when I was a kid."

He thought of the "One-Way Universe". An ugly, though not unreasonable, suspicion rose up in his mind again. But he made an effort to appear composed.

"John's a good fellow. I'm very fond of him."

Mrs. Chaddlewick, however, was not deceived. She knew well enough that she had shot a poisoned arrow.

## 5

And now the conduct of Robert Arthur was really abominable. Sheer brutality was too exhausting, but he nagged and wrangled, he jeered and quibbled, he barked and he bickered from morning to night. His inside was evidently deteriorating. He complained of pains and of spasms, of headaches, dizziness, vertigo, staggers, nausea. Very often he went up to his father's room, and there the two men sat together, talking in a querulous vague way about the rottenness of things, the rottenness of everything, in fact.

The old man, who blamed his daughter-in-law for the discomfort of Robert Arthur, became even more frigidly and rigidly aloof. But he renewed his oblique attacks.

He wrote the most unpleasant quotations on slips of paper, and put them in Bertha's work-basket. Sometimes he handed them to her with affected courtesy. It seemed as if he knew by heart all the bitter and perverse things which have ever been written about women, all the hollow, sentimental cantings and rantings in praise of chastity, prudence, motherhood, mother love, duty and faith—all the shoddy gibble-gabble by which righteous men have tried to keep their females in order. In these literary assaults he made a masterly use of Shakespeare and the Bible, and it was extraordinary how he knew where to go for the most rancid morsels of libel or satire.

Doctor Wilson Bagge visited the house more frequently and more professionally. He looked gravely at Robert and begged him to be careful.

"You smoke too much, my dear fellow," said the doctor. "You don't get enough exercise. I shall have to keep an eye on you. We can't have you going on like this—tut, no! We shall have to do something about it. Now look here!—I'm going to give you a new medicine, and you must promise to take it regularly. Then we shall see a difference, I think."

And he smiled brightly, tilting his little head on one side and looking for all the world like a small, intelligent sparrow.

Not perceiving clearly all the causes of his disorder, Robert was inclined to believe it purely intestinal. He thanked the doctor with genuine warmth.

It's very good of you, Bagge," he said. "Really, I don't know where I should be if it wasn't for you. It is particularly unfortunate that I should be feeling unwell, just when I am considering a new venture." He told the doctor all about Sundale and his wonderful sharks.

As for the doctor, he listened with his unwavering bright gravity.

"Not a bad idea, Kewdingham—speaking with due reserve, of course. But you mustn't go too fast. You will have to stay at home for a considerable time—oh, yes! for quite a considerable time, let me assure you, my dear fellow. We shall have to brace you up. We shall have to give you a tonic—oh, indeed we shall! Leave it to me. I know exactly what I intend to give you, and I shall make it up myself. I propose to give you a very special and a very considered treatment. In the meantime, the diet—eh?—come, come, now! The diet…"

So Robert wrote to Mr. Sundale, and Mr. Sundale answered him at considerable length, and even suggested an early meeting in London.

"Nonsense, Robert!" said the old man. "How can you think of such a thing at your time of life? And what would happen to me?"

And when the Poundle-Quaintons were told of the shark business they were filled with dismay.

"My dear Bobby!" cried Aunt Bella, "you are building castles in the air. I'm sure this man is not to be trusted. Dear Phoebe does know such very peculiar people. You had better make enquiries. It doesn't sound at all right. Sharks, indeed!"

But the more he was opposed, the more obstinately he clung to his idea. It was, he kept on saying, the chance of a lifetime, and he would be a fool if he let it go by. After all, he did not propose to end his days in the Pacific. In a few years he would be able to retire with an ample fortune and with a large holding in the company. Those who were first in the field would naturally get most out of it, and there was no doubt that Sundale was a remarkably shrewd man who knew what he was doing. (That, indeed, was true enough.) Even the Rule Britannia League and the great collection were matters of secondary interest. (But pray consider what a collection a man could form in those remote islands—what a stupendous or stupefying variety of objects!) And Athu-na-Shulah, the Priest of Atlantis, retired into the shade of his vast antiquity.

Of course, Mrs. Chaddlewick encouraged him. By flattery of a kind most acceptable to the middle-aged she persuaded him that he was a man fitted for adventure. She egged him on—though knowing well that he would never go—as a lady of the Romantic Age might have egged on her dashing knight.

Rosy coral and blue lagoons, white cargoes and wailing ukuleles—how simply thrilling! The mere thought of it quite melted Mrs. Chaddlewick. Her attitude, frivolous as it may seem, was not without importance in the unwinding of the drama. She urged Robert to see Mr. Sundale again, and by so doing became the unwitting instrument of destiny. Without this persuasion it is probable that Robert would have contented himself with exchanging letters until everything had fizzled out.

So things went on until near the end of January. Locked in Bertha's private box were seventeen unopened packets of lead acetate, like a supply of ammunition in reserve. Although her resolution was unshaken, she hesitated a little before making the first move. Something might happen…

Late at night, Doctor Wilson Bagge worked in his dispensary, a trim, busy little figure in a white jacket. Atropos clicked her shears.

Then, on a Wednesday morning, there came a big envelope from Mr. Sundale addressed to Robert. Inside the envelope were a lot of thin papers, Roneo copies of a prospectus, a number of perplexing diagrams, and a blue document with "Confidential" written across the top of it.

Mr. Sundale had sent a covering letter, in which he explained that he was receiving more applications than he could deal with at present, and so he was moving to a larger office in the Kingsway. He felt, however, that Mr. Kewdingham had a prior claim. He was glad to say that he could now offer him a quite exceptionally good post as a manager, though he could not say precisely when he would be called on to attend to his preliminary duties, or where he would be eventually dispatched.

If he would read carefully the enclosures, he would see…In view of the tremendous number of applicants, the company had decided that no appointments were to be made without the deposit of a small premium. The stipulated premium was the absurdly low figure of one thousand pounds, in exchange for which the applicant was to receive five hundred cumulative preference shares in the company.

But since Mr. Kewdingham was a man of such exceptional value, in view of his technical knowledge, Mr. Sundale had induced his brother directors to accept, in this case, a premium of a mere five hundred pounds, carrying with it, none the less, an allotment of five hundred preference shares. Mr. Kewdingham would be good enough to say nothing about this to anyone who might take advantage of the information.

Mr. Kewdingham would be interested to observe so distinguished a name as that of General Sir Hashall Mewken on the list of directors. Mr. Sundale would beg Mr. Kewdingham to think it over carefully after reading the prospectus—he did not want him to lack the most complete information—and he had no doubt that he would appreciate the wonderful opportunity which presented itself.

Also, Mr. Sundale hoped that he might be allowed to say that he was acting as a friend of the family, since he had known the Misses Kewdingham for many years, and he asked Mr. Kewdingham to treat the offer in strict confidence. If, after consideration, he decided that he would rather not take up any active duties, but would prefer to be an ordinary shareholder, they might possibly come to terms which would be highly to Mr. Kewdingham's advantage. At the same time he would point out that a factory manager had the almost certain prospect of making a substantial fortune. The life in the islands might be described as idyllic, and the duties were not onerous.

If Mr. Kewdingham would like to discuss any further details, Mr. Sundale would urge him to come immediately to London, as all the shares would be allotted and all the appointments confirmed within ten days' time.

This, of course, was much too long and much too explanatory for a straightforward business letter. But Kewdingham treated it as a striking proof of his own importance.

"Bertha! Sew this button on my grey coat, will you? I'm going up to London to-morrow."

# Chapter VII

## 1

John Harrigall had lunched with a friend at the Athenaeum. There had been a long conference in the smoking-room, and it was about four o'clock when he crossed Pall Mall, intending to go to the London Library.

It was a horrible tempestuous afternoon. A stiff north-westerly gale, slapping and buffeting the people in the street, came blasting along with showers of cold, stinging rain. As John reached the pavement on the north side of Pall Mall a squall made him duck his head and blew him off his course. While he was thus bending to the storm he bumped into someone who was coming towards him.

"Sorry!" cried John without looking round, and he was about to proceed on his way when the other man touched his arm.

"Hullo! Why—don't you know me?"

John slewed round in a jiffy, tottering a little as the tempest whanged him on the back. He saw Robert Arthur Kewdingham.

It could be seen at once that Kewdingham was violently agitated. It was not so easy to say whether he was angry or surprised or frightened, or for what reason he was in such a pother. He was loose, disarticulate, without purpose or stability, a shivering phantasm of a man, a patched-up sort of thing, a thing which might be expected to fall to pieces or dissolve at any moment, blowing about like a wisp of a soul in limbo.

"Why—John!" Robert Arthur clutched his crumpled hat as the wind whipped and whistled along the street, and it seemed as if hat and head might blow away together. "Look here—I particularly want to see you."

Poor Robert had come up to Phoebe's flat on the previous evening, and he had just had a talk with Mr. Sundale. Things were not so jolly after all, and Mr. Sundale had been curiously insistent about the premium. Kewdingham said that he could not possibly get hold of five hundred pounds, and Mr. Sundale said that he could arrange for a loan, if that was the only difficulty. But, of course, it was not the only difficulty. There were many things a man had to consider before he engaged himself in such a venture. Mr. Sundale was very friendly, but he was obviously disappointed about the premium, though Kewdingham did all he could to show this excellent man how much he appreciated his generosity. Yes; he did realise the extraordinary kindness of Mr. Sundale...a great opportunity...oh, quite! And then Mr. Sundale kept breaking off his conversation in order to speak on the telephone, for he was tremendously busy, talking in the coolest way about hundreds of thousands of pounds. It was curious that he thought so much about a mere five hundred; but then, as he pointed out, he had to observe the rules of the company. At last he said he was sorry, but several people were waiting to see him: would Mr. Kewdingham ring up, or send him a telegram, if he decided to join in? There were still a few days...No, no! Not at all!...He had been delighted! And yet there was a touch of petulance in the twitching black eyebrows (or was it a touch of regret?)

which puzzled Robert and gave him a nasty feeling inside. He came away from Sundale's office in a flurry of disjointed ideas. The more he thought of the interview, the more he was flurried, and the darker the assemblage of perplexing notions which tumbled in his brain.

At the moment of his collision with John, Robert had decided, after half an hour of aimless wandering, to walk up to Piccadilly for a bus. But now fate took charge of the poor man, forcing him to an encounter which he dreaded and yet desired. Well!—the sooner the better. They might as well get it over and have done with it.

The two men did not shake hands with each other. Kewdingham drew up the collar of his coat, while John set his hat more firmly on his head. In both gestures there was a hint of preparation for combat.

"Hullo, Bobby! I had no idea you were in town. Here—let's turn up Waterloo Place, out of this confounded gale."

They both knew they were on the edge of a crisis, for John had perceived Robert's jealousy, and Bertha had told him that she believed his letter had been confiscated.

Of course, John was not seriously disturbed, he took heart from the evident uneasiness of the other, and he believed himself in a good position to receive the attack—if there was one. He had been a bit startled, it is true, by the unexpected appearance of Robert, but now he was rapidly organising a line of defence. He would simply make a flat denial. Why on earth hadn't Bertha told him that Bobby was coming to town?

"I have been wanting to see you for some time," cried Robert hoarsely, as they turned into the shelter of Waterloo Place. "A family matter of some importance—perhaps you can guess what it is. Eh?—How are you getting on with your new book?"

"Oh, pretty well, I think. It's not easy for a man to judge his own work, you know. Will you come to my rooms?"

"No, thanks. I'm in rather a hurry. Only a few words—Brr!" He scowled and shivered as the rain trickled down his neck, and again he tugged up his collar.

For a few seconds they walked in silence. The gale rushed whooping and booming overhead. Above the uncouth masses of London architecture the low clouds tore apart, disclosing a strip of jagged, pale watery sky. There was a spluther of hail. A shaft of greenish light fell on the Victory of the Crimea, making her look like a figure of polished ebony.

"We will head for the Park, if you like," said John, and presently they swung round the corner into Jermyn Street.

Had they been of a more resolute complexion they might now have been compared to a brace of duelling rivals, marching to the field of honour. And, indeed, the fact that they were marching to a given place, and for a given, though unspoken, purpose, had a steadying effect upon the nerves of Robert Arthur. There was a comforting sense of order and inevitability in what they were doing, and the walk to the Park would give him a respite and enable him to prepare himself. It is so much easier to prepare yourself than to plunge into action. Thus, he thought, a man feels when he is going up to the front line—cool, determined. He had never been to the front line, but he knew what it must be like. He talked in a rambling way of trivial family affairs, and John answered him carelessly.

Evidently Robert had made up his mind to have it out within the sight and hearing of passers-by. He did not wish to be left alone with John. But he did wish the weather had not been so devilish.

The wind blew sharply along the Ritz Arcade as they passed through it. They were tossed about in the loud commotion of the storm.

## 2

Cuffed, thumped, shaken, deafened, lashed, harried by the violence of the gale, Robert Arthur and his cousin entered the Green Park.

Inside the Park, twigs were being snapped off the bare black trees and whisked and whirled through the air and over the ground. Bits of paper, sticks and leaves were dancing on the asphalt in a scurrying rattle. A few people were scattered along the walks, all stooping and staggering, either fighting up into the wind or driven before it.

What with the roar of the gale and the still audible thunder of Piccadilly traffic, Robert had much difficulty in assembling his thoughts and in giving them expression. They had walked for some time, and had reached the desolate fountain of soft and mouldering stone at the cross-ways, when he opened the attack:

"As a matter of fact, I wish to speak to you on the subject of Bertha."

"Bertha?" said John. "Ah, yes! She's quite well, I hope."

"You know what I mean," shouted Robert, giving himself the order to advance while the storm howled about them. "Let me put it in this way—let me ask you a question. I want you to suppose—"

A furious puff of wind, lifting dead leaves and a gritty dust, lashed him full in the face.

"Suppose a man discovers that someone is making love to his wife. I am not thinking of myself. I want you to understand that I am not thinking of myself at all. Impossible! But just suppose—what would you advise him to do?"

"Well," replied John, raising his voice in the hurricane, "it would rather depend on the other man, wouldn't it? As you are not personally concerned, you must forgive me if I appear cynical. There's money to be considered, the social point of view, and all sorts of things—if you mean to imply criminal intimacy. But why do you ask me such an extraordinary question? I thought you had something to say about Bertha."

"What! Do you mean to say you wouldn't advise him to thrash the cad?"

He scudded over to the edge of the grass and then rolled back into the fairway.

John smiled. "My dear chap! Without overwhelming proof—and even then I shouldn't recommend violence: it's obsolete, and expensive, too. As for a mere flirtation, if that's what you mean—why not leave it alone?"

Kewdingham wavered. Then he decided to attack more openly. His check with Mr. Sundale had made it necessary for him to assert himself. They were in sight of Constitution Hill, and he looked up at the monstrous winged lady in the chariot. The top of an arch, he thought, is a curious place for a chariot exercise, but if you have a pair of good wings you are safe enough.

"Look here, John; you're getting away from the point. You know perfectly well what I'm referring to. I am not the man to play fast and loose with. I say what I think. It is not my custom to beat about the bush."

John had made up his mind that he would fight on the defensive as long as he could, and turn the tables if he got a chance. He was an easy-going man, he did not positively hate Kewdingham, and he would avoid a quarrel if he could.

But the heart of John was capable of hardening. The last observations of Kewdingham made him feel angry. He would not allow Robert to bully him. A sense of outrage began to quicken his pulse. He shouted in a louder voice:

"I have not the least idea of what you are driving at. I never said you were a man to be trifled with, did I? No doubt you would make short work of anyone who crossed your path. But that is neither here nor there. You tell me you have something to say about Bertha. Well; out with it! Is anything wrong? Do you want my help or advice?"

"Oh, go to blazes!" roared Kewdingham, giving way to a gust of rage. "Will you have the decency to behave like a man, and own up? Why do you persist in dodging the question? This is not the time for your silly jokes. It's the time for straight speaking. A man doesn't make silly jokes about honour."

They had turned about on Constitution Hill, and were now scurrying back over the Park with the wind rattling and booming astern. They could hear each other with less effort.

"Good Lord! I'm not trying to make silly jokes about honour or anything else. But what has honour to do with all this nonsense? I'm sorry to say it, but you *are* talking nonsense, as you know very well. I wish you would come to the point, if there is one. It's not a very pleasant evening for a stroll, and I have some work to do. What are you talking about? What do you mean by owning up? Will you be so kind as to tell me? I ask you again, is there anything wrong?"

"Confound you!—you—you damned Dutchman!" Robert's temper was getting out of hand. Yet he observed that several people were passing within hailing distance.

John stiffened like a porcupine. His policy was forgotten as he retorted sharply:

"I will not allow you to insult me."

"I'm not insulting you. Can't I say what I think? I am trying to make you understand—make you understand—"

"Then perhaps you will be good enough to speak plainly."

"I've been speaking plainly enough in all conscience. If you were half a man you would have answered me. You would have been straight with me, as I am with you. Straight—English—that's what I want. Do you want me to come to the point, as you call it? Very well, then—here's the point. What do you imagine my wife is, eh? Answer me, will you?"

John turned his head towards the blunt mass of Buckingham Palace, the dim towers of Westminster. Upon my word! he thought, this man is a crazy fool—I can't stand very much more of it. And he really did feel, for a moment, as though he would like to kill him. With a considerable jerk of the will he recovered his balance.

"Do be more sensible, Bobby. I am fond of Bertha, as you know. I hope we are good friends. As for what I think of her—since you ask me—I think she's a very intelligent and a very charming woman, and a very good one. But what is the point of your question?"

"We'll have no more of this, if you please. Things have gone too far. People are talking. You come to my house and receive my hospitality, and now you have the damned impudence to tell me to my face that you're fond of my wife."

"What is the matter?" cried John. "Why are you trying to pick a quarrel with me? We have always been friends; but I tell you frankly, there are limits to my patience."

"Oh, very fine!" yelled Kewdingham, making an effort to walk steadily. "You go on with your pretences, like a sly lying Dutchman, and you know quite well what I am talking about. Can't you see—"

This was more than John could stand.

"Get at it and have done with it! If I am a lying Dutchman, then what are you? A muddled, pigheaded Irishman! Put an end to these futile insinuations of yours. I won't have any more of this ridiculous ambiguity and these foolish insults. You have sworn at me and called me names. Now then!—Will you explain your conduct?"

He knew that his temper was getting out of control, but he did not care. He felt the grand exhilaration of a man discovering his own powers. He had never imagined that he could be in such a splendid temper, such a tuning-up of body and soul in the glory of battle. A lovely pervading warmth ran like a soft fire through his limbs, such a glow as may be felt after hard though healthy exercise. Suddenly he sprang in front of Robert and forced him to look him in the face. There they stood, slanting in the gale like a pair of ruffled chickens. Three girls, hurrying past, looked at them with amusement.

"Listen to me, Bobby. You are willing enough to talk of being a man and all that, but instead of daring to speak honestly you bluster and call names, and you insist on this idiotic prevarication. If you really have anything to say—in God's name, say it!"

Kewdingham recoiled. He glanced angrily at John, but he backed away from him.

John noticed the movement and saw its meaning in a flash. Now was the time to strike hard. Kewdingham was afraid of him.

"Do you dare to insinuate that I have been trying to seduce your wife? Is that the filthy thought which has come into your muddled brain? Out with it, then! Out with it!"

A scurry of icy sleet drove in their faces. It was growing dark. The pale white fires of the lamps began to shine in the stormy twilight.

"You have been playing with her," said Kewdingham vehemently, but with signs of weakening morale.

"Staying with her?" roared John, deafened by the noise of the tempest. "What do you mean?" He moved fiercely towards Robert, staring in his face. "What the devil do you mean?"

"No! I said—*playing*," cried Robert, staggered by John's violence and by the horrid implications of the word.

John saw that he had got the upper hand. He smiled.

But a wonderful change had taken place in him. It seemed as if his blood was thicker, as if the naked fire of anger had licked him into a new shape and given him a new impulse. And he was already sharpening the edge of retaliation. He would get his own back. Any lingering scruples were blown away like the dry sticks in the gale. He swung round again, and they walked on to the fountain at the cross-ways.

"I ask you once more," said John, completely under control, "do you imagine that I would accept your hospitality and then make love to your wife? Is that what you have been getting at, or trying to get at, all the time?"

"I say that you have been flirting. And I am going to put a stop to it. Do you understand?"

"Don't be a fool. Who, or what, has put these outrageous ideas into your head?"

"I know perfectly well—"

"If you are going to say that you know I have been flirting with Bertha, then I tell you that you know nothing of the sort. I think if any other man had dared to insinuate—"

"That's mere bluff. You think you can deceive me."

"Someone has deceived you right enough. You said just now that people had been talking. Good heavens! Can you really suppose that she—your wife—Bertha—is the sort of woman who would—? Well; you remember what you said. As for myself, I have never pretended to be a saint; but do you believe that I would come sneaking into your house to play the dirty game you have suggested? For my own part, I would not care so much. But I can't allow you to wrong a woman who is so loyal to you. And, look here: if people have been stuffing you with nonsense, just let me know who they are, will you?"

He spoke loudly and rapidly. Poor Robert felt a sudden liquefaction of ideas, a dissolution of confidence.

So, jarring and wrangling, but with John definitely on top, they reached again the crest of Constitution Hill and again they turned. By this time the storm was dying down, with a shuddering among the trees and a more spasmodic rattling of twigs. A silver ghost of a moon rode up through the clouds, and was then swallowed in a black mist of advancing hail.

"Yes, yes!" cried Robert Arthur, obscurely feeling himself lost in the meshes of doom. "I see your game. You're trying to slip away from me. You won't look at the facts of the case."

"Nothing of the sort. And what *are* the facts of the case? What *is* the case, anyhow? What has come over you? Are you determined to believe a falsehood, or to wreck your happiness because of some ridiculous mistake, mere lying gossip or malicious invention? I don't know, of course. I don't even know what I am supposed to have done. But you have been wickedly bamboozled."

Kewdingham was being worn down. His main attack was broken, yet he was not without reserves.

"Why should I believe you? I have a right to think as I please."

"You have no right to do an unforgivable injury—"

"I have a right to do and think as I please. What I think about my wife is no business of yours. There is no need for you to interfere, thank you."

"If it comes to rights, then I have an unquestionable right to intervene when I see that you are the victim of a dangerous error—and one that concerns my own honour, too. You have no proof, you have not a scrap of evidence to support your fantastic accusation. Who has forced you to swallow all this nonsense? Will you tell me?"

"Proof! I tell you I've got the proof in my own hands, and if I see fit I will produce it. I will produce it—do you hear? You hardly expected that, did you?"

John did not flinch. He knew that Kewdingham was using idle words, for there was not merely no proof—there was nothing to be proved. Still, it was desirable to be extremely cautious, extremely vigilant.

"You have evidence, you say? If this evidence is at all concerned with me, I will ask you to produce it now—if you can. It is as good a time as any."

Robert promptly changed his front:

"Let us come to a plain understanding. I don't want you to see her again. Or at least, only in a social sort of way. You have been behaving very imprudently, and in such a manner as to encourage a grave scandal—and I won't have it! If you are really Bertha's friend, and mine, you can prove your friendship by keeping at a distance."

"Indeed! I don't see why. That would be lending countenance to all this damned rot. It wouldn't prove any friendship, either for you or for her. It would only prove cowardice and folly."

"I don't say that you are not to call, when I'm there myself." He thought, with a tingle of regret, of John's interest in the great collection. "You may come in for a meal now and then when you're in Shufflecester. But I won't have any more motor drives and all that sort of thing. And I won't have you writing to her and asking her to your rooms and so forth."

He glanced aside at John, and he saw dimly in the twilight the flicker of a smile. Another gust of anger shook him.

"None of your tricks—you little blackguard!"

The sky was clearing. The wings of the lady in the quadriga pricked up over the trees like monstrous black ears, the lights of the traffic gyrated merrily around Hyde Park Corner.

Blackguard! John said nothing. He stiffened himself in a final resolve. He thought of Bertha with her fine appealing eyes, her promise of passion. And he made up his mind. He would not fail Bertha in the hour of need; he would rise up as a willing champion. He was ominously composed.

"Very well, Bobby," he said. "Do as you please."

"Of course I shall." Robert spoke less gruffly and with something like a groan of relief. "You might as well have seen that before. It's a family matter—what?"

Newsboys were bawling, the bowler-hat brigade was hurrying back to suburban quarters, taxi-cabs went swishing down Grosvenor Place. London roared and rumbled all about them as Robert Arthur and his cousin parted company outside the Park.

## 3

When John got back to his Chelsea rooms he felt excited though chilly. He shivered a little, and there was a dry, gritty sensation in his mouth, as though his tongue was being gently galvanised. Perhaps he was going to have an attack of influenza. Or was he shaken up by his row with Kewdingham?

He rang the bell for his landlady, Mrs. Appleton.

"Mrs. Appleton, could you let me have supper at home to-night? I am not going out after all."

The landlady, who was pale, genteel and motherly, looked at John with visible concern.

"Yes, that will be all right, Mr. Harrigall. Excuse me—but are you feeling quite well?"

"Oh, I think so, Mrs. Appleton; I think so. I was foolish enough to walk part of the way back, and it really was frightfully cold."

Still wearing his overcoat he stood with his back to the fire, smiling with reassurance at Mrs. Appleton, who, after a few words about the meal, softly padded out of the room in her discreet slippers.

He had intended to go to the *Chauves Souris* with Jellibun, who writes those delightful bits in the *London Argus*, but he rang up and told him that he was not feeling well.

Actually, after supper, he did feel curiously exalted. The chill had gone, but the excitement remained. Nor was this excitement at all unpleasing. He had never known anything like it before. For the first time in his life he was feeling like a really murderous man. If there is anything which is convincingly virile it is the desire to kill; a desire planted imperishably in the fundamental nature of man, never to be uprooted by laws or punishments or the attitude of society.

Not that John had made up his mind to kill Robert Arthur. No such thing. He was merely in a murderous condition. With proper provocation he would have killed anyone. The new current of hatred was hardening and stiffening a hitherto pliable, indulgent character. When John walked out of the Green Park he was not by any means the John who had walked into it. When he came out he was converted. The devil makes a convert now and then, as well as the other party.

He asked Mr. Appleton (who was not quite as genteel as his wife) if he would be so good as to go out and get him a bottle of brandy.

At half-past ten John was sitting by the fire, thinking.

He thought of Bertha. He thought of the scene in the Park. As he remembered Robert's yellow, contorted face, all puckering up in spasms of idiotic rage, he felt again the hot rush of his own anger flooding through his body like a torrent of life.

Robert had revealed himself. He had shown John something unsuspected, terrifying and ugly; for below his ridiculous bluster there could be seen—so John imagined—the stark menace of the insane. And now John could realise what Bertha had to endure, to apprehend. It was a shocking realisation. It was more—it was intolerable. Mere philandering might be very well on occasion, but now he was thinking (not unheroically) of a rescue.

## 4

"I am not surprised that you are worried, my dear chap," said Doctor Bagge to Mr. Kewdingham. "You are extremely unwell. I have been thinking about it, I can assure you. And here is an astringent with tonic properties which I have made up after the most careful consideration—the most careful consideration. Tut-a-tut! We can't have you going on like this! It will never do. Not that I want to alarm you; certainly not. All I want you to do is to take this mixture three times a day in water, with an additional dose at bedtime if you feel any discomfort. Pray take it regularly: the effect is accumulative."

"It is very good of you to take so much trouble," said Robert Arthur.

"My job is to cure you," replied the doctor cheerily. "But a cure, in this case, is not possible without the intelligent co-operation of the patient—and that, I know, you will give me."

Robert Arthur smiled, with an air of torpid resignation. He carefully pushed into alignment, on the table in front of him, a series of impaled butterflies.

"You really must promise to do as I tell you," the doctor continued, not without a trace of annoyance. "Be regular. If you go away, take a bottle with you. I shall ask Mrs. Kewdingham to see that you don't forget it—I'm sure that she will be ready to help me. Eh?"

"Oh, I won't forget, I won't forget! I'm not a child. Of course, I shall take the stuff regularly. Is that it?—That big bottle you've got there?"

"Yes, that's it. And I shall call occasionally, just to see how you are getting on. I have taken a great deal of trouble with that medicine, and I am anxious to see how it works. One more bottle will probably do the trick. I shall be surprised if we have to continue the treatment for any length of time."

"I'm extremely grateful." And still the annoying man examined minutely his row of butterflies.

"And, look here!"—the doctor was emphatic—"no more playing about with your quack medicines and your drugs and all that!"

Robert Arthur merely exhaled a powerful breath, pushing out his lips and frowning a little.

"Did I show you this bit of a bronze brooch, doctor? Probably Roman. Got it on Gunter's Hill yesterday…"

"If you interfere with the action of this medicine," said the doctor, who knew Robert's irritating ways, "I cannot answer for the consequences. How can I do you any good if you will persist in dosing yourself with heaven knows what?"

"Probably Roman," Robert Arthur repeated. "I wouldn't like to call it anything else—Yes; I shall not forget what you have said."

## 5

It is not necessary to follow in detail Bertha's plan of action, nor is it necessary to explain or defend her conduct. We are only concerned, in this narrative, with a record of events. Bertha knew perfectly well what she was doing: she was killing her husband, or trying to kill him, with lead acetate.

There was no difficulty in giving him the stuff. Bertha did most of the cooking, and she was, therefore, able to put suitable doses of acetate into a great variety of substances. She had not undertaken her task in blind ignorance of toxicology. She knew that she would have to be patient, observant, methodical. Heavy doses would have defeated her purpose. A mere pinch in a rock bun, a mere powdering over the porridge, a mere suspicion in a jam tart, a bit here and a bit there, given as the occasion presented itself, but given steadily and with confidence—that was the correct procedure.

As a result of lead poisoning a shooting pain in the limbs may be anticipated, followed by unsteadiness and a sensation of cramp. This will be normally followed by a blackening of the teeth and gums, and by that peculiar drooping of the wrist which is so characteristic of the poison. Afterwards come the traces of symmetrical paralysis. Finally, in a typical case, you get the more interesting phenomena of plumbism—illusions, or the mental disorder which goes by the frightful and appropriate name of "saturnine lunacy".

But not one of these symptoms was discovered in the singular case of Mr. Kewdingham—not even the arthralgia.

On the contrary, there was a marked improvement in health after a fortnight's course of acetate. The patient was brighter, more vigorous, less irritable. How was it possible to explain such perversity?

Something must have gone wrong. But no!—It was out of the question. Whatever he was or was not taking, it was certain that he was taking poisonous doses of lead. Yet he was taking it with no result, or with a result exactly contrary to general experience. It was like a nightmare. Such absurd, unaccountable frustration is out of the natural order of things. It was like shooting at a ghost, trying to destroy some indestructible phantasm.

Mr. Kewdingham attributed his improvement partly to the medicine of Doctor Bagge and partly to his own knowledge of the pharmacopoeia. His opinion of Bagge naturally rose to a higher level, and he took the mixture with scrupulous regularity. He took other things as well, but he trusted mainly in the mixture.

This phenomenal recovery of health stimulated Robert's general activity. He was busily occupied with his collection, to which he was now adding an extensive biological department. He got an enormous glass tank which he filled with detestable slime, into which he dropped unsightly creatures. In the silence of the evening his poor, disheartened wife could hear the soft exgurgitation as the bubbles broke on the top of the filmy water, or the occasional plosh of a minnow.

And as Robert grew more industrious and even cheerful, his wife became more pale and apprehensive.

"I don't like the look of Bertha at all," said Mrs. Poundle-Quainton to her daughter. "You would think she had something on her mind."

"Yes, indeed," replied Miss Ethel, clicking her bright steel needles. "I expect she is worrying about Michael. And you know, Bobby is rather selfish, I'm afraid."

"Oh, he's just a man!" The old lady tilted her sharp little chin. She had been engaged more than once, so she knew what she was talking about. "And he might be worse. I think it's a good thing he is able to take such an interest in science. Besides, it was very brave of him to see that man about the—the South Sea business, you know."

Ethel counted her stitches. "Twenty-one, twenty-two... He's a regular Kewdingham." And she left it at that.

It was about the middle of February.

Then Robert began to get a little restless. He was not ill, but he felt uncomfortable. When he sat with his wife in the evening, she noticed a very singular tense, dense perplexity in his face, such as you may see in the face of a tired bull. He fiddled about with his boxes, his corks or cards, in a more disjointed way. Every now and then he gave out a long windy groan.

"Are you feeling all right, Bobby?"

"I feel tremendously better. That stuff of Bagge's is doing me a lot of good."

"No pain?"

"Absolutely. Only a sort of—"

"Something like rheumatism?"

"No; not at all. I don't think I feel anything, really. I don't know what it is. I'm a hundred times better than I was before Christmas. Jenkins was remarking on it—said he'd never seen me looking so fit."

Bertha stared at him with bewilderment, with a kind of terror. Was he really indestructible? Was Athu-na-Shulah more than a match for any ordinary poison? Nonsense!

She increased the dosage. And then—explain it as you can—he got better again.

Certainly Bertha had some difficulty in believing it. But the evidence was clear enough. Having swallowed enough lead to make a charge of duck-shot, this peculiar man was going about, not merely in his ordinary manner, but with a new appearance of alacrity. No one, not even a toxicologist of wide experience, could have detected a symptom of poisoning.

She was being defeated—by whom or by what?

After all, she *knew* he took the acetate. He took every morning, in his porridge alone, a very considerable amount of heavy metal. He took it also, throughout the day, in pies, pastry, cakes, muffins, custard, puddings, and so forth. She watched him putting it down. There could not be the slightest doubt of it. And yet, so far as results were concerned, he might have been taking so much ordinary sugar.

Yes; it was unreal, terrifying, this diabolical frustration; it was a thing outside the region of ordinary experience, like a miracle. What, in the name of goodness, could account for Bobby's immunity? A man is a man, lead is lead, and when you combine the two in definite proportions you ought to get a definite result.

## 6

Tumbling one night on a most uneasy bed, and half listening for the fatal call, poor Bertha had a dream which frightened her very much indeed.

She was in the midst of a desert. Instead of being covered with sand in the ordinary way, this desert was covered with a soft, black, fluffy dust, such as you find lying on the tops of old books in London. She was quite alone, dressed like an explorer in tunic, shorts and a sun-helmet, with a big pistol on one side of her belt and a bag full of enormous bullets—lead bullets—on the other.

At every step in the black, fluffy subsiding dust her feet sank a little deeper. The air was very hot and there was a smell of dead things, although nothing could be seen but the sooty expanse of the wilderness, unbroken, unlighted, unshadowed, fluffy and silent. Her own footfalls were inaudible, she was like a fly walking in dust. And then—oh, horror!—she began to sink into this deadly though almost intangible sooty and fuscous deposit.

She had already sunk to her knees, she could feel already the awful warm dust between her thighs and her shorts, when a most obscene yellow chimpanzee rose from nowhere and waggled himself about ten paces away. He was on the top of the dust, capering as if it was an asphalt platform. She took her pistol and fired—ploff!—right into his guts. But the awful chimpanzee merely grinned; he jabbed a bit of glass into his left eye and came closer. Two shots now, two deadly smacks of lead—ploff! plaff!—full in his middle. He gave a crackle of demonic laughter and came so close that she could see all the hairs on his obscene body. Still three shots left, and it was impossible to miss him. She would give him the final and fatal dose. Now—ram the muzzle right into that swagging belly of his!—ploff! ploff! plang!—a great mass of lead has gone tearing and plunging into his vitals. He must be dead, he must be crumpled up like a punctured bladder. No! He is actually laughing again! He is coming…

And then, suddenly appearing from nowhere (like the chimpanzee), John was on the scene. He appeared in the full magnitude of a hero, skimming lightly over the black face of the desert, though in his ordinary clothes and with no weapon.

"Oh, John!—dear John!—save me!"

With this cry actually on her lips, Bertha woke.

"Eh, what? What's matter?" said Robert drowsily. As luck would have it, he had been sleeping extremely well.

"It's—it's nothing, Bobby. Only a nightmare. I'm so sorry if I disturbed you."

But Robert only mumbled in somnolence, rolled himself round on the squeaking mattress and fell asleep again.

# Chapter VIII

## 1

Bertha was not the only one to be troubled by the unaccountable resistance of Robert. Doctor Wilson Bagge had been for some time on the look-out for symptoms. He had called once or twice in a friendly and hopeful way, and was not a little disconcerted by the appearance of his patient. Of course he behaved in the most irreproachable manner.

Robert looked up with his peculiar, twisted, excruciating smile. "Your medicine appears to suit me very well. I notice a marked improvement." He had never made such an admission before.

Doctor Bagge stared at him with a prim fixity. He was at a loss.

"No trace of the colic, eh?"

"No pains at all, doctor. I don't eat a great deal, you know. I never did. But—all things considered—I feel remarkably well."

"Well; keep it up, keep it up," said the doctor rather testily. "Take larger doses if you like. Take the extra dose at bedtime. Splendid, eh? Positively splendid result!"

In spite of himself, he could not help speaking in a snappy, irritated, precise way. After all the trouble he had taken, he was not merely disappointed, he was bewildered. He could hardly believe that Robert was taking his medicine. He would have to find out.

Another week passed. The doctor called again. Robert Arthur had gone to a meeting of his Rule Britannia League, as fit as a fiddle. Bertha, however, was in the drawing-room. She was looking ill.

"Ah-h!" cried the little man, twinkling with dapper vivacity. "Good afternoon, my dear Mrs. Kewdingham. How delightful to see you." He made the primmest of little bows. "The new rugs have arrived only this morning from Heal's, and I do hope you will come and give me your opinion of them. I depend entirely upon your impeccable judgment."

"I should love to." But there was no eagerness in her voice. "Do sit down. I wanted to ask you—about Bobby. I am feeling rather anxious."

"Why—he's very well, isn't he?"

"Unnaturally well."

"Unnaturally well! My dear lady!—whatever do you mean?"

"He can't really be well."

"And why not?" He was in a twitter of curiosity.

"It's not so easy to explain. For one thing—hasn't he got a very weak heart?"

"Yes: but there's no reason why it shouldn't last for years."

"And kidney trouble?"

"Chronic nephritis. Yes."

"Then, you see, he gets those awful gastric attacks from time to time. So you can hardly expect him to be very well, can you?"

"Still, he's much better?"

"He appears to be better."

"To be frank with you, Mrs. Kewdingham, I will admit that I certainly am surprised to find him as well as he is. I had not anticipated so rapid an improvement. The ways of Nature are incalculable."

"You are very modest. He puts it down to your medicine."

The devil he does! thought Doctor Bagge. But he said:

"That is very kind of him, but I don't think I can take all the credit. Nature, I repeat, is always baffling or surprising us. I must say that I had not expected—well, I had expected a change, of course. Can you tell me whether he really does take the medicine regularly?"

"Yes. I think he wants another bottle."

"He shall have it. I shall see that he is not kept waiting. And I'll stiffen it up a bit." As he spoke the last words a transient though savage gleam flickered in his eyes. "I shall make it up this evening."

Then he said again:

"Are you *quite* sure that he takes it regularly?"

"Quite. I usually get the medicine-glass and the water for him."

The doctor pressed his lips together demurely and lowered his eyelids. He was trying to conceal his perplexity.

"It's very peculiar," he said.

Bertha, whose nerves were on edge, replied a little sharply:

"What is peculiar? I don't understand."

Instantly the little man recovered himself. He cocked his head on one side and twinkled at her like a perky though amiable little sparrow.

"A purely professional matter, my dear lady. In ordinary practice one would not anticipate such a marked reaction to the drug in so short a time. But as it suits him, let us carry on; and let us hope for even greater improvement."

Then, hearing the slippers of his enemy, old father Kewdingham, shuffling over the oil-cloth on the landing, he rose to take his leave.

The old man, a grim, tall figure in his grey and black clothes, entered the room. He looked sternly at the doctor and bowed with tight, exaggerated formality. He did not lack intuition. It was like an encounter between a venerable sardonic jackdaw and a bright little pitter-pattering sparrow.

"Good afternoon, Doctor Bagge. Cold, is it not? Yeh. I suppose this weather keeps you busy. What does Dickens say in one of his books?—I can't remember which one, but it don't matter. Very fine thought. He says: 'There's something good in all weathers…something good in all weathers…' I forget how he goes on. I should like your opinion of Dickens. I suppose you will admit there's no one like him now? What?" He frowned fiercely. "But I won't keep you now—I see you're busy."

## 2

That evening the doctor bounced into his dispensary in a flutter of keen vexation. He ran nimbly from bottle to bottle, preparing for his irritated nerves a pharmaceutical cocktail. It was his custom, when tired or depressed, to run for relief to his materia medica, as a less enlightened man would run to his whisky or some other crude intoxicant.

Quickly he mixed for himself an exciting compound of strychnine, phosphoric acid, calcium carbonate, manganese dioxide, cannabis indica and acetum cantharidis. After swallowing his ingenious concoction he felt very much happier.

Now then! said Doctor Bagge to himself—what about this Kewdingham fellow? What's the matter with him? Why does he fail to react as he should to my alum chlorate? It is damnable: it is enough to make a man lose faith in his own knowledge. And yet—knowledge, truth, science—these things eventually *must* prevail! They must and they will prevail!

He had chosen aluminium for several reasons. There is considerable diversity of opinion in regard to the toxic properties of this metal, and there are some who deny that it has any toxic properties at all. Bagge knew better. He had carried out a little experiment. But he was not obliged to give away his knowledge; and if, in given circumstances, there were any questions about the medicine he gave to Kewdingham, he would at once invoke the respectable opinions of those who believed that aluminium was perfectly harmless. What is more, he had taken the precaution of falsifying his prescription-book, in order to explain, if necessary, his liberal use of alum chlorate.

And it would be correct to say that the doctor's vexation was rather professional than personal. After all—good Lord!—he was a man of science, he knew what he was doing, he was no bungling amateur. He knew what would happen, what was bound to happen, if you gave a man an aluminium lining. But it wasn't happening—that was the trouble. There was a hitch, a resistance. Or miraculous immunity.

No, it was physically impossible! It would only be a matter of time and a heavier dosage, a much heavier dosage, an overwhelming percentage of metal. He was only at the beginning of his resources, and he was too moderate. That was it—a mere freak of the constitution, a physiological curiosity.

In all his medical experience he had never come across anything like Robert. Probably the case was unique. It was a shame that, for purely personal reasons, he would be unable to send a report to the *Lancet*. Still, he might carry out another experiment on rabbits or something like that. The possibility of being thwarted by another chemical, administered by Robert himself, did come into his mind; but the chances of such a thing being the case were about ten thousand to one.

Very good then, said he—the best thing is to increase the amount of the toxin, for it *is* a toxin, whatever they may say.

The doctor also thought he might make up an additional medicine, to be taken between meals. He could, moreover, carry out a flank attack on the heart, which might be helpful. Indeed, there were all sorts of things he might do without spoiling the main experiment. Cheer up! said this clever little Doctor Bagge; we are only at the beginning after all! So he might comfort himself, but he could not understand—no, he could not for the life of him understand…

## 3

The explanation of this tragic dilemma is purely chemical.

Doctor Bagge and Mrs. Kewdingham, though bravely and patiently working for the same result, were defeating each other's purposes. The subtle aluminium of Doctor Bagge was counteracted by the obtuse lead of Mrs. Kewdingham. The acetate of the one was hurried away by the impetuous chlorate of the other. Nothing, or next to nothing, was left behind. Each of these people was giving a poison, and each was giving an antidote. What is more, the doses were so graduated that the only consequence, at first, was a gentle stimulus to the peristaltic movement, beneficial rather than otherwise. At the odds of twenty thousand to one, the almost incredible was happening.

It was a game of cross purposes, no doubt unique in the history of medicine. Had there been a lag, an irregularity, a disproportion, then the acetate or the chlorate, as the case might have been, would have had a chance of winning. But their own admirable care and vigilance, their own thoughtful preparation and excellent method, actually prevented both Doctor Bagge and Mrs. Kewdingham from making any headway. By their very persistence in a common design they were acting at variance with each other: co-operating, yet rivals; united in purpose, yet mutually obstructive; criminal in thought and innocent in action.

For the time being, therefore, matters were at a deadlock.

# 4

Then, towards the end of February, John Harrigall came to Shufflecester for the day—at the very time when our puzzled poisoners were beginning to realise that something was wrong.

He had lunch with Uncle Richard, who grumbled savagely about his nephew Robert.

"What the devil's the matter with him, eh? Pecking about over that rubbish of his. Collection, he calls it; and it *is* a collection too, by gad! Did you ever see anything like it? Trash, trash. Anyone can see that. I've as good as told him so, but he only grins at me. I suppose he thinks I'm a poor ignorant old buffer. If you ask me, I should say he's a bit—" Uncle Richard smartly tapped the shining top of his head.

He continued, grimly:

"I don't know what's come over him these last few weeks. Of course, we're talking of family matters, and so I may as well be frank with you. But since he went up to London the other day...did you meet him?"

"We had a little walk together."

"Well, something must have gone pretty wrong, I should think. There was a yarn about some Dutch company or other—"

"It came to nothing, I believe."

"Pssh! Came to nothing? Of course it came to nothing. If there was any stuff in the fellow do you think he would go muddling along as he does? Damned if I understand him. At one time he was doing well enough. But now—and the way he treats that poor girl—"

"Bertha?"

"Yes, Bertha. She has a sharp tongue, I know, and I dare say she makes good use of it—or bad use of it, perhaps. But he's outrageous. Orders her about, snubs her in front of other people. Asking for trouble, I call it. She's a fine handsome woman."

"Unwise of him, certainly."

John twiddled his fingers round the stem of his port glass. He looked thoughtful. He had come to Shufflecester with a definite design.

"I think I shall run round and call on them presently."

At half-past three he was walking up Wellington Avenue. Uncle Richard's account had prepared him for the possibility of a stormy encounter. He had not written to Bertha; he now regarded letters—rightly—as highly imprudent; but he had resolved to see her at all costs.

Robert Arthur was at home. He received John with an air in which enmity, a stiff politeness and a real desire for compromise were strangely combined in various degrees and alternations. To his chaotic mind there was nothing unreasonable in the idea of being friendly with John without abandoning totally his misgivings.

For a few moments, as luck would have it, John found himself alone with Bertha. Robert had gone to look for something.

"My dear," she said, "have you quarrelled with him?"

"Yes—in a way. He's jealous. I was afraid of writing."

"John, John! This is too dreadful! Will you promise—"

"Yes, Bertha, of course I will. You may depend upon me."

It sounded very sententious and formal, but he meant what he said. Certainly, John had never been so fond of any other woman as he was of Bertha. He continued more happily:

"I could meet you with the car. At Eastbourne, for example."

Bertha looked rather perplexed and uneasy. She did not feel quite sure of him.

"I will write to you," she said. "But, John, you must promise—"

Robert Arthur, with an enormous cardboard box in his arms, appeared in the doorway. Nothing can prevail against the pride, the pertinacity of the born collector. And obviously Robert did desire a compromise or a state of suspended hostility. Besides, he had obtained a fibula, a hairpin, a pair of tweezers and a bit of an ivory comb, all of which were probably Roman.

# Chapter IX

## 1

After further study of the Kewdingham problem, Doctor Bagge prepared carefully a new mixture. It was pinkish, opaque, viscous, and it smelt agreeably of roses. In his tiny, meticulous hand the doctor wrote a label: "R. A. Kewdingham, Esq. Three times a day as before."

As he licked the label in his dispensary, the blue eyes of Doctor Bagge flickered up for a moment like the eyes of a little demon.

"There you are, my boy!" he said.

He took up the large bottle lovingly and shook it with a gentle sideways motion. Then he put it down on the table. Filmy coils of an exquisite cloudy pink were softly curling and falling in the darker pink of the mixture. Coils neither of oil nor of powder, and yet both oily and powdery, wreathing and curling and falling like a plume, a cloud, a living flush in marble. It was very pretty indeed. Of course, when the mixture was properly shaken, these clouds all ran together and made a homogeneous opacity in the bottle. Pink and milky, like an ideal union of strawberries and cream.

The doctor himself carried his masterpiece to Wellington Avenue.

"Now, my dear chap," he said to Robert, "if this doesn't work I shall be very much astonished. It's the same as the other," he added quite truthfully, "only stronger and with a less objectionable taste. You may take longer doses if you like. Take one in the morning, before breakfast."

## 2

Mrs. Kewdingham was keeping pace with the doctor. Two or three packets of acetate were being administered every week. The pink mixture and the acetate hurried each other away; but now they were causing a more painful disturbance.

By the middle of March, Robert was decidedly unwell. He was fretful, captious, and occasionally brutal. In the secret councils of the Rule Britannia League he talked more fiercely and extravagantly about his flying bombers, his machine-guns. He talked like an arm-chair soldier. In the home, his behaviour was too shocking for words. He snapped, he blustered, he bullied, he sulked, he scattered petulantly over carpets or tables the rubbish of his collection. It was hardly possible to walk across the drawing-room without kicking the trays or crushing upon the floor a dusty assortment of beetles. And before sitting down, the visitor had to remove from his chair a tottering pylon of boxes or a heap of junk.

Even the old father was a little dismayed by this encroachment, and he was almost inclined to sympathise with his unhappy daughter-in-law.

The strain of this very singular position was beginning to tell on Bertha. She was reckoning upon the affection, the generosity of John Harrigall. She was reckoning upon the final success of her experiment. It was a grim job. She had need of all her courage and resolution. And so she went on, persevering from day to day, never allowing herself to despair. Now, in view of what had happened, it was more than ever necessary for her to accomplish her purpose—by some means or other. If she failed with acetate, she would have to consider a new method. It might be said that she was displaying a perverse kind of heroism.

Must we talk of perversity? Perhaps Mrs. Kewdingham was a real heroine, like Jael or Judith; certainly she was a much finer woman than Delilah. In any case, are there not heroes of evil as well as heroes of good?

Such was the state of affairs, a state of high tension and of dreadful uncertainties, at the middle of March.

### 3

Whether it was prudent of him to do so, or not, the doctor could not refrain from calling at Wellington Avenue three or four times a week. Just running in for a minute or so in the course of a round. And Mrs. Kewdingham continued her friendly practice of going down to the doctor's house and giving him the benefit of her excellent advice on the subject of his new decorations, his rugs, his carpets and papers.

And why was the doctor so anxious to arrange his house to the liking of Mrs. Kewdingham? Why did he look at her so closely, so professionally, when she tried the fit of a new chair-cover, or shook with her graceful arm the long folds of a curtain?

If you had seen him—the dapper, slim, alert little man— you would have been reminded, not so much of a lover gazing at his mistress as of an ex-jockey admiring the lines of a thoroughbred. He looked as if he was calculating, making a valuation, fixing a price or guessing a pedigree. Doctors— particularly elderly doctors—are not like other people. Very often, of course, they talked about Robert.

Mrs. Kewdingham could not help deploring the irritability of her husband and his wilful disregard of good manners. He was talking more frequently of his Atlantis life: always a bad sign.

"Illusions?" The doctor was interested.

"Well, I hardly know what to call them."

"I mean, he doesn't see apparitions or anything like that?"

"Not as far as I know. He keeps on muttering about a temple and a pyramid and the wisdom of the Israelite. It all sounds to me like utter nonsense."

"So it is, of course," said the doctor. "I will call professionally this afternoon."

And when the doctor did call he was very much interested by Robert's appearance. The colour of the poor man's face was like that of yellow ash, and he appeared to be racked by a painful and unremitting anxiety. Now this look of anxiety, as the doctor knew, is a symptom of metallic poisoning. Of course, it may just as well be the symptom of something else, but in this case you can hardly blame the doctor for jumping to a conclusion.

"Acidity!" cried the hopeful Bagge, shaking his forefinger with a gesture of reproach. "Oh, come, come!—we can't have this. What have you been eating?"

Ah, yes! What *had* he been eating? That was the point.

"Oh, just the ordinary things, as far as I know."

"Well, I should be careful. Go on with your mixture, and I'll send you a little corrective as well. Touch of acidity; there's no doubt about it. You are not worried over anything, are you?"

"No, certainly not."

And then Robert suddenly turned upon the doctor a fearful gelatinous eye, magnified by the shimmering disc of his monocle.

"I say, Bagge, have you ever heard the voice of the ages?"

The doctor suddenly stiffened himself in his chair. "No," he said, "I haven't." He froze up in a rigid professional concentration, his eyes like two little bits of blue, irradiating steel.

"Wonderful—wonderful!" Robert's chin was drooping over his crumpled neck-tie. He was not looking at the doctor, but apparently at a heap of pearly oyster-shells on the hearthrug. "Wonderful! The voice of ancient wisdom!"

"You had better not think about it," said the doctor, staring hard at Robert's neck and forehead.

Cerebral disturbance—most interesting.

"Why should I not think about it? Time is lost in the stream of the ages; wisdom remains. Atlantis, Egypt, Israel. Do you understand? We are one with Israel in the keeping of wisdom. The High Priest of Atlantis…No; of course, you don't understand. You think I am talking nonsense."

"By no means. Not at all, my dear chap. On the contrary I am very much interested, very deeply interested. Look here—" the doctor snatched up a folded newspaper from the table—"can you read this?" He pushed the paper in front of Robert's face and pointed at random with his finger.

It was a critical experiment.

Robert Arthur proceeded to read:

"Firm conditions ruled in the stock markets yesterday. Although business remained small, the tendency of prices was favourable to holders, and there were indications that more active conditions may develop after the holidays. A slight improvement—"

Doctor Bagge suddenly jerked the paper up and down, peering closely into Robert's eyes.

Robert was disagreeably startled. He blinked.

"Here, Bagge! What on earth are you doing?"

"Only testing your eyesight, my dear fellow. There's no reason for you to be worried, I can assure you. As for the acidity, we can easily cure it."

Five minutes later, the doctor left the house.

"Well, I'm damned!" he said to himself as he walked up the Avenue. He had never been more completely puzzled. Kewdingham had mental symptoms, but he was able to concentrate and his reactions were normal. He was not in the accepted sense of the term a lunatic. There was evidently a slight gastric disorder—nothing of any consequence. There was nothing which could be attributed to the enormous doses of alum chlorate that he was swallowing, presumably, every day. How could this be explained? Was it the result of interference, neglect, or physical idiosyncrasy? Close observation was desirable. There might be a collapse at any moment. But how the dickens did he manage to hold out for so long?

"He's enough to drive any decent ordinary practitioner out of his wits, indeed he is. Poor Mrs. Kew—poor Bertha!—poor dear Bertha!"

## 4

At the end of March John paid a flying visit to Shufflecester. He went there for the purpose of assisting his aunt, Mrs. Pyke, in the settlement of certain family matters. Casually, he asked her how the Kewdinghams were getting on.

"Well, John—I never could abide that woman, as we used to say." The angular dame sniffed sharply out of her long carinated nose.

"She looks very cross, and talks very roughly to poor old Bobby. I don't know how he can put up with it at all. I often feel like giving her a bit of my mind."

"Oh, come! I think Robert knows very well how to answer for himself. If it is a matter of mere rudeness—"

"It's not only that. The whole town is talking about her—the way she goes running round to Doctor Bagge's house and spending hours alone with him."

"Oh?" said John.

"Yes. Not very nice for the family, is it? We've been here for thirty-seven years, and there's never been a breath of scandal until now."

"Hardly a scandal, I should say. Bagge is a queer little fellow, but he's a respectable practitioner, and he wouldn't risk his reputation. And I should certainly trust Bertha. I think she advises him about the affairs of his house. You will probably find that everything is grossly exaggerated—about her visits, I mean."

The formidable aunt rose up stiffly out of her chair with a cracking of hip-joints.

"I make allowances for exaggeration. Even then it's bad enough. I have told Bobby quite frankly that I should go to another doctor."

"Really! And did he agree with you?"

"All the Kewdinghams are as obstinate as mules. He said that he had entire confidence in Doctor Bagge."

John, trying to feel that he, too, had entire confidence in Doctor Bagge, ran round to Wellington Avenue. And here he committed a fatal indiscretion.

Robert Arthur, not anticipating this call, had gone out to walk over some ploughed fields, where he was no doubt looking for things probably Roman. Bertha was at home, but she was going, at four o'clock, to have tea with the Poundle-Quaintons: it was unavoidable.

Now John had a suggestion to make. Could not Bertha go with him some afternoon to Crawley?—It was only about ten miles from Shufflecester, and he would pick her up with the car. It would be very pleasant, surely. Or why only an afternoon? Why not make a day of it, taking their lunch and exploring the hills and woods? But she refused to give him a definite answer. She would write to him. He thought her nervy, capricious. As they stood by the open door of the drawing-room he gave her a final kiss.

He should have known better. There was a rustling, obscure movement in the darkness of the landing, and he caught a glimpse of the maid Martha descending the stairs.

## 5

April came. April with all her symphonic variations of blue and green, her pretty gambols of youth.

But spring had no message for Robert Arthur. He was very unwell. Nothing could induce him to follow Mrs. Pyke's excellent advice and see another doctor; he went on doggedly swallowing Bagge's mixture, and the mixture got pinker and pinker and Robert got worse and worse.

The doctor now anticipated a sudden collapse. He could not explain Robert's phenomenal resistance. Had it not been for the scientific interest of the experiment he would have tried something else. But he was quite as dogged as Robert himself. He was giving him an aluminium compound of extraordinary strength; he could hardly make it stronger or give him any more. Surely the end was near.

It was; but not the end anticipated by Dr. Bagge.

Mrs. Kewdingham, on her part, was equally persistent; and so the awful bombardment went on—more lead, more aluminium; acetate, chlorate; ounces, packets, bottles.

In spite of this effective neutralisation, Robert was ill. Perhaps he was not being poisoned in the strict sense of the word, but he was being put out of gear. If there was no toxic result from these preposterous doses, there was a very definite mechanical result. Too much time and too much space were taken up by this internal wrestling-match; even though the match ended, and was likely to end always, in a draw—or more properly, in a withdrawal.

On one occasion it was touch and go. Kewdingham, although he had such confidence in Doctor Bagge, decided that he had taken enough of the mixture. The doses were discontinued for a whole day. Whereupon the acetate, finding a free field, rioted about in the most disastrous manner.

"But, my dear chap, are you taking your medicine? No! Good gracious! What are you thinking about?"

So the aluminium, only just in time, came hurrying back to the arena. Murderous Bagge again rescued a threatened life. It was the strangest of situations, and the most bewildering for all concerned.

This episode very naturally restored Robert's faith in his pink medicine and in the professional ability of Dr. Bagge.

Again the situation was a deadlock. It would be interesting to speculate on the probable course of events if things had been different. Let us assume that Kewdingham had gone away—as he actually suggested—for a change. Would he have taken a bottle of Bagge's mixture away with him? On the other hand, suppose that he did listen to Mrs. Pyke and threw over the family doctor? Indeed, there is no end to these conjectures. But the Kewdingham drama was to follow a strange and a most unexpected course. It was to follow a course which led, by grim stages, to the transcendent region of pure mystery.

# 6

On a Sunday afternoon, early in April, the Poundle-Quaintons called at Number Six. Kewdingham had not been to see them as frequently as usual, and they were disturbed by his appearance of ill health, and also by some very uncharitable rumours.

The old man was asleep upstairs. Bertha was out for a walk with Michael. As for Robert, he was peering in a disconsolate way over the odds and ends of his vast collection. He came down to open the door, and as soon as the Poundle-Quaintons saw his face they were filled with alarm.

"Bobby! What's the matter?"

To this chirruping anxiety Robert answered:

"Oh, nothing! Come upstairs."

His manner was testy, rude; his voice rough, unmodulated. In his face there was a blending of surliness and vacancy.

"Hadn't you better see another doctor?" said Aunt Bella as they stumped up slowly over the oil-cloth.

Robert gave her no answer. Never before had he behaved like this.

The poor ladies were chilled, puzzled and rather frightened. They followed him silently into the littered drawing-room. Robert lifted peevishly from a couple of chairs a box, a tray and several packages and let them fall noisily upon the table.

"Are we disturbing you, Bobby?"

"Well—I'm classifying some of these things."

"We were anxious to see how you were getting on."

"Getting on? From what I can see, people would be better pleased if I got off and had done with it."

The wretched man turned upon them the same awful gelatinous eye which had roused the fears, or the hopes, of Doctor Bagge.

"My dear!" cried Ethel, pressing her thin fingers on her breast in a spasm of horror.

Kewdingham merely grunted.

"What do you mean?" said Aunt Bella, not without indignation. "I had no idea that you were so ill. Why don't you go up to London to see a really first-rate doctor?"

"Why should I? Can you show any reason why I should go dragging on like this? What's the use of it?"

Ethel turned pale. "Oh, Bobby!—"

But Aunt Bella, who was older and wiser, and who despised weakness in a man, raised her brittle hand, commanding silence.

"What you need, Bobby, is a bottle or two of good port, less medicine, and a change of air. It is not impossible that Doctor Bagge is giving you the wrong treatment."

"If it was not for Bagge I should have been dead weeks ago," said Kewdingham, not realising the literal truth of his words. "Whether I should be grateful to him is another matter."

Tears filled the gentle eyes of Miss Ethel. "You have no right to say such awful things."

"Look here, Bobby." Aunt Bella, shaken though she was, decided to have no more nonsense. "Look here, Bobby! What you are saying is absurd. Do, for goodness' sake, be a man. You are out of sorts, and you are just giving way, as though you were a silly child. I won't listen to such stuff any longer. Either you change the conversation, or we go."

"You—you ought to think of the family," said Ethel with a jerking sob. "You ought to think of others."

"Oh, very well then!" cried Robert in a shrill, serrated voice. "Oh, certainly! Have it your own way. Talk about anything you like."

He was obviously demented.

The Poundle-Quaintons, full of dismay, ran off to Mrs. Pyke.

Mrs. Pyke listened rather grimly. "It's all the fault of that woman," she said. Aunt Bella decided immediately that she would have a word with Bertha—without alarming her, of course.

So much may be done by a word in due season.

### 7

While the old lady was deploring the awful decay of her nephew, John was arranging to spend an afternoon with Bertha, in accordance with his suggestion. On the appointed day he would come to Shufflecester, with his car, at two o'clock.

When the day came it was dull and showery, though fortunately not cold.

Bertha looked ill, nervous and over-strained.

"John! There are two women from Shufflecester on the road just behind us. I'm sure they know me."

"Oh, never mind!" replied John. "They are of no account."

"No, but—"

"Come along, come along! How fine it is to see you! I have got tea in the car, and rugs, and all that we need. We shall reach the woods in a few minutes. Why do you look so unhappy?"

She smiled, but said nothing, as she stepped into the car.

A trackway, sandy and furrowed, led from the main road through the woods. John turned up the trackway and came to a stop on a patch of dusty grass by the side of it. They walked into a coppice of young firs and larches, put their rugs on a layer of dry brown leaves and sat down.

Bertha took off her hat, and then she looked at herself in a little mirror, patting her hair. Then she looked at John.

"Are you angry with me?"

"Angry! My dear woman!"

He felt embarrassed. There was something tragic, restrained, about her which he could not fathom.

"Listen to me, John. I want to talk to you. There are so many things I want to say."

"Well?" It was best to be patient.

"I am afraid of something. Bobby has been very strange lately. I don't understand him."

"Is he ill?"

"He is very ill. John—he is dying."

"Dying! How on earth do you know? What do you mean? Why didn't you write to me? What are they doing about it?" He did not believe her. "Why, there was nothing wrong when I saw him the other day."

"He does not know it. The others do not know it. But I am positively certain."

"And what does the doctor think?"

"The doctor thinks I am wrong."

"Well—I should be inclined to believe him."

"No, John. I tell you he is bound to die, he *must* die—very soon." She spoke in a low voice, but with harsh intensity.

"Bertha! You cannot possibly know."

"I do know."

"No, you don't! How can you? What you mean is that you observe a certain change—"

"After all," she said, brusquely jerking her head and shoulders with a vigorous, liberating movement, as if she was throwing off a load, "who would blame me if I did something desperate?"

"My dear!" cried John, deliberately shutting the door on a horrible thought.

# Chapter X

## 1

The Chaddlewicks, when they called at Number Six Wellington Avenue, noticed the change in Robert Arthur. He put on the airs of a martyr, and told them with rasping intensity that he was extremely unwell.

"Oh, but you will have to be careful!" Mrs. Chaddlewick tootled in a gush of warm solicitude. "You will have to take the most dreadful care of yourself—won't he, Mrs. Kewdingham?"

Bertha did not think it necessary to reply.

"I was telling George as we came along—wasn't I, George?—I saw a pig looking through a gate; and I said at once to George—didn't I, George?—I said, 'There!—I know that means a friend of mine is ill: not a dangerous illness, but something quite nasty.' I'm very odd in that way, you know. I sort of understand what things mean. The other day I dropped my hairbrush twice—you remember, George, don't you?—and of course that meant that I would get a letter from Susan; and when I came down, sure enough, there it was on the table.—Oh, George! Why don't you stop me chattering away like this? I'm frightfully 'shamed of myself, truly I am. Do forgive me, Mrs. Kewdingham." She smiled in her adorably vacant way, opening her big dolly eyes and slowly pivoting her fluffy head until she had beamed in turn, like a revolving light, on each of the company; that is, on Mr. and Mrs. Kewdingham, old father Kewdingham, and Mr. Chaddlewick himself.

There was a pause. They waited for the airy lady to speak.

It was hard to say what she did exactly, but Pamela had a way of taking command or of snuffing out the ordinary conversational impulse. She floated always on the top of her social *milieu*, obliging other people, whatever they might think, to keep in their proper places.

"But really, Mr. Kewdingham, I'm worried to see you looking so ill. Doesn't he look ill, George? I do hope your doctor is looking after you properly. Doctor Bagge, isn't it?"

"Yes. I think he knows his job very well."

"He's frightfully popular, I know. But can you really trust these ordinary doctors? They're so materialistic. I wish you'd go and see my dear little Doctor Dibworthy in Wigmore Street. These London men are so intelligent. He's an occult healer. Quite one of the new sort. He doesn't believe in medicine or surgery or anything horrid like that—only perhaps just the tiniest little teeny pill now and then. He believes in thought."

Robert Arthur smiled faintly. Personally, he believed in drugs. "Deep thinking, deep breathing, and all that?"

"Oh, no! The stars. Doctor Dibworthy goes by your horoscope. He won't look at you without a horoscope. Astro-therapy. *So* much better, I think. Everything is ruled by the stars."

"Then what can Doctor Dibworthy do?" said Bertha.

"Oh, shut up!" snapped Robert rudely. "You don't understand."

Mrs. Chaddlewick, cooing like a turtle-dove, ballooned over the obstacle. "It's all a matter of occult knowledge. The aura—"

"Ah!" said old father Kewdingham, himself coming under the spell of the airy fairy. "There are more things in heaven and earth—"

"Indeed there are!" fluted Mrs. Chaddlewick. "Many things—oh, many, many things!"

"I should rather like to see this Doctor Sipworthy," said Robert. "He would probably be interested in my own experience of the occult. In fact, I might be able to tell him something—"

Tea arrived, so Kewdingham was fortunately obliged to give his attention to the shifting and shuffling of boxes, bags, trays, drawers, papers, bottles, and all the rest of it. A more general conversation was begun.

But they were dominated by the airy lady, ballooning away over their heads and every now and then bouncing lightly into the field of their conversation. She was feeling dreadfully psychic, she told them. "George knows what I mean. He knows when I'm sort of excited, don't you, George?"

"Do you know?" she cried in her most piccolo manner, "I've got a sort of 'lectric feeling, like I had in church the other day just before Canon Heppledon fainted. Mr. Kewdingham, you simply must let me have a look at your teacup."

"What? Look in my teacup?" Compared with Atlantean mysteries, this was rather footling. But Robert, smiling indulgently and adoringly, handed her the cup.

"Now, please, everybody—don't talk for a minute. I shall have to think most terrific'ly hard."

The lady took the cup, holding it daintily in her pretty fingers, and then she rested it on her knee. The men watched her with amused attention, while Bertha glowered with tight lips and a darkening brow.

"May I just tip out a teeny drop into the basin? Thank you, Mrs. Kewdingham. Please take it again, Mr. Kewding-ham, and give it one little wiggle. That's right. Oh, yes! There really is something here. Now I shall be able to tell you—"

She held the cup lightly on her knee again.

"Oo-o! It's going to be frightfully exciting!"

"And what have you discovered?" said Robert, not with-out a shade of apprehension. Even the most intelligent men are apt to be disturbed by these parlour fooleries.

"It's too fearfully thrilling for words! I've never seen such a marvellous teacup in my life. It makes me feel quite spook-ish, George—like the one I saw at Wapsey Manor, but ever so much more interesting. Wait a moment. Yes—I thought so! Really, I don't think I ought to tell you."

"Oh, come!—That's too bad!" said Robert, beginning to feel both uneasy and ridiculous.

"No; I don't think I ought to." Pamela shook her fluffy head with a smile of mystery, as though to intimate her knowledge of some awful doom and her friendly desire to conceal it. "You see, it's a teeny bit frightening. When I saw that pig looking through the gate, I knew something odd would happen this afternoon. I said so, didn't I? And now I rather wish I hadn't looked at your teacup after all."

"Nonsense, Pam!" said Mr. Chaddlewick in a somewhat irreverent manner. "We all know your little game. You don't really see anything but a few tea-leaves, a little sugar—"

"Don't be so absurdly commonplace, George. Why, it was only last week I told you about those dud shares of yours; and the next day you heard from the broker—"

"All right, all right!" said Mr. Chaddlewick hurriedly. "Never mind that. Go ahead if you want to, and if you think the others will be amused—"

"Shall I really tell you, Mr. Kewdingham? It's not alto-gether nice, I'm afraid."

"Of course, Mrs. Chaddlewick! Please do—by all means!"

Bertha looked at them rather wearily. The old man was greatly interested. Mr. Chaddlewick was embarrassed, he did not like these infantile diversions. Robert was trying to appear as if he enjoyed the joke. The lady with the teacup was inscrutably vacant. At last she spoke in the muted voice of an oracle:

"You are in danger, Mr. Kewdingham. You have two enemies, a man and a woman. Real danger. There's a black speck in the middle. It would be hardly fair of me to tell you—"

"Not very cheerful," said Robert, uneasily twitching the cord of his eyeglass. "Can't you see any—any money, or something like that?" He cackled sharply, making a desperate effort to appear jocular.

"No," said Mrs. Chaddlewick, in the accent of genuine regret. "I mustn't invent anything. I can see the woman quite distinctly—she's a dark woman, rather tall. And there's the man!—he might be a doctor or a lawyer or a writer—he looks professional somehow. He's not so clear as the woman. But he's terribly dangerous. I wish I didn't see things like this. Yes; I wish I'd never looked at this cup: it's too upsetting. I won't look at it any more. No, indeed, I won't. There!" She slapped the cup over the basin and then put it down on the tray. "Isn't I an absurd little person? But I simply can't help it. Please forgive me, Mrs. Kewdingham."

There was a moment of painful and foolish silence. Bertha, unaccountably pale, stared at Mrs. Chaddlewick in angry bewilderment. What was her game? What was she actually thinking about—or guessing? Or was it simple idiocy?

Old Kewdingham, with an air of genial banter, said loudly:

"You think it may be a doctor—yeh?"

"Oh, please don't ask me anything more about it. You may think it's awfully silly of me, but I'm not quite like other people. I do see things. I can't help it. Motoyoshi told me I ought to be a medium. You'd never think it to look at me, would you? Such an ordinary little person! Do let's talk about something else. It makes me feel just a teeny bit sick, you know."

"Well," said Robert, affecting a sportive manner, "I shall obviously have to be on my guard. I suppose it's not poor old Bagge, is it? The dangerous professional man—ha!"

"There, George! Didn't I say it was a B?" cried Mrs. Chaddlewick.

This curious question was not answered, nor did the lady explain herself.

"M'yeh!" cackled the old man suddenly in a sputter of senile merriment. "Bagge!—Of course it is! You'll have to be very careful, Bobby."

"Don't you think," said Bertha, "that we might begin a more rational conversation?"

Robert looked up angrily. But he was recovering himself. Athu-na-Shulah was not the man to be afraid of a teacup. "And a tall dark woman—" he said with pointed malice.

Bertha, her chalky pallor giving place to a bright flush, could endure the strain no longer.

"Bobby—how can you be such a fool?"

Mr. Chaddlewick, deeply grieved, raised a protesting hand as Robert sprang out of his chair. But he could not avert the explosion.

"This is perfectly intolerable!"

"It is you who make it intolerable. You cannot even behave in the presence of visitors."

"Bertha, Bertha! I beg you—" The old man wobbled unsteadily to his feet. He spoke quietly, but he was crimson with rage. Very deliberately Bertha rose and faced the two men. The Chaddlewicks alone remained in their chairs; Mr. Chaddlewick scratching the top of his head and looking miserable, and Mrs. Chaddlewick masking her intense pleasure under an air of concern. Who could have known that a pig looking through a gate meant so much?

"It is hardly for you to talk of behaviour. You have grossly insulted Mrs. Chaddlewick, who has been so kindly trying to amuse us—"

"Mrs. Chaddlewick can speak for herself. I only wish that her ridiculous vision might prove to be true. A black speck in a teacup represents a coffin, doesn't it, Mrs. Chaddlewick?"

"Oh!—Mrs. Kewdingham!—"

"Bertha is occasionally hysterical," said Robert Arthur, turning pale, though shocked into a sudden recovery of balance. "She does not consider my own wretched health or the feelings of others. I can only say that I regret this unpleasant scene, and that I hope you will make allowances for—for circumstances. Bertha has a grim sense of humour. She does not bother about the taste or meaning of what she says."

"Please don't say anything more," said Mr. Chaddlewick, getting up. "All in good part, eh?—I hope you will soon be quite well again.—Now, Pamela, we shall have to go. That fellow is coming to see me about the fence at half-past five."

And when the Chaddlewicks, after a most uncomfortable leave-taking, had got away in their car, Mr. Chaddlewick observed:

"I say!—I wish you hadn't looked into that teacup, you know!"

And Mrs. Chaddlewick, all innocence, replied:

"But who could have told?"

And she added, as Mrs. Pyke might have added: "I tell you what, George—there's something wrong about that woman."

"There's something wrong about both of them, if you ask me," said George.

## 2

The teacup scene occurred on a Wednesday. On the following day John Harrigall was to dine with the Kewdinghams, according to plan. Robert Arthur, if he was not positively anxious to see John, was at least agreeable; he was glad to have an opportunity for showing the latest additions to his collection; and he was also glad to be relieved, even for an hour or two, from the infernal strain of his domestic tragedy.

Now, on the morning of this momentous day (as it proved to be) Mrs. Kewdingham went out into the town to do some shopping. It was her custom to do so, and there were certain things to be ordered for dinner.

In the first place, she ordered a bottle of burgundy—not one of your cheap commercial decoctions, but a real wine.

Burgundy was occasionally drunk by Robert Arthur, who believed that it was good for him, but he did not usually demand such an excellent vintage. It was doubtless in honour of John that Mrs. Kewdingham ordered a 1921 Pommard.

And perhaps it was also in honour of John (or was it in honour of the Pommard?) that she made her next purchase.

She went into the shop of Mr. Hickey, who described himself as "Antique Dealer and Repairer", and said that she wanted a set of green glasses—port-glasses, not expensive.

"Ah, yes!" said Mr. Hickey, a soft, urbane person with an apron of blue baize. "You mean Bristol glasses. A good set of two dozen or so is not very cheap, I'm afraid. Let me think a minute…"

Having thought a minute, Mr. Hickey remembered a set of half a dozen glasses, two of them odd, and one with a chip out of the foot, but all of a beautifully dark green.

"A lovely colour, mem; but not much good to me, to tell you the truth. They are not really old, and a bit too short in the stem. I could let you have them at a shilling each—or shall we say five shillings the lot?"

"Will you promise to send them round this morning? Thanks very much. Here is my address. No—I'll pay now."

"They're pretty glasses, mem. Them four would look well on any dinner-table. About 1870, I should say. The two odd 'uns would be a bit later—and likely enough German. Yes, mem; you shall have them by twelve o'clock. People don't fancy those glasses now, for some reason—except the real antiques. That's a fine set over there—Regency pattern—only four pound the lot. Good morning, mem—and thank you!"

## 3

John arrived at Shufflecester in the afternoon. He was to stay for a few days with Uncle Richard, who promised him some trout-fishing on that famous river, the Little Shuff.

"I was up there on Monday," said the cheery old boy, "and I got a brace of two-pounders on a blue dun. If the wind keeps where it is, we ought to do well. I shall give you that bit under the Priory garden; there was a big fellow rising close to the alders, and I missed him twice."

John was keenly interested in the news of the river.

"Thanks very much, Uncle Richard. It ought to be great fun. I was thinking of a little dark fly with a red hackle—"

"I've tried a red spinner," said Uncle Richard seriously, "but they don't seem to like it. I think the duns are best at this time of year. Of course, there's no reason why you should not do well with a fair-sized Butler's Glory."

Presently John explained that he was going to dinner with his cousin.

"Ah, yes. I saw Bertha in the town this morning, and she told me they were expecting you. He's in a poor way."

"Really ill?"

"I think so. Groggy heart, they tell me. Other things as well. Gastric trouble and all that."

"Temper rather bad, I suppose?"

"Oh, vile! I went round there the other day—not that I care much about going, but I feel that I ought to occasionally. He did nothing but growl and grumble and snap and snarl and talk the most frightful damned rot, until I very nearly lost my own temper as well. Then old Robert came in with his proverbs and poetry and all the rest of it, and poor Bertha was looking so grim. I didn't stay long, I can tell you."

Having announced his intention of going early to Wellington Avenue, John was there at six o'clock.

Robert Arthur himself opened the door—it was Martha's day off, and Bertha was upstairs changing her dress. There was a flicker of amiability on his face as he greeted his cousin. John could see at once that he was really ill; he was looking ashen, worried, unsteady.

"Come along up. Bertha's powdering her nose. Michael went back to school this morning. Father's having a game of chess with old Ampiter—he'll be back before long."

"And how are you, Bobby? I must say, you're not looking too well."

John was ascending the stairs. He had noticed, in passing the open door of the dining-room, that the table was laid for dinner. Somehow, this interested him particularly.

"Rotten!" said the other, shuffling and lumbering up the stairs behind his guest.

"Let's hope you will soon be better again."

They had reached the landing. John paused.

"But, look here," he said, "before the others come I want to have a word with you about those brooches. There are some in the British Museum which are distinctly similar."

"The brooches?" replied Kewdingham with a groan. "Some fellow saw them the other day, and he said they were probably Roman, I think."

"Yes; but are you sure?"

With astounding patience John turned over the bits and pieces of that odd collection. He could hear the creaking of the bedroom floor as Bertha moved about.

Presently he looked up at the clock on the mantelpiece. Ten minutes past six.

"I believe you are quite right, Bobby. But there are Saxon affinities, if I am not mistaken. Hullo! I nearly forgot. Will you excuse me? I must run out to the pillar-box and post this letter. It's been in my pocket all day. Rather urgent. Don't bother to come down; I'll put the door on the latch."

The pillar-box was only a few yards away.

Leaving Robert with his bits of brass, John ran down the staircase and out of the front door. It was a pleasant warm evening, though cloudy. He posted the letter. Then he looked up and down the Avenue. Not a sign of old father Kewdingham.

Quickly he was back at Number Six.

For one moment he stood in the hall. He could hear, coming from the drawing-room upstairs, the tiny clatter of brass handles—Robert pushing the trays in a cabinet. The door leading to the kitchen was open; he could not tell if there was anyone on the ground floor.

Apparently with no object, he lightly tripped into the dining-room. He observed on the table, among other things, a handsome decanter full of wine, and four green glasses—one at each place. He had not seen those glasses before, and he could not help looking at them with curiosity. There they stood: green, shining and elegant, neatly outlined on the white table-cloth, beautiful in form and colour, chaste, aristocratic and pleasing. He lifted the glass from the place at the head of the table—Robert's place—and held it up to the light. Yes; a lovely colour. And then something startled him. He put the glass down again abruptly. Perhaps it was only an illusion after all. At any rate, he did not wish to investigate…

Back with Robert. The awful rubble.

"Yes. It's a pretty series. Perhaps the periods are not clear in every case—"

At half-past six Bertha came in, looking very pale, to greet John, and then she went down to the kitchen. The old man came back soon afterwards and went upstairs. John said that he would like to wash his hands, and Robert conducted him to the bathroom.

After John had left the bathroom, Robert went there in his turn, and he was absent for about ten minutes. The time and order of these simple movements became later of considerable interest.

Bertha came upstairs at half-past seven to tell them that dinner was ready. Presently they were seated in the dining-room: Mr. and Mrs. Kewdingham, old Robert Kewdingham, and John Harrigall.

## 4

The dinner was not exactly cheerful. It seemed as if the company was affected by a feeling of high tension in the air, a sort of physical uneasiness, such as one may feel on the approach of a thunderstorm. They sat down in the warm, grey twilight.

Kewdingham was peevish. He grunted fiercely at the food, sighed, emitted his peculiar rasping groan, pushed about the morsels on his plate with a horrid squeaking and rattling of knife and fork. The old father attempted a literary conversation, which fluttered for a time in the close atmosphere, and was then asphyxiated. Bertha said little. As for John, looking at the tremulous, irascible, joggling head of Robert Arthur, he felt that something dreadful (he could not say what) was going to happen before the evening was over. He could not talk easily; the most that he could do was an occasional spurt of trivial chatter. It was an awful strain, a most unexpected and unaccountable strain.

"Have some burgundy?" said Robert, pushing the decanter towards John. "It's all I can offer you. Pommard, though—a good vintage. I'm rather fond of a good burgundy myself."

"Thank you," said John.

The blood was tinkling in his ears, and he observed with dismay a perceptible tremor in his legs and arms, a prickle of cold moisture on his brow. What on earth was the matter? Why did he feel the presence of something uncanny in the room, the unseen threatening of something malignant?

He filled his green glass with a wobbling hand, and then passed the decanter to the old man. Bertha, he knew, did not drink wine. Father Kewdingham filled his glass, and the decanter came back to Robert, who filled his own.

And as Robert Arthur poured the wine into his glass, John and Bertha looked at him and then glanced at each other. Doubtless a freak of telepathy.

With a jerk of the head, Kewdingham raised his glass.

"Here's health," he said.

It seemed to John that Bertha started, and that she was trembling.

"Good health!" said John.

After a curious preliminary groan Robert sipped his burgundy.

"Ha!" he said, "that's devilish bitter. It's a very harsh wine for a good vintage year. Still, it helps one to wash down this filthy underdone beef. Eh? Switch on the light, Bertha."

John also sipped his wine. It was bland, mellow and satisfying.

"I think it's a very fine burgundy—very good indeed."

The same opinion was expressed by the old father.

Robert grunted. He finished his glass but he did not have another. He muttered something about the wretched state of his digestion, a disordered palate, and so forth.

When dinner was over, Bertha cleared the table, the old man retired, while John and Robert carried on a flickering conversation in the drawing-room.

They were talking about family matters when John noticed that Robert was becoming exhilarated. Instead of drawling and groaning, as he usually did in those latter days, he began to shout in a hoarse, peculiar voice, somewhat unearthly. His eyes were fully open, dilated, brilliant. He was uncouthly jocular, and soon he was braying and laughing as if he had drunk a whole bottle of burgundy instead of one glass. It was a terrifying change. John was unprepared and rather frightened. He wondered if there was any danger of violence. He had never seen Robert in such a state before. The very character of the man appeared to have altered. Even in the prime of his life Robert had been dour, sedate, unemotional, avoiding demonstration or boisterous gaiety.

Bertha, when she came up from the kitchen, with coffee on a tray, was immediately alarmed. She gave John a dark interrogative glance, as much as to say—"Can you explain this? What have you been doing?"

"Old Muriel, eh?—Ha, ha-a-a!" Robert was husky but garrulous and full of demonic merriment. "Why, she fell in love with a missionary—ha, ha, ha!—a proper prayer-book missionary—blue glasses and a golden cross and all the rest of it! Yes—that's a fact—didn't you know it? Ha-a-a-a! And the best of it is, *he* fell in love with *her*. Incredible—what? Now then—why didn't she marry this proper prayer-book missionary, eh? Why—he'd got a wife in the Solomon Islands! Ha, ha! So there was poor old Muriel—" He went off into a sputtering cackle of merriment, a choking, rasping, agonising laugh, with tears of real pain in his eyes. This horrid laughter was uncontrollable. A dusky flush came over his twitching face; the veins of his neck, temples and brow looked as if they would burst under the tight skin.

All at once, the laughter came to an end. He made a diving, clutching movement with his hand.

"Ah, ha!" he cried, unclosing his fingers. "Did I get him?"

"Get what?" said John, feeling shivery.

"Why, that little green what's-a-name. You saw him, didn't you? One of those little green—ha, ha-a-a!"

And again there came a shrill, whinnying laugh.

"Well, I could have sworn I'd got him. There—there!—That's him, isn't it?—down on the hearth-rug."

Robert was chuckling with a dry throaty rattle, but the sound must have been automatic. He stared at the hearthrug with an expression of utter dismay. Then he shot out his foot over the carpet with a movement so powerful and spasmodic that he nearly pitched himself on to the floor.

"There!—He's gone!"

He bounced back on the chirruping springs of the chair, a pitiful, uncanny sight.

Then he began to chatter again. He paid no attention to the others. It was a stuttering flow of sheer nonsense, broken by shrill neighs of laughter. Family matters and family characters, all fearsomely distorted, were jumbled up in a shocking phantasmagoria.

This went on for some time, John and Bertha sitting as pale as corpses. Bertha, with a shaking hand, endeavoured to pour out some coffee for John.

Abruptly, for no apparent reason, the flow ceased.

"Bobby—hadn't I better send for Doctor Bagge?"

For a moment, the name recalled him.

"Bagge? Bagge? No, of course not. Why should I want to see Bagge? He's coming to-morrow."

Then he went off again. He was looking with his dilated eyes at the space in the middle of the room. He was looking, not with terror, but with insane curiosity. There was an intermittent giggling cluck in his throat, like a dry gargle.

"How very strange!" he whispered. "It must be an illusion. I say it must be an illusion. There's nothing there, is there? You see where I mean? Just there—" He wagged a shaking hand vaguely. "It can't be anything but an illusion, mere illusion." The hand fell and he sagged back loosely in the chair. "Of course it is, my dear fellow. I know that as well as you do. You needn't think you're so clever. To begin with, no such thing could possibly have got into the room. How could it—eh?"

"No!" said John soothingly. "It would be impossible."

"Impossible. That's the word. Quite impossible."

His mood was changing. He was getting drowsy, and he talked in a thin husky whisper.

"Obviously quite impossible," he observed gravely. "I should be sorry if you thought I was drunk or anything of that sort, but I could have sworn there was a—"

"John," said Bertha, "I wish you would run round for Doctor Bagge. I'm frightened." There was no telephone in the house.

"Is it safe to leave you?" said John. "Wouldn't it be better if you went yourself?"

But the scene was nearly over. Robert got up on his feet, swaying, as though he was trying to balance himself on a moving surface like the sliding deck of a ship in a heavy sea.

"It was *there*—"

He shuffled unsteadily forward, lifting his feet high and stretching his arms.

"Why—why—confound it! Look! It *is* there. It's there all the time. No!—it's impossible. Look—look out! It's moving. Oh, good Lord!—it's moving. I tell you, I saw it move quite distinctly. Stop it, can't you? Give me a—"

John rose; he was nearly as unsteady as the other.

"I don't think you are very well, Bobby. Hadn't you better go to bed?"

Robert stared at him. A sudden gust of rage blew up into the hollows of his tottering mind. It was a final rallying of energy. He raised his fluttering hands above his head.

"You damned little Dutchman! You're trying to frighten me. You, with your dirty little tricks! Crocodiles, eh? But I know it's an illusion. It's a dirty trick—dirty—"

Those were the last words of that sad automatism Athuna-Shulah in his Kewdingham form. He fell crash on the floor in a sprawling bunch.

## 5

Fortunately, Doctor Bagge's house was not far from Wellington Avenue. It was about ten o'clock when John rang furiously the doctor's bell.

"John Harrigall. You remember me, doctor? Please come round at once to see Kewdingham. He's gone down in a fit or something. It looks pretty bad. We've put him on the sofa—"

"I'm not surprised to hear that," said Doctor Bagge, snatching up a grey felt hat. "Poisoned, I should think."

"What!"

"Well, you know his habits, don't you? Always fooling about with drugs that he ought never to have had in his possession. Come along—this way—through the dispensary. I shall need one or two things, though I doubt if there's much to be done."

When Doctor Bagge saw the patient he shook his head and said that he must have a nurse at once. He gave John the necessary particulars and John went off and presently returned with Nurse Cundle. Between them, they put Robert to bed; and then, seeing that he could do nothing more, John returned to Uncle Richard with his alarming news.

Kewdingham died at one o'clock in the morning. He had lapsed into coma, and death was due to failure of the heart.

The old man, who had been disturbed by the noise in the house, was ominously calm. He wandered about in a heavy overcoat, as if he was looking for something, but nobody observed his movements. His air was not so much sorrowful as grim and inquisitive. Bertha gave him a cup of tea, which he took without a word.

Doctor Bagge left the house at two o'clock. He returned at half-past ten.

The doctor, like the old man, was evidently looking for something. He was puzzled. He had a long talk with Bertha about the circumstances of the previous night, and he asked her many questions. She was pale, though steady.

"Very painful, Mrs. Kewdingham," said the doctor, "very painful indeed. I had not anticipated anything of the sort. There is no doubt as to the cause of death, none at all. But there are one or two things I should like to know before I give the certificate. Do you happen to know if he was taking the mixture? The bottle used to be on the table in the bedroom, but I can't see it anywhere. If you could get hold of it for me—" He did not explain his request.

"I will have a look for it," said Bertha, not paying much attention to him. "He was taking the stuff regularly, as far as I know."

"You have communicated with the members of the family?"

"Yes. Mr. Harrigall has just been here and he is going to inform the members of the family in Shufflecester. He is also going to send a telegram to Phoebe Kewdingham."

There were some more questions, and then the doctor wrote out the certificate:

(1) Cardiac failure due to acute gastro-enteritis.
(2) Chronic nephritis.

# Chapter XI

## 1

Phoebe Kewdingham arrived at Shufflecester on Friday afternoon. She had put on a black dress which suited both her and the occasion extremely well; but she caused inexpressible offence to the Poundle-Quaintons by her brightly incarnadined lips. "It might be all right for those nasty detrimentals in London," they said, "but she ought to show more respect for her poor brother—and, indeed, for the Family."

Phoebe, who knew perfectly well that Robert and his wife had lived in perpetual discord, assumed an air of sorrow and reserve tempered by vigilance. She did not dislike Bertha and had always appreciated her dramatic qualities, but she did feel that poor Robert had not been altogether in the wrong.

The family assembled in gloomy conclave. Uncle Richard was impenetrably neutral. Father Kewdingham looked as though he was brooding over a secret: he mumbled furtively into Phoebe's ear. Mrs. Poundle-Quainton was a model of bereaved respectability. Mrs. Pyke glowered at Bertha in a way that was definitely suspicious. Bertha herself was tired, resigned and a little irritable; she could not even affect an overwhelming sorrow.

John had returned to London. He would, of course, come back for the funeral.

It was arranged that Phoebe should spend the next few melancholy days with Mrs. Pyke. Michael would arrive on Saturday afternoon and the funeral was to take place on Monday.

When she was over at Number Six, helping Bertha, Phoebe could not help being surprised by her father's manner. He kept on shaking his head and muttering, avoided conversation as much as possible, and appeared to be occupied with some problem of an intricate nature. He did not emerge from his rooms, except when it was necessary for him to do so.

Phoebe was also puzzled by the demeanour of Martha Tuke, the maid. This demeanour was not unlike that of the old man. Martha had a strange air of preoccupation; she looked as if she was trying to make up her mind to say something.

But there was a lot to be done, and Phoebe could not give much attention to the vagaries of others.

By the day of the funeral, suspicion was on the point of begetting rumour.

As for the funeral, it was an exclusive family affair, carried out in the best possible taste. Miss Phoebe Kewdingham was greatly admired. John was also a distinguished figure, easily the smartest of the men. Doctor Bagge, so well known at the cemetery, looked as neat as a pin, though when you compared him with John you saw that he was decidedly provincial. They were all there except the old man, who stayed at home.

Michael, in his little black suit, was proud to find himself, for the first time, in a position of some importance. He could not regard the experience as wholly disagreeable. His only embarrassment was caused by his gloves—they were too large, and he was continually trying to push back the tips of the fingers.

The curious march of events, totally unexpected by everyone concerned, does not allow us to record the impressions and manoeuvres of the family after their return from the ceremony. Some of them were obviously relieved and others were still unsettled. There was a certain amount of regret, and there was a great deal of unaccountable whispering.

## 2

On Tuesday morning, while she was having breakfast with Mrs. Pyke, Phoebe was astonished to hear that Martha Tuke was at the front door, and requested to have a word with her. Phoebe was leaving by an afternoon train, but she would naturally call at Number Six before going to the station. She could only imagine that Bertha had sent an urgent message.

But Martha, standing in the hall, begged for a private interview. Evidently she had been crying. Phoebe, after apologising to Mrs. Pyke, took Martha into the morning-room and closed the door.

"I'm leaving Mrs. Kewdingham," said Martha. "I've been up since four getting my things ready. My boy's coming round at dinner-time to fetch my box, and I'm going home by the bus this afternoon. I can't stay there no longer."

"But, good gracious!—Why?" asked Phoebe, recalling with sudden alarm Martha's odd behaviour at Number Six.

"I tell you, Miss Kewdingham, there's things been going on at that house as people ought to know about—and they will know about 'em, too, before long."

"Please tell me what you mean."

"I'm not educated like you are, Miss Kewdingham, but I can't help seeing what's going on; and maybe I can think a bit." Martha, knowing that she might be severely rebuked, was inclined to be defiant, after the manner of such people.

Phoebe, whose gravity was not assumed, understood her.

"If you have anything to say, please be quite frank with me. I am not criticising you."

"I'm an honest girl," said Martha, feeling more confident, "and I try to do my duty, and I think it's my duty to tell you as I don't believe Mr. Kewdingham come to a natural end."

"What makes you believe such a thing?"

"It's a scandal, the way Mrs. Kewdingham has been carrying on with Mr. Harrigall all this time—kissing, and that sort of thing. And running round to Doctor Bagge, until the whole town's talking about it. Well, the less said the better! There's many as think Doctor Bagge a very proper sort of gentleman, I know. But see here, Miss Kewdingham—"

Phoebe could not restrain a little start of alarm and surprise. "Please go on," she said quietly.

"Now, on Thursday night Mrs. Kewdingham says to me, 'You need not be back till eleven, Martha. I can do most of the washing-up myself,' she says. Never before had she offered to do such a thing—never. She'd got some new green glasses and she'd got a bottle of burgundy, and I could see she was all in a flutter about something. I come in at half-past ten, when they'd got Mr. Kewdingham on the sofa and the doctor was there. When I'd done what I was told to do, I went downstairs and had a look at the dining-room. The green glasses had been took away and washed and put away—all the other things was just piled up anyhow and anywhere. You may say it's only my ignorance, Mrs. Kewdingham, but I know there was something wrong, and I believe them glasses had something to do with it. You see, it was my evening off; and so Mrs. Kewdingham laid the table. I've been thinking about it ever since, and I know *positive* there was something wrong about them glasses. Then there's a bottle gone from the bedroom…I would have spoke to the old gentleman, but then he's that curious and ancient—I couldn't tell how he would take it, you see. Then, there's another thing, Miss Kewdingham—Perhaps I ought not to have done it—"

Martha hesitated. She knew that she would have to be careful.

"You may trust me," said Phoebe.

"Well, it's like this. Mr. Harrigall left after the funeral yesterday, as you know, miss. In the evening, about half-past eight, Mrs. Kewdingham gave me a letter addressed to Mr. Harrigall. 'Here, Martha,' she says, 'just run out and post this for me, will you—I'm terribly busy.' I took the letter and went out with it, but before I got to the pillar-box I felt it was wrong somehow, and so I—I—I thought I would give it to you instead. Here it is, Miss Kewdingham; and, of course, if you like to blame me you're free to do so."

Opening her smart little hand-bag, Martha produced the letter.

For a moment Phoebe paused. Then she took the letter and turned it over in her hand.

"No, Miss Kewdingham!" said Martha, in a glow of hot reproach, "I've not opened it; if that's what you think."

"I don't think anything of the sort," Phoebe replied. A whole multitude of new, disquieting ideas filled her mind. She recalled a number of sinister fragments in the conversation of Mrs. Pyke. She remembered what she herself had observed on different occasions. Tolerant by nature and with no disposition to meddle or pry, she was unaffected by the prevailing rumours. But here she was confronted by a definite responsibility, by something more substantial and more redoubtable than mere suspicion. She was a woman of quick resolve, and she now decided that she would act on her own initiative, with secrecy and with considered method. Having thanked Martha and obtained her address, she impressed upon her the desirability of absolute silence. Then she went back to Mrs. Pyke, who was grimly finishing her breakfast.

"Martha tells me that she is leaving. Evidently there's a lot to be done, a lot to be cleared up; and I should like to stay here until to-morrow, if you can manage—"

"Certainly, my dear. I am very glad to hear you say so. I am not at all surprised. Indeed, I think it is your duty. Robert is much too old, and Richard is too easy-going; and as for Bella and Ethel—what do they know about business? And then, you know, *that woman* has never taken the slightest interest in family matters."

## 3

The Chief Constable of the Shufflecester City Police, Colonel Henry Dowser Drayford, D.S.O., was a burly, boisterous man with a flashing red moustache and a sharp staccato manner. He had a constitutional grin upon his face, which, combined with his bristling hot moustache, gave him the appearance of a tiger-man.

On the afternoon of the 1st of May, Colonel Drayford received in his office a tall, venerable gentleman who was carrying a brown-paper parcel.

"Mr. Robert Henry Kewdingham? Pray take that chair, sir."

The old man sat down, not without dignity, putting his parcel on the edge of the colonel's desk. He had come up a flight of stairs to the office and he was out of breath.

"Bitter constraint—" he mumbled.

"Eh? What's that? Please explain your reasons for coming here." The Chief Constable tapped a pencil sharply on his blotter.

"I will be as brief as I can," said old father Kewdingham. "I have come to see you about the death of my poor son, Mr. Robert Arthur Kewdingham." On hearing these words, Colonel Drayford could not refrain from uttering a quick explosive sound, though it would have been hard to say whether he was thus giving expression to surprise or annoyance.

"That is what I have come to see you about," the old gentleman continued, fixing his eyes upon the colonel in a melancholy though resolute manner. "I am very dissatisfied, very uneasy. You will appreciate, sir, the difficulties of my situation. It is by no means pleasant to have to say what I am about to say—a terrible duty, sir, I can assure you. I must ask you to listen with all your sympathy, my dear sir, and with all your consideration. You will understand, I know, the extreme delicacy—my great sorrow—"

Colonel Drayford impatiently twiddled a rubber date-stamp on the corner of his desk. His fiery face did not promise the understanding of anything delicate.

"My great sorrow—of course, you have heard the talk about my daughter-in-law and Doctor Wilson Bagge. I very much regret having to mention this. I fear it is necessary."

"Talk, talk, talk, sir!" replied the colonel, chopping out his words like a ventriloquist. "Talk, did you say? Gad, sir! I've no time for listening to talk. Please let us come to the point."

"I believe my son was poisoned."

Again Colonel Drayford made a sudden explosive noise. He looked up sharply. "Poisoned? Why, and by whom? What makes you think it? Why have you waited so long? Have you said anything about it? What is your evidence? Why didn't you speak to the doctor?" He shot out his questions like a burst of rapid fire.

"I suspect the doctor himself."

"What! Do you understand what you are saying, sir? Doctor Bagge? Why, sir, Bagge is a friend of mine, and a man of excellent reputation, a most popular man. What you say, if repeated elsewhere, would be highly scandalous. You had better be careful, sir; you had better be careful. Here, of course, it's a privileged communication. But positively absurd—"

"Pray listen, Colonel Drayford. The illness which led to my son's death undoubtedly began when Doctor Bagge gave him a certain medicine. Never mind, for the moment, what made me suspicious. Here is a bottle of the medicine. What has occurred since the death of my poor son has confirmed my suspicions. If you would rather that I communicated with the Home Office—" He was rigid, firm, insistent, even harsh. He now faced the grinning tiger-face of the colonel with a stern determination.

"Quite absurd, Mr. Kewdingham. Let me look at the bottle."

After much fumbling and fiddling with a disordered mass of string and of crackling paper, the bottle was produced. It was half full of a cloudy pink mixture.

"You had better leave it here, perhaps. But how can I tell where you got it from, eh? You ought to have called in the police, my good sir. I will make one or two enquiries. And I warn you—not a word. Not a word to anyone. I shall communicate with you in due course."

He struck a metal bell on his desk. A policeman entered.

"Now, sir, I must attend to other matters. Good morning, sir. Mackey, show this gentleman out, and then tell Inspector Miles that I want to see him—tell him to bring those papers about the Sibley Hall case."

A few minutes later, the chief was writing a memorandum. He looked up at the clock as the inspector came into the room.

"Look here, Miles—this Kewdingham affair.—We shall have to do something about it. You remember that young lady who came here this morning?"

"Miss Phoebe Kewdingham, sir?"

"Phoebe. Yes; that's right. Her father has just been here. It's really very odd, the ideas these people have got into their heads. Tuh! Just listen to this…Now I want you to run over to Wyveldon this evening, taking Sergeant Hopkey with you, and get a statement from that girl Miss Kewdingham told us about—Martha—Martha something or other—"

"Very good, sir."

"And look here, Miles. Caution her—put the fear of God into her. You never can tell what's behind these rumours. There *has* been a lot of talk about the death of this man Kewdingham. I've heard it myself."

"Yes, sir; there's been some very dangerous talk, too. Bound to be trouble before long, if I'm not mistaken."

## 4

On the 2nd of May, Doctor Bagge was talking to Mrs. Kewdingham. They were in the drawing-room of Number Six. Bertha was looking somewhat haggard, though very graceful in her black clothes.

"That mixture, by the way. Did you find the bottle? No? Well, I must say it's rather odd. I wonder if he was taking any dope, or quack medicine, or anything of that sort. You see, I remember noticing that bottle in the bedroom. Please don't imagine that I have been worrying about a trifle. But I should like to know—"

Bertha looked at him sharply. Did he suspect anything? Of course not!

"Perhaps you would like to see the medicine cupboard."

"Well, well! I don't want to seem inquisitive. Still, if you would allow me—"

"Yes, do. It would relieve my own mind, after what you have been saying."

They went up to the bathroom and the doctor opened the cupboard.

"Ah!" The little man gave a chirp of astonishment. "Good gracious! What an amazing collection! I've never seen anything like it."

He deftly poked among the tinkling bottles, the innumerable packages and boxes. Some he merely lifted up and put down again, and some he took out and examined carefully. The bottles made a faint crystalline sound as he moved them, jars rattled, corks plopped, the lids of boxes grated or squeaked; and still he went on, shaking the bottles, holding them up to the light, smelling them, reading the labels. He dipped his finger daintily in powders or pastes, occasionally sniffing and even tasting. Bertha watched him grimly. He was fumbling among the discarded lotions with a tush-tush! of disapproval.

"I don't like the look of some of these things—not at all! This may be arsenic…And what's this?—Sugar of lead? How very extraordinary!" He frowned. "I had no idea he had such a deadly assortment."

He went on, fumbling in the secret recesses of the top shelf.

"Hullo! What on earth is this?"

He had fished out a little cylindrical object, wrapped in an outer cylinder of paper which was bound with a piece of thin ribbon. From the paper wrapping he now withdrew a very striking object: a blue glass phial with a silver filigree mounting.

"I'm sure I don't know what it is," said Bertha. "I've never seen it before. It looks like one of those old-fashioned scent-bottles."

The doctor pressed open the silver top of the phial, a kind of hollow stopper with a cork lining which fitted very tightly; it worked on a hinge and was held in position by a snap fastening. He sniffed lightly. A subtle, peculiar smell, not unlike the scent of a warm cherry-orchard when the trees are in blossom.

"Ah!"

He drew himself up very rigidly, holding the phial in one hand and looking at Bertha.

"Well?" said Bertha, twitching her eyebrows.

Doctor Bagge could see that she was not particularly interested. Instead of replying he put the phial to his nose again, and then he slowly walked over to the window. He looked closely at the filigree pattern—unmistakably oriental. He shook the little flask up and down. He held it to the light, as though he was admiring the lovely blue. Then he saw a medicine-glass on the window-ledge, and into this he tipped a few drops out of the phial. He sniffed again.

"Bless me! This is most extraordinary!"

He took the glass to the basin and rinsed it out with a more than usual degree of thoroughness. Holding the pretty blue flask in his hand, he looked again at Mrs. Kewdingham.

"You are sure that you have never seen this before?"

"No. I have just told you so. I had my orders to leave the cupboard alone."

"And the cupboard was never locked?"

"Not so far as I know."

The doctor stood there for a minute in prim, irritating silence. He kept the phial in his hand and stared at it with an air of pure abstraction. He was thinking hard. Indeed, the cupboard had now given him more than enough to think about.

"What is it?" said Bertha. "Can you tell?"

"A form of atropine, I should imagine. Enough to kill a whole family."

The paper cylinder, with its band of pink ribbon, lay on the window-ledge. Bertha took it up.

"Look here," she said, "this is a letter or something of the sort. We had better read it."

Pinching the cylinder lightly, she slipped off the ribbon. On the paper, written in faded brownish ink, she read the following remarkable words:

"This phial was given to me by the Rajah of Pyzaribad. It is one of the many curious gifts presented to me by His Royal Highness in 1863, as tokens (he assured me) of gratitude and esteem. I had been successful in treating the indisposition of one of his favourite ladies, under circumstances which were certainly delicate and possibly dangerous. He did not tell me precisely what the phial contains, but gave me to understand that it would enable me to remove any person who was troublesome to me, without exposing me to the risk of a painful investigation. A few drops, he told me, would be enough. Such gifts are by no means uncommon, as many Englishmen can testify, and of course I could not dream of refusing it. I told the Rajah, with a smile, that it was not likely to be of any use to me, but that I appreciated his kind thought and greatly admired the pretty workmanship of the silver mounting. There can be little doubt that the phial contains a preparation of Dhatoora (*datura stramonium*) with a more than usually high percentage of hyoscyamine and other poisonous alkaloids. Of its taste I have no knowledge, but it has a slightly acrid smell and is almost colourless. I need hardly say that I keep it merely as a curiosity! Many of my friends have told me that I ought to throw the stuff away, merely retaining the flask; but somehow it would seem a pity to do so.

"Lionel Tighe Howard, Surgeon, Bombay, June 17, 1881."

The writing was that of Robert Arthur's grandfather, that famous and eccentric Indian surgeon, known to everyone in the Presidency as Bombay Howard.

# 5

The doctor continued his morning round, precise, discreet, friendly and careful as ever. And yet, inside his impenetrable shell of decorum, the doctor was profoundly uneasy.

He knew well enough that ugly rumours concerning the death of Kewdingham, originating he could not say how or why, had already come to the ears of the police. Now his adventure in the medicine cupboard had given him a whole series of unexpected shocks. There was no limit to the amount of mischief a man might do, either to himself or to others, with such an assortment of deadly drugs. The blue phial was a startling discovery, but it was only one among other discoveries equally strange. If you began to speculate on all the possible uses and abuses of the drugs in that cupboard, the imagination recoiled in hopeless bewilderment.

Bagge was chiefly disturbed by the loss of the medicine-bottle, the bottle containing his pink invention. Who had taken it away? And why had it been taken away? He had noticed it on the table at the time of Kewdingham's fatal illness, and then—he could not say precisely when—it had disappeared. Doctor Bagge was a subtle fellow, and he knew how much old father Kewdingham disliked him. Aged men are generally suspicious, incapable of drawing the ordinary line between fantasy and reasonable conjecture. Hence they often arrive at a true conclusion by working on a theory which a vigorous normal mind would never entertain. Suppose the old man had taken the bottle for sinister reasons of his own? He could easily make trouble. The doctor was not so wide of the mark; indeed, he was much closer than he imagined. Then, when he found the blue phial, he saw a possible cause of Kewdingham's death. He recalled the symptoms; his new suspicion became almost a certainty. Wisely or unwisely, he had persuaded Bertha to let him take the phial. He decided to forestall any enquiry…If his prescription was called in question, he had an excellent defence, and he would be able to produce evidence which pointed to suicide. He did not know the real strength of his position; he was led by a fortunate instinct.

# 6

Colonel Drayford, the Chief Constable of Shufflecester, was at his desk. He had just been having a talk with Inspector Miles. A case of assault was giving them a lot of trouble. The colonel was in a glow of exasperation, his red moustache flickered like a flame under the deeper red of his angry countenance. He was fiercely snapping away in a long chitter-chatter of questions, instructions and cursings when the telephone bell cut him short.

"Yes, yes…Bagge?…Well, look here; I'm frightfully busy just now…Urgent?…Oh! I see…Can you make it eleven-thirty?…Very good then. Right you are."

And at the half-hour exactly the neat little man tripped into Drayford's office.

"I see you're busy, colonel; but you know I wouldn't bother you unless it was necessary. And it is. Very necessary, if I'm not mistaken."

"Sit down, Bagge. I suppose it's one of your usual cases."

"No, it isn't. I wish it was."

"Well, fire away, there's a good chap. I have to be in the court by twelve, and we're not quite ready."

"It's about the death of a patient of mine. You have probably heard of him. Kewdingham. I believe he was poisoned."

The Chief Constable fairly bounced in his chair. He could not get any redder, but he went all of a cloudy purple. He struck violently the bell on his desk.

"Miles! Miles!" he roared.

The inspector, one of those over-acute, heavy, insinuating men, came into the room.

"Sir?"

"I want you to listen to what Doctor Bagge has to say, and be ready to make notes if I want 'em. Go on, Bagge; go on. The inspector is my confidential secretary, so to speak. You have often met him before."

"As a matter of fact," said the doctor, speaking very distinctly and slowly, "the case is one which certainly does require investigation. I am very glad my friend the inspector is here. I will be brief.

"This is about the death of Mr. Robert Arthur Kewdingham, inspector. His name cannot be unfamiliar to you, because you have doubtless, in the course of your duty, heard of the various rumours which are now circulating in the town. Mr. Kewdingham died early in the morning of the 28th of last month, at his own house, Number Six Wellington Avenue. I attended him. At the time of the death I was in no doubt as to the cause. Kewdingham had a very weak heart, and he also suffered from an incurable disease of the kidneys. He was, moreover, subject to violent attacks of dysentery. His general health was deplorable, he was a wreck, liable to collapse at any moment. On the day of his death, and on the previous day, he was suffering from a recurrence of dysentery; he was exhausted, weak and irritable. His death was due to cardiac failure, which might have been predicted with confidence by anyone who knew the state of his organs. But I will admit, honestly, that I was at a loss to account for one or two rather unusual symptoms."

"Make a note of that, Miles," said the Chief. "He could not account for one or two symptoms. Put it down, Miles."

"Those symptoms were delirium (which I did not see personally) followed by a very deep coma, while the pupils of the eyes were abnormally dilated. Of course, these symptoms might have been produced in the ordinary course of his illness, and I may as well say frankly that I did suspect a definite disease of the brain. We know now that symptoms are extremely variable, and are seldom, in themselves, a reliable guide in diagnosis. Then, finding that I was unable to get this case out of my mind, and hearing the distant echo of certain rumours, it occurred to me (only yesterday) that

I would run round to the house and ask Mrs. Kewdingham, the widow, if she would allow me to look at the medicine-cupboard. I had some curiosity to see this, because I knew very well that Kewdingham was a wretched hypochondriac, fond of purchasing drugs and of making various mixtures—I cannot call them medicines—for his own use. I had repeatedly warned him against this dangerous practice, and he had finally promised to be more careful. Indeed, I told him that I would give him up unless he gave my own medicines a proper chance. Well; I saw the cupboard, and I got more than I bargained for. I got this."

He took the blue phial and the covering letter out of his case and handed them to the colonel.

"You had better be careful: it's full of a deadly poison."

"Poison! Good heavens, man! What poison?"

"Can't say exactly. But here's the history of the thing—on this bit of paper." He read aloud, quickly, the account of Surgeon Howard. "Probably that's quite correct. I had identified the main substance, by smell, before I saw the description. Atropine, hyoscyamine, stramonium, belladonna…"

"Miles! Have you got that?" cried the Chief, peculiarly excited.

"I'm not very sure about the spelling, sir."

"Never mind the spelling. Say that he spotted the poison by the smell. Very smart of you, Bagge. Mrs. Kewdingham was there all the time, eh? Yes? Very good. Go on, Bagge; go on, go on. Do you suppose he took it with intention—"

"I have no wish to evolve a theory. All I can say is that acute poisoning by the mydriatic alkaloids which I have mentioned would produce dilation of the pupils, delirium and coma, followed by paralysis of the respiratory mechanism, causing death."

"Stop, stop, stop!" The Chief was more and more agitated. "Don't be so damn' technical. It would cause death.

Poison would cause death, with symptoms. Put it down, Miles. Did you think he was likely to poison himself? Did you warn him? Did you see him on the day of his death? Did you know that he was playing about with these drugs all the time? Miles!—Are you noting this, eh?"

Dr. Bagge looked at the Chief Constable with a blue glitter in his eye, but he spoke with his customary precision.

"Kewdingham was not quite an ordinary man. He was liable to extreme depression, and also to singular fantasies about himself. Had I been told that he had committed suicide I should not have been at all surprised. But the point I want to make is that poisoning by a mydriatic alkaloid would have produced all the symptoms which were observed, either by myself or by others, in this particular case. That is not to say, of course, that he was actually poisoned by such an alkaloid. In my opinion, however, an enquiry may be desirable."

"Well, Bagge, this is a damned odd business. I hardly know what to say. I think I had better say nothing. It's very odd, very odd indeed. It looks to me as though you may be right. He was a funny chap, you say, and he may have taken a dose of poison. And so you bring me this little blue flask, and you tell me what you suspect. I think you have acted in a very proper manner. Either he took it, or he didn't; or somebody gave it to him, or didn't give it to him. That's as much as I care to say at present. It's a remarkable coincidence—I mean—well, it's a devilish odd affair. We shall have to investigate. I shall inform the coroner."

The inspector shifted his large body as if he was adjusting himself for mental concentration. He bent his head, puckering the skin of his jaw over the stiff collar of his tunic. His little grey eyes turned obliquely towards the Chief.

"Very odd, sir."

"Very odd. Yes, precisely. Your conclusion, inspector, is the same as my own. We shall certainly have to do something. Look here, Bagge; you had better leave that thing with me, in case they—in case we decide to do something. Probably I shall want to see you again. I shall send you a message. Now I have got to prepare for the court."

# Chapter XII

## 1

On a morning in the second week of May, John Harrigall received a telephone message from New Scotland Yard. He was asked if it would be convenient for him to be at home between half-past eleven and half-past twelve. If so, an officer would like to see him. If not, perhaps he would be so good as to name some other time later in the day.

John was not altogether surprised. He knew something about the Shufflecester rumours, and he guessed why the officer wanted to see him. He said that he would be at home all morning. Soon after eleven a nicely dressed man came to the house and gave his name as Detective Inspector Boskell.

The inspector was very smooth in manner, almost cajoling, and he apologised in the most urbane way for putting John to so much trouble. A duty by no means agreeable! he said. But he would merely ask John to answer a few simple questions, and he would be as brief as possible.

As for the questions, they were fairly obvious. First of all, the inspector wanted to know what John could tell him about the late Mr. Robert Arthur Kewdingham, of Shufflecester.

John described his cousin with singular impartiality. He had been a moody, irritable man, he said, who was often frightfully depressed. Yes; Mr. Kewdingham was evidently worried about health and money, and things of that sort. A bit queer, perhaps? Decidedly queer, said John, if not positively mad. He had some curious fancies, had he not, said the inspector—reincarnation or something? John replied that such was indeed the case. He saw that a theory of suicide was in the air, and he naturally did all he could do to strengthen it. As for Mr. Kewdingham's relations with his wife, they were quite ordinary, as far as he knew. Well; there might have been an occasional quarrel, but he had never seen anything worthy of mention.

Now—in regard to a certain meal on the 27th of April?

John remembered it very well indeed…Yes, they all ate from the same dishes, and all except Mrs. Kewdingham had some burgundy. Yes, yes!—from the same decanter, the only one on the table.—Did Mr. Kewdingham partake of anything which the others did not partake of?—No, certainly not. Was there anything strange about Mr. Kewdingham's behaviour during the meal, or just before?—He was extremely depressed, looking ill, and inclined to be quarrelsome.—For how long, previous to the meal, had Mr. Harrigall been able to observe him?—For nearly an hour and a half.—And he had noticed this peculiarity, illness, depression, and so forth?—Yes, he was very much alarmed, he had never seen his cousin looking so ill before.

The inspector then asked a number of questions about the movements of John and of the other people in the house between six o'clock and supper-time. When did he post his letter? When did he go to the bathroom? When did Mr. Kewdingham go to the bathroom?—and so on.

After supper, the inspector continued, there was a very painful scene? John described the events preceding the collapse of Mr. Kewdingham. Without knowing that he was doing so, he described all the symptoms of datura poisoning with the accuracy and precision of a text-book. Then he gave an account of all that happened until his return to Uncle Richard's house.

"Next morning, Mr. Harrigall, you went back to Wellington Avenue?"

"I did."

"And you saw nothing unusual?"

"I don't quite follow your meaning, inspector."

"Let me put it in another way." The inspector looked at him with a soothing and reassuring smile. "Were they all behaving as you would have expected them to behave in the circumstances?"

"Most emphatically they were. Why not?"

"Now, sir, think a minute. You write books, Mr. Harrigall. You observe things. Tell me—you didn't see or hear anything which struck you as odd?" Inspector Boskell flipped a page of his note-book.

"No, I didn't. We were all very much upset."

"Quite. I'm sorry to remind you of the sad occasion. Of course, nobody suggested the death was anything but natural?"

"Good God, inspector!" John drew himself back in his chair. "You don't mean to say—"

"No, sir. I don't mean to say anything. And now—will you be so good as to hear me run through these notes, and correct me if I have misrepresented you in any way? I will send you a typed copy for signature."

## 2

John guessed, and he guessed correctly, that similar enquiries were being made at Shufflecester, with apparently similar results.

Detectives were taking statements from old Kewdingham, Bertha Kewdingham, Doctor Bagge, the maid Martha, the two Poundle-Quaintons, and the nurse who attended Kewdingham when he was dying.

Horror! Disgrace! Such a thing had never been known in the family. What had become of the special providence?

And rumour, with her brazen voice, spread the awful tale. Have you heard? Mr. Kewdingham was poisoned—yes, *poisoned!* The police are investigating. They were in the house all day yesterday? Suicide? Well, my dear, I'm not surprised to hear it. Look at the woman—you can see she's half a foreigner. Mixed marriages, you know, are *such* a mistake! Of course, it must have been suicide. What—what did you say? Oh, no! I can't imagine how you could even think of such a thing.

So rumour spoke and so the tale of horror spread. And every now and then voices were lowered and a sinister word came in a whisper, a little word of two grim syllables.

Pamela Chaddlewick was full of twittering sorrow, and yet she was not unpleasantly excited.

"George, George! What did I tell you? Didn't I see it in the poor man's teacup? Didn't I tell you it was a coffin? You remember? Coffin in the teacup! A little teeny spickly speck, right in the middle. As soon as ever I saw it, I said to myself: That's a coffin in the teacup, that's what that is. I knew it meant something."

Doctor Wilson Bagge never turned a hair. He was prim, inscrutable, withdrawn. He would answer no questions, except those of the police. To none of his acquaintances would he say a word about the Kewdingham affair, and he neatly rebuked those who attempted to express opinions. Even with Mrs. Kewdingham he was terribly reticent, but that was because he wanted to spare her feelings. Also, he realised the importance of discretion until matters had been cleared up. People admired his exemplary behaviour. They felt rather sorry for him.

Father Kewdingham (to whom Phoebe, of course, had said nothing) isolated himself as much as possible. In his occasional conversations with Bertha he was exceedingly dry and cautious, though implying a disbelief in the notion of suicide. The state of affairs in the house, though outwardly quiet, was anything but happy.

They all knew that something awful was about to fall upon them.

## 3

On the day after his interview with Inspector Boskell, John came up to Shufflecester for the day.

He, like the others, believed in being discreet, but he could not abandon Bertha in her present awful situation. She had sent him the most appealing letters, telling him of her loneliness, her dismay, her knowledge of hostility and suspicion. He could not have known, any more than Bertha herself knew, that one of her letters had been intercepted and was then in the hands of the police.

When John arrived he went straight to Wellington Avenue. It was about twelve o'clock on a Thursday morning. Bertha opened the door.

"Oh, John, I'm so glad to see you! Doctor Bagge is here, and I should very much like you to have a talk with him—with both of us. Please do, my dear! He is doing his best to help us."

After permitting himself to kiss Bertha very chastely and quietly, John followed her into the drawing-room.

Here was a very odd situation.

Boxes and cabinets, already pushed into the corners, were still dominating the scene, the more so as they were piled one on top of the other. Even now, poor Robert was making himself felt, almost as if he was there watching them.

"Good morning, Mr. Harrigall," said the doctor, making one of his prim little bows. "I am glad that you have come. Mrs. Kewdingham has been telling me—"

They discussed the whole position. The doctor, who was really glad to have the opportunity, asked John some further questions in regard to the fatal 27th. John told the doctor precisely what he wanted to know and what he expected to hear.

"Do you suppose the police are going to take any further action?" said John.

"Well, Mr. Harrigall, that is hard to say. Evidently the matter has been referred to the Home Office."

"But—" said Bertha nervously, "what can they do?"

"They may consider it advisable to hold an inquest."

"Surely they would not do that," said John, "unless they suspected foul play. And foul play is out of the question."

"Oh, quite!—Of course."

It seemed to John as if the doctor spoke with a certain grim reserve, and with a lack of satisfying emphasis.

"But, my dear doctor! Well!—I mean to say—the mere suggestion is fantastic."

"Quite fantastic, my dear Mr. Harrigall, quite fantastic! That is, to you and me. Only, you must remember, the police are not as well acquainted with the circumstances as we are."

"Yes, but even on the face of it—"

"On the face of it, there were at least three people in the house who might have poisoned Mr. Kewdingham. That is how the police have to look at it." The doctor spoke in the gentlest way imaginable, as if he was conveying to a child some unpleasant but necessary truth. "You yourself were here, Mr. Harrigall; Mrs. Kewdingham was here; Mr. Kewdingham's father was here. Perhaps we may rule out the maid, because she left the house at three o'clock and did not return until ten-thirty. Of course, *we* know that a theory of foul play would be—as you have so pertinently observed, Mr. Harrigall—quite fantastic. That is because we know all the people concerned, and we know it would be an absurd theory. But, you see, the police know nothing of the sort. No theory is too fantastic from the police point of view. Indeed, it is their duty to be imaginative."

He suddenly looked full in the face of John with a glittering blue stare, though his expression was perfectly amiable.

"For example, they might suspect *you*, Mr. Harrigall. They might say—"

"Really, doctor! This is a bit thick. It is hardly an occasion for joking."

"I am not joking. I am only trying to answer your question about the police, and I suggest that it is just as well to look at things from their point of view."

"But if they suspect any such thing, they would be more likely to suspect me, wouldn't they?" said Bertha.

Doctor Bagge nodded his head very gravely. "Yes, they would," he replied.

There was a moment of impressive silence.

John, pulling himself up with a sidelong jerk of the shoulders, brightly said:

"By Jove! This is a grim conversation, and not very pleasant for you, Ber—Mrs. Kewdingham. And anyhow, doctor, such theories as you have mentioned would not bear examination."

"Wouldn't they?" said the horrid little man. "Why not?"

"But—I say!—"

"They would bear examination, Mr. Harrigall. They are probably being examined at this moment, and the examination will doubtless prove them incorrect in a very little time."

Something in the tone of the man's voice, or in the defiant urbanity of his manner, exasperated John. He forgot, or he disregarded, the peculiar delicacy of the circumstances.

"Well," he said, "while they are about it, they might also work on the hypothesis that it was *you* who killed him—with a bottle of medicine."

"Indeed, sir!" There was a wicked flicker in the blue eyes. "You were talking about the impropriety of a joke—"

"I am only trying to look at it from the police point of view. Nothing is too fantastic for the police. It's their business to be rather imaginative, you know."

John grinned. He saw that he had knocked the other, for one second, off his little dicky-bird perch. He could not say exactly why, but he was beginning to hate the doctor. Perhaps he regarded him as a rival. It is impossible to record the subtle impressions which may influence a man in such a way.

"Do let us be sensible, if you please," said Bertha, wrinkling her brow as though in pain, while at the same time she could not help feeling faintly amused. "This is terrible for me—"

"It's a damnable affair," said John warmly.

"I hope you don't blame me," said Dr. Bagge. "No medical man, in the circumstances, could have done anything else. And after all, if he *did* take the stuff—"

"Oh, it's awful, awful!" moaned Bertha.

"You could not possibly have foreseen such a thing," said the doctor.

"No one could have foreseen such a thing," said John.

"Though it is not surprising," said Bagge.

"How, not surprising?"

"Suicide would not have surprised me in such a case."

"Then you think—?"

"I think, if he swallowed the poison, it might be suicide."

"It could not be anything else."

"Why?"

"Surely that is evident."

"Not at all, Mr. Harrigall. It might have been an accident. Such things do happen, you know."

"But everything would indicate suicide—"

"Quite so, Mr. Harrigall. If the police come to the same conclusion they will probably decide to go no farther."

"And if they are not satisfied?"

"They will continue their enquiries."

"It's a painful situation, Doctor Bagge."

"A very painful situation, Mr. Harrigall. A painfully delicate situation. But I do not think we need be apprehensive."

"Why, no! What on earth should we apprehend?"

"Nothing worse than a little inconvenience, I hope, sir." And again the doctor looked at John with his peculiar metallic stare. It was a singular, inhuman stare; John felt it like the impact of a penetrating ray.

"But you are no doubt anxious to have a talk with Mrs. Kewdingham. In any case, it is time for me to go. Believe me, Mr. Harrigall, I have no wish to thrust myself impertinently into the discussion of private business, or to be concerned, beyond the limits of professional obligation, in family matters."

## 4

Then came the blow.

It was a few days after the conversation recorded above. Bertha, who had not succeeded in replacing Martha, and who was doing most of the housework herself, heard the door-bell ring at about eleven o'clock in the morning. When she opened the door she saw standing before her a grave, though amiable, gentleman with a ruddy face. A slim subordinate, in a dark blue uniform, stood behind him. In the background, by the edge of the kerb, there was a big saloon car. Bertha could also observe a number of people who were looking towards the house with evident curiosity.

"Mrs. Kewdingham?" said the grave personage. "Ah, yes! My name is Hubert Mills. I am the Borough Coroner. This is Police Superintendent Lee. I deeply regret that we are obliged to trouble you. Lee—tell those people to disperse immediately."

Mr. Hubert Mills was a lawyer. His manner was kindly and quiet, though extremely business-like. Having entered the house with Superintendent Lee, he explained that he was to hold an inquest on Mr. Robert Arthur Kewdingham. It would be necessary, for the purpose of the inquest, to examine certain parts of the house and also to remove certain objects. In this procedure he was merely carrying out his duty, and it was very distressing, etc.

Bertha was calm. By this time she had realised that anything was preferable to uncertainty. With a gravity quite equal to that of Mr. Mills, she assisted him in his round of exploration.

Her attitude, of course, made things far easier for Mr. Mills. There were no questions, there was no unnecessary talk. They were associated, you would have said, in the friendliest way imaginable. Even the hovering presence of old father Kewdingham was disregarded, and he presently retired to his room, quivering with excitement.

Apparently imperturbable, serene, Bertha conducted Mr. Mills from room to room.

When he saw the medicine-cupboard, Mr. Mills decided that it would be necessary to remove practically the whole of its contents. At first it did not seem as though he was going to take much besides; but presently he said that he would like to see the things in the kitchen, the scullery and the tool-shed. Evidently (as Doctor Bagge had foreseen) there was a definite line of research.

In the kitchen there was a cupboard full of glasses, jugs, jars, tins and so forth.

"Ah!" said Mr. Mills, looking into the cupboard. "Now here is a set of half a dozen green wineglasses. Am I right in assuming that four of those glasses were placed on the dinner-table on the evening of the twenty-seventh of April?"

"Yes," replied Bertha in a tone of mild surprise, "four of those glasses were on the table. I cannot say precisely which four, of course."

"No, no—naturally!" Mr. Mills himself appeared to be surprised by something. "Take these glasses, Lee, and pack them with great care. Thank you, Mrs. Kewdingham; some of that paper will do very nicely. Thank you."

The burgundy of the twenty-seventh had gone—old Mr. Kewdingham had drunk it—but Mr. Mills looked at the cut-glass decanter with a certain curiosity.

Then, when he came to the tool-shed, Mr. Mills was obviously puzzled. He had the air of a man looking for something which ought to be immediately visible, but which he cannot see. He could not refrain from exchanging glances with the Superintendent, and they poked and pried into every corner. Finally, with a trace of keen disappointment on his face, he selected a watering-can.

Soon after this, the investigation was concluded.

In full view of at least fifty gratified persons, Mr. Mills and the Superintendent conveyed to the car seven enormous packages. A curious intercepting move by father Kewdingham, who came shuffling down into the hall, was parried by Mr. Mills with an unexpected flash of severity. No! he said, he could not discuss the case with anyone; those who had evidence to give would be required to give it at the proper time and in the proper manner. His change of demeanour was remarkable. His gentleness gave way, in spite of himself, to an appearance of real hostility. Bertha, completely baffled by more than one feature of this investigation, felt more bewildered than ever. Recovering his grave courtesy,

Mr. Mills bade her farewell, and again apologised for the extremely painful, etc., etc.

It now occurred to Mrs. Kewdingham that the police might be on the wrong track altogether. It also occurred to her that there might eventually be some doubt as to the cause of poor Robert's death. The finding of the blue phial had certainly complicated matters in the most extraordinary way. These reflections were a source of comfort.

## 5

Mrs. Chaddlewick emitted a shrill cry of excitement, of delight and of horror.

"George, listen! Isn't this too awful?"

She was holding the day's issue of the *Shufflecester Gazette*. In a thin, eager, piping voice she read as follows:

### EXHUMATION ORDER
### *A Shufflecester Sensation*
### Mystery Move by Police

We understand, and our readers will be at one with us in sympathising with a well-known Shufflecester family, resident in the town for nearly forty years, that the Home Secretary has issued an order for the exhumation of the body of Mr. Robert Arthur Kewdingham, 47, who died on the 28th of April last, and who was connected for several years with the local branch of the Rule Britannia League, and a very distinguished engineer as well as a member of the Shufflecester Conservative Association, being very much interested in the preservation of Shufflecester antiquities and other curios, where his activities were of unusual value. He had been for

some time in bad health and had not
been able to continue so actively as
for some time in the past. He was a
highly respected, and we may truly say,
having regard to his varied interests
and loyal devotion to all that is most
British and most dear in our national
life, esteemed citizen. The Chief Constable of Shufflecester, Colonel Drayford, D.S.O., etc., has very properly
declined to make any statement to our
representative, though receiving him
with his universal and appreciated
courtesy. It is, however, understood
in authoritative quarters, meanwhile,
that investigations are being made in
the town and elsewhere, and that certain results have already resulted. We
shall, consistent with our invariable
regard for the *bono publico* and the
sanctity of private affairs, keep our
readers *en courant* of all developments
in this, as we may well term it, painful mystery, although it is unlikely
that there will be anything to report
beyond the usual formal proceedings
for some time. It is probable that an
inquest will be held in the Coroner's
Court this morning.

Mr. Chaddlewick, in spite of his customary reserve, was
flustered.

"Good heavens!" he said. "Who would ever have thought
of such a thing?"

Mrs. Chaddlewick could make no immediate reply. She
blinked in a dumb ecstasy of pleasurable excitement. The
paper, loosely held in her trembling hand, rustled on the
edge of the table-cloth.

"Oh!—it's too—"

But no! She could not rise to an adequate strength of superlative. No human speech could meet her need, she had gone beyond the limits of mere verbal expression.

## 6

Of the opening of the inquest little need be said. It was, as the *Shufflecester Gazette* had so accurately foreseen, purely formal.

The coroner briefly explained to the jury that there had been "certain suspicions" in regard to the death of Mr. Kewdingham. An order for exhumation had been issued, and it had now been carried into effect. There had been a post-mortem examination, and in due course there would be a report from the Home Office. Until that report was received there would be an adjournment of the inquest. For the time being, there was nothing more to be done. But the coroner reminded the jury of the extreme impropriety of listening to rumours or of helping to circulate them, and he warned them to avoid getting into conversation with persons who might be suspected of acting for newspapers.

It was observed with surprise that Doctor Bagge was not one of the four doctors concerned in the post-mortem examination—a fact which Doctor Bagge himself deeply regretted.

As for the effect of this alarming move upon the Kewdingham family, it was by no means alike in every case.

Father Kewdingham was curiously undisturbed. The venerable Mrs. Poundle-Quainton felt herself disgraced for ever, poor dear lady! Uncle Richard growled fiercely, and even said something quite unpardonable about the fellow giving more trouble than he was worth. Mrs. Pyke observed sternly, though obscurely, "I always knew there was something wrong about that woman."

Bertha, for her part, appeared to be desperately calm. She knew that she was up against it, and that she might find herself in a difficult situation. She imagined, of course, that her lead acetate had left unmistakable traces, probably visible to the naked eye; and no one could imagine that lead would be used as a vehicle for suicide. True, the issue would be complicated by Bobby's habit of drugging himself—and she had wisely placed a few packets of acetate in the cupboard. But that was not all…Many things were hidden from her; and she would have given a great deal to know if the police had any evidence of her affair with John Harrigall.

Bewilderment, irritation, anxiety for Bertha, and a most unreasonable suspicion of Doctor Bagge, filled the uneasy mind of John Harrigall himself. Of course, he would have to give a lot of evidence at the resumed inquest, and that was a damned nuisance, and he wished to heaven the police had not been so officious. He could not account for his suspicion of the doctor. It must have been due, he thought, to his disagreeable memories of the conference at Shufflecester, when the doctor had looked at him in such a peculiar way.

And as for Doctor Bagge, there was no change in his prim demeanour. He pattered in and out of his patients' houses, generally a welcome little presence, with a kind hint, a timely suggestion, a word of hope.

It may be doubted if there was another man in Shufflecester for whom so many people had so much respect. Nearly everyone felt sorry for Doctor Bagge, sorry that he was involved in this unhappy Kewdingham affair; and he received many gratifying proofs of friendship and of confidence. Indeed, he had not realised the extent of his popularity. But now all sorts of people, from the Dean to the dustman, told him how glad they would be when the wretched business was ended, and how shocked and astonished they were by the action of the police.

Bagge was naturally pleased by these tributes from the high and the humble alike. He could almost regard the Kewdingham affair as a blessing in disguise, a kind of advertisement. If only he could foresee the result of the laboratory investigations by the formidable Professor Pulverbatch, the Home Office expert! Never mind; he could wriggle out; he was preparing a defence, in case it was needed, and it was a very good one.

# 7

As a matter of fact, the redoubtable Professor Pulverbatch was terribly puzzled. Even after a long discussion with Doctor (now Sir Paul) Dinham, the official pathologist, there were certain features not easily explained.

Pulverbatch was a thin, pale man, with an expression like that of a highly intellectual saint. He appeared to be in ceaseless communion with a fount of inner knowledge. When he spoke, he had a way of drawing back his thin lips, showing two rows of very small natural teeth, and occasionally giving a short whispering whistle. In the seclusion of his fine Bayswater home he attempted, with no great success, to play jigs upon the violin for the entertainment of Mrs. Pulverbatch.

"Hyaline deterioration?" said the Professor to his eminent colleague. "Yes, my dear chap—I quite agree with you. But look here…This poor Kewdingham must have been fairly bombarded with poisons, he must have been overwhelmed by a lethal barrage. I never saw anything like it. I wish we had Chesterton here. But I think we shall ultimately come to the conclusion which I ventured to put forward as a working hypothesis at the start."

He delicately adjusted the shining brass tube of his microscope.

"Just have a look at this, my dear chap. Smith has taken a lot of trouble with the slide, and it's really beautiful, one of the loveliest little things I ever saw. Quite equal to anything done by those fellows in Vienna."

Pulverbatch looked up with a saintly smile at the broad, brown face of Doctor Paul Dinham.

Without a word, Doctor Dinham applied his eye to the microscope.

"Yes, Pulverbatch," he said, after a pause, "you are right. A positively exquisite preparation. By Jove, though!—It won't be so easy to decide, eh?"

"A final application of the Hauser-Moroni ought to help us."

They were standing in the laboratory, surrounded by sights and smells of the most nauseating description. Pulverbatch, looking like a middle-aged angel in his white coat, smiled again at the burly Dinham. They were among the few men in London who were capable of applying a test so delicate as the Hauser-Moroni.

"It's a remarkably fine piece of work, Pulverbatch. Now what do you say to having a word with old Heagh-Spoffer? He's a hopeless imbecile, of course, but we can't deny that he has a special knowledge of such cases."

"By all means, my dear chap. I had been thinking of Spoffer. We may as well ask the secretary. Tu-tu-tu-tu!"

He called a meek, laborious young man, who was cutting up a piece of something which looked very unpleasant.

"Mr. Smith! We have both greatly admired your beautiful slide. I shall certainly display it to Sir William. Very good, Mr. Smith, very good indeed. And now, Mr. Smith, would you be so good as to get me the secretary on the telephone?"

Mr. Smith, well pleased by the compliment, drew off his rubber gloves.

## 8

In the meanwhile, two eminent men of another sort had come to the town of Shufflecester, and the public were totally unaware of their presence. These eminent men were Chief-Inspector Villiers and Detective-Sergeant Massey of New Scotland Yard. Working rapidly and with most ingenious disguises, they discovered, pursued, unravelled or discarded a whole series of Kewdingham clues.

# Chapter XIII

## 1

The inquest on Robert Arthur Kewdingham was resumed in the Coroner's Court at Shufflecester on the 17th of July.

There are courts of all sorts, but none could be more dreary and squalid, more infernally bleak and hideous, than the Coroner's Court of Shufflecester. It is only possible to find this extreme degree of squalor, of neglect and of ugliness, in courts of law—places where the sane influence of women has not yet penetrated and where men still have it all their own way. This particular court was a room adjoining the Town Hall, with a door opening immediately on Frog Street.

When you entered the Court from the street you found yourself in a dusty pen, separated from the main part of the room by a wooden barrier with little wicket-gates at each end of it. By each of these gates there was a chair for a policeman. Apart from these chairs there was no furniture in the pen. A big rusty stove was placed in one corner, and behind it there was a stack of brooms and buckets, a fire extinguisher of obsolete pattern, a bicycle, a sheet of corrugated iron and a derelict bird-cage. In the other corner there was a stretcher on wheels. The floor of the pen was uncovered, and you saw beneath you the rough, dirty boards, overlaid by a deposit of dust, mud and bits of plaster. This was the accommodation provided for a hundred members of the public.

At the far end of the room, opposite the street door, there was a small raised platform or dais. Above it, fastened to the wall, a yellow-faced clock. To the right of the dais there was a door leading to the jurymen's room; to the left, a door leading to the coroner's room and the waiting-room. On the dais itself was a handsome desk with a chair upholstered in shabby green plush by the side of it, and another chair close to the edge of the platform. A raised wooden enclosure stood on the right of the platform, with a chair for the witness. When you sat or stood inside this box you were close to the coroner's desk, and it was possible for the coroner to whisper to you without being heard by the public.

Down the right side of the court (looking towards the street door) was a row of about sixteen chairs to accommodate the jury.

Along the opposite side were more chairs, intended for relatives of the deceased, witnesses (after they had been heard), and other privileged people. The number of these chairs varied according to the nature of the inquest.

The centre of the court was occupied by two large tables with plenty of space between them. All the leading people in the case—counsel and experts—were placed at these tables, with all their papers and paraphernalia before them. A special table, guarded by a policeman, was provided for exhibits.

Between the central space and the public pen were long deal benches for less important folk, pressmen, court attendants and so forth.

There were three windows in the court: one in the same wall as the street door; one behind the jurymen, looking out on the Corporation's garage; and one in the opposite wall, permitting a distant view of the gas-works.

As for the walls of this ghastly chamber, they were painted a thick anchovy-paste red, a colour which fell heavily upon the ambient gloom, choking the very daylight and adding to the general impression of tawdry horror.

This filthy room, on the morning of the 17th of July, was full of people. Seated upon his mournful eminence was Mr. Hubert Mills, the coroner. Below him, at the head of one of the tables, was Mr. Keynes Yelford, the Assistant Director of Prosecutions, representing the police. Mr. Yelford had a tough, supercilious face and a harsh manner. At the same table, on the right of Mr. Yelford and facing the court, was Mr. Folliard Ellwright, a local solicitor, watching the proceedings on behalf of Doctor Bagge. Next to Mr. Ellwright was Mr. David Williams, engaged by Uncle Richard on behalf of Mrs. Kewdingham.

These were important men, but everyone knew that the result of the inquest would depend upon the little group seated at the other table, almost exactly in the middle of the court. There was the great Pulverbatch, smiling in his saintly way at nothing in particular; and there was the burly form of Doctor Paul Dinham, with his enormous rough head and his disorderly moustache. There was also a tall, old gentleman with tidy white hair and a most elegant frock coat—it was Colonel Wilbert Heagh-Spoffer (I.M.S.), C.B., C.M.G., the authority on oriental poisons.

And there were the jurymen, owlish and imperturbable, in whose dull faces you would have looked in vain for the signs of intelligence. Except, perhaps, in the case of Mr. John Quatt, who owned seven public houses; and possibly in the case of Mr. Bimble, tobacconist.

Looking across towards the jury were the privileged people on the other side. These were members of the family, including Uncle Richard and several cousins, and there were also a number of Shufflecester worthies who were acquainted with the coroner. Chairs were reserved for witnesses who were to remain in court after giving their evidence.

A mixed lot of pressmen and of hangers-on occupied the benches, and behind them, on the other side of the barrier, at least 120 members of the public were tightly compressed. Policemen were stationed by the doors, by the coroner's platform and by the witness-box. Inspector Miles, like a monument of civic dignity, was planted immediately below the coroner, facing the court.

The witnesses were now waiting in their grim, dingy room, not greatly cheered by the distant view of the gas-works, and their conversation was of a scrappy, disjointed nature. Chief among these were Dr. Bagge, old Kewding-ham, Phoebe Kewdingham, Nurse Cundle, Martha Tuke, and Mr. John Harrigall: the others will be mentioned in due course. All of them were trying to seem indifferent. The nurse alone was perfectly unemotional and was enjoying her temporary importance. Doctor Bagge looked about him with a more than ordinary number of blue flashes, but he said very little. Father Kewdingham mumbled some carefully selected quotations, of which no one took the least notice. Phoebe was cool, inscrutable; she avoided speaking to John, in a manner which, coupled with her strange behaviour in London during the previous few weeks, made him feel extremely uncomfortable. As for John, he kept moving about from one part of the room to another, studying the print of Queen Caroline's trial which hung over the fire-place, or reading the notices on the wall. They were all the time under the eye of a discreet though not unfriendly policeman who stood by the door leading to the court.

Bertha Kewdingham was not present. Acting on the best legal advice, she had chosen to be represented by her solici-tor, Mr. David Williams.

## 2

At half-past ten, after the usual formalities, the coroner addressed the jury:

"Gentlemen," he said, "I am about to place before you evidence of a peculiar nature, requiring your close attention. After we have listened to this evidence I shall set before you the main features of the case, as I perceive them, and you will then consider your verdict. Here I will only remind you that you will be called on to decide one thing, and one thing only—the manner in which Robert Arthur Kewdingham met his death. I propose to call, in the first place, Sergeant William Fawley, who will speak as to the taking of a blue flask and a bottle, and afterwards a number of sealed jars, and certain packages, to London, handing them over to the Home Office analyst, Professor Pulverbatch, at St. Audrey's Hospital, and getting a receipt for them. Then, in order that he may have an opportunity for hearing the medical evidence, I shall call Doctor Wilson Bagge, the physician who attended the deceased. After that, you will have the privilege of hearing three eminent authorities: Professor Quintin Pulverbatch, who has just been mentioned; Doctor Paul Dinham, pathologist to the Home Office; and Colonel Wilbert Vauban Heagh-Spoffer, formerly of the Indian Medical Service. The evidence of a gentleman who saw the deceased within a few hours of his death, and the evidence of the nurse who was in attendance, will also be taken. Other witnesses have been warned to appear, including Mr. Robert Henry Kewdingham, the father of the deceased. I am told that all these people are now in the waiting-room, and I hope it will not be necessary to adjourn the inquest."

After the formal police evidence, Doctor Bagge was called.

He entered the witness-box, trim, correct, responsible. Looking at the coroner, he bowed, and the coroner replied with a friendly jerk of the head: it was their custom on these occasions.

Then came the first surprise.

"Before taking your evidence, Doctor Bagge, there is a certain matter to be considered. Inspector Miles, will you show Doctor Bagge exhibit number one."

The inspector produced from a package a large medicine-bottle. Inside the bottle there was a pink mixture with a heavy sediment.

"That bottle comes from your dispensary, Doctor Bagge, and that is your writing on the label?"

Very slowly, very deliberately, the doctor turned the bottle in his hands. He was evidently prepared for this.

"Yes," he said.

"It contains the medicine prepared by you for Mr. Robert Arthur Kewdingham?"

"I have no idea what it contains now. When I last saw it, it contained medicine for Mr. Kewdingham."

Mr. Ellwright, counsel for Doctor Bagge, jumped up and addressed the coroner:

"This is a very exceptional procedure. May I ask, sir, whether that bottle was removed by the police, and, if so, why?"

"It was not removed by the police. I shall call further evidence regarding it. For the present it is enough that Doctor Bagge recognises the bottle as one which contained medicine for Mr. Kewdingham."

"I do not know why you are producing that bottle, sir, or what it has to do with your enquiry," Mr. Ellwright said, appearing to be extremely angry, "but if it was not removed from Mr. Kewdingham's house by the police it would appear to me to have no significance whatever."

"Be so good as to wait for a moment, Mr. Ellwright. Inspector, will you now hand the bottle to Professor

Pulverbatch? Thank you. If I am not mistaken, professor, you have seen that bottle before?"

"Eh, surely!" replied the professor. "I brought it with me from London this morning."

Mr. Ellwright shrugged his shoulders impatiently. Doctor Bagge was quite unconcerned; he flicked a little dust off the sleeve of his neat grey coat.

Professor Pulverbatch explained that he had originally received the bottle from the police, and that he was instructed to make an analysis of the contents. He had done so, and had found an extraordinarily high percentage of aluminium, together with *morphinae hydrochloridum* and other drugs of an astringent nature. In reply to a question conveyed from Doctor Bagge to Mr. Ellwright, the professor gave the exact composition of the medicine.

The coroner: "Does that conform to your prescription, Doctor Bagge?"

The witness (in a clear, steady voice): "Most decidedly not. I cannot question the analysis of so eminent a chemist as Professor Pulverbatch, but I may say with confidence that no doctor in his senses would ever make up such a prescription. The amount of alum chlorate found in the analysis is about five times as great as the amount which I used in preparing the medicine for Mr. Kewdingham."

Mr. Keynes Yelford (for the police): "How do you account for that, Doctor Bagge?"

The witness (with a smile): "I don't account for it. Either the stuff now in the bottle is not my medicine at all, or else the bottle was never shaken by the patient, in which case the chlorate would remain at the bottom and would there form a thick deposit, such as you actually see in the bottle at present. But even in the latter case it would be almost impossible to explain the result obtained by the analysis."

Questioned further by Mr. Keynes Yelford, the doctor said that he did not agree that aluminium salts, in any quantity, were poisonous; he accepted the views of Schlangenhausen and of Aldenstein, though he was not unaware of the results obtained on rabbits by Sychoff at Lausanne. (Doctor Paul Dinham smiled appreciatively.) Yes; his prescription book could be produced if they cared to send for it; he could easily explain to any of the court officials where it was to be found.

Mr. Ellwright (to the coroner): "May I be allowed to ask, sir, what we are trying to prove? I do not quite follow this enquiry. I object very strongly to these questions being put to my client, nor do I see in what way they can be of the slightest use. I am in the dark, and I should be very much obliged if you, or any of these gentlemen, would enlighten me."

Mr. Keynes Yelford: "I am only too willing to help my learned friend to the best of my ability. I will ask Professor Pulverbatch to tell us whether, if the mixture now contained in this bottle had been taken by Mr. Kewdingham, or by anyone else, it was likely to have a harmful effect."

Professor Pulverbatch: "Eh, well! I think it would produce immediate vomiting. If taken regularly, there would, of course, be certain consequences."

Mr. Keynes Yelford: "Possibly fatal consequences?"

Professor Pulverbatch: "That would all depend…No; I should not like to say so."

Mr. Ellwright (to the coroner): "Sir, this is really intolerable. I never heard of such a thing in my life. A scandalous, a grossly improper suggestion has now been made in the hearing of the public. It is imperative that I should ask a question without delay." (To Professor Pulverbatch): "Did you, sir, find anything attributable in any way to the action of this, or of a similar medicine, in your examination of the organs which were submitted to you?"

Professor Pulverbatch: "No; I found no change or injury which could be attributed to such a medicine. That is what you want to know, is it not?"

Mr. Ellwright: "You did not find a trace of this medicine?"

Professor Pulverbatch: "A barely perceptible trace in the lower intestinal passages."

Mr. Ellwright: "Now please tell us definitely whether you attached any importance to this?"

Professor Pulverbatch: "None whatever."

Mr. Ellwright (to the coroner, with indignation): "Now, sir, may I ask why we have wasted so much time in discussing a matter to which the expert himself attaches no importance? I wish to claim—"

The coroner: "Pray be calm, Mr. Ellwright. You will see, before the enquiry is over, that we had a very good reason for introducing this matter. We may now proceed. I will request Doctor Bagge to give his evidence in regard to the general health of the deceased, and then in regard to the particular circumstances of the death."

While Mr. Ellwright blew a fierce breath over his papers, Doctor Bagge began to give his evidence in a plain, precise, unhesitating manner. He was immensely relieved, though at the same time extremely puzzled. When he came to the death of Mr. Kewdingham, he said that he had then formed a definite opinion as to the causes, but he now believed that he might have been mistaken. He described his investigation of the medicine-cupboard, the astonishing discovery of many dangerous drugs and of the blue phial.

By the coroner: "Gentlemen of the jury, it is necessary for me to inform you that the contents of this cupboard have been examined by the police, and you will hear more about them presently."

The witness proceeded to identify the blue phial (exhibit number seven) and the coroner read aloud the paper which had been wrapped round it. This produced a great sensation in the court.

Mr. Keynes Yelford (to the witness): "After this discovery, you recalled certain symptoms—dilation of the pupils, for example—which led you to suspect the action of a mydriatic alkaloid, such as belladonna?"

The witness: "Yes."

Mr. Keynes Yelford: "But at the time of the death you were quite satisfied with your diagnosis?" The witness (tartly): "Of course."

Mr. Keynes Yelford: "Though your search in the medicine-cupboard was due to a certain anxiety?"

The witness: "No. A certain curiosity."

The general impression made by the doctor's evidence was entirely satisfactory, though everyone was puzzled by the introduction of the pink mixture. Yet no one could have been more puzzled than the doctor himself was by the answers of Professor Pulverbatch. What the devil! Only a barely perceptible trace of the chlorate? Lucky in the circumstances, no doubt; but how could you account for it? He took his place among the privileged people, waiting to hear Dinham and Pulverbatch, and hoping that he would be enlightened.

## 3

There was a ghoulish excitement among the reporters, a fluttering and rustling and shuffling of papers, a twitching of elbows and a scraping of boots, a mumbling and movement among the public (restrained by a severe glance from the coroner), a general adjustment and expectancy as Doctor Paul Dinham was called.

Doctor Paul described in detail the heart and the visceral organs of poor Kewdingham. There was no doubt as to the disease of the heart and the kidneys. He noted a venous congestion which indicated the condition known as asphyxia.

In one place he had observed a slight blackening of the mucous membrane, due, it was discovered later, to a minute deposit of lead sulphide. (On hearing this, Doctor Bagge could not refrain from making an audible clucking sound, though he quickly controlled himself.) But, said the eminent pathologist, the most important discovery was made in the stomach. "Here," he said, "I was at once struck by a bright red arborescent extravasation and by the emphysematous condition of the membrane."

Mr. Keynes Yelford: "Naturally, when you saw that, you were led to a certain conclusion?"

Then came a bombshell.

"Yes," said Dr. Paul, speaking very deliberately, "I came to the conclusion that I was dealing with a typical case of acute poisoning by arsenic."

# Chapter XIV

## 1

No sooner had the word "arsenic" fallen from the lips of Doctor Dinham than a reaction of surprise, curiosity and horror was evident throughout the entire court. Clearly Doctor Bagge had not expected to hear anything of the kind. He sat bolt upright in his chair, petrified with amazement. Uncle Richard, and all the Kewdingham relatives, fairly gasped. A gleam of savage delight passed over the faces of the reporters. The public swayed and murmured. Only the jury, conscious of their superb isolation, remained owlish and imperturbable.

Mr. Keynes Yelford paused for a moment, allowing the emotion to subside. Then he continued his examination:

"You have seen many similar cases?"

"Yes, hundreds of cases."

The coroner: "I will now call Professor Pulverbatch, and afterwards Colonel Heagh-Spoffer. These gentlemen are anxious to return to London this evening if possible, and I hope there will be no reason for detaining them."

The eminent professor was examined in a masterly way by Mr. Keynes Yelford. He smiled benevolently upon the court, and gave his evidence in a soft though audible voice, with many whistlings and ejaculations. First of all, he said, the post-mortem appearances had justified him in testing the various organs for the presence of arsenic, and he had found it in all of them. He gave the details of his analysis, and showed that he had obtained, in all, 2.079 grains of arsenic. A dose of at least 4 grains must have been swallowed by Mr. Kewdingham within a few hours of his death. Two grains, in ordinary circumstances, would constitute a fatal dose. Having revealed these sensational facts, the professor was cross-examined by Mr. David Williams, on behalf of Mrs. Kewdingham. Mr. Williams had considerable knowledge of arsenical poisoning, and he now observed that none of the ordinary symptoms had been recorded in the early stages of the fatal illness. To this the professor replied that in exceptional cases, which were known as "nervous cases", the well-known symptoms did not occur.

Having established the presence of arsenic, said Pulverbatch, he had then carried out a very delicate and a very prolonged experiment, having for its object the detection of a certain vegetable alkaloid. This experiment was known as the Hauser-Moroni test, and it required, he might be allowed to say, very considerable skill in the use of microscopic apparatus. Eh, well!…

Mr. Keynes Yelford: "Will you tell us why you should have tested for this particular alkaloid?"

The witness: "A blue phial with a mounting of silver filigree had been handed to me in connection with this case—"

The coroner: "It is exhibit number seven, produced when Doctor Bagge was giving his evidence. Inspector, will you now show this exhibit to Professor Pulverbatch, so that he may identify it? The jury had better see it as well."

The witness (resuming his evidence after the phial had been identified): "In this phial, which is of Indian origin, I found a powerful preparation of the alkaloids belonging to what we call the atropine group—in this instance, the alkaloids of stramonium. My colleague, Colonel Heagh-Spoffer, will presently describe to you the use—I should, of course, say the former use—of such poisons among the upper classes in India. Daturine is a term occasionally employed. The preparation in that phial is one of the most concentrated forms of poison which I have ever come across; it is a deadly preparation." (The jury, after nervously examining the phial, return it quickly to the inspector.)

Mr. Keynes Yelford: "How much would be sufficient to cause death?"

The witness: "About three drops. Death would certainly take place within six hours of swallowing such a dose."

Mr. Keynes Yelford: "Did you find any trace of this poison in the organs taken from the body of Mr. Kewdingham?"

Speaking clearly and emphatically, the witness replied: "I did."

"Now, professor," said Mr. Yelford, aware of the intense excitement in the court and uttering his words in the gravest and most impressive manner, "I want you to say whether you found the traces of a fatal dose of this poison."

"Certainly I did. At least half a teaspoonful had been taken."

In the course of his examination by Mr. Yelford, the professor said that the symptoms noted by Doctor Bagge, and others, which, he understood, would be described by another witness, were highly characteristic of poisoning by atropine.

Mr. David Williams: "And by no means characteristic of poisoning by arsenic?"

The witness: "That is so."

Mr. Keynes Yelford: "It amounts to this—he had taken a fatal dose of arsenic and he had also taken a fatal dose of atropine?"

The witness: "Precisely."

Mr. David Williams: "But you cannot, in such a case, assign any priority of action in the matter of causing death?"

The witness: "That is quite true. It is, if I may say so, as if a man had been stabbed through the heart and shot through the brain at the same moment."

Mr. Keynes Yelford: "Or as if a man had been murdered at the very moment of committing suicide?"

Mr. David Williams: "I take exception to that question."

Mr. Keynes Yelford: "It is only by way of illustration, for the benefit of the jury."

After some further legal and medical argument, the coroner called an unexpected witness. This was a local chemist, Mr. Brown, who said that he had sold a half-gallon tin of Dragon Weed-killer to Mr. Kewdingham personally on the 3rd of March. This weed-killer contained a high proportion of arsenic in a liquid form. Mr. Kewdingham had, of course, signed the poison-book, which was produced in court.

Mr. David Williams: "Have the police succeeded in tracing this particular tin?"

The coroner: "No, sir, they have not."

Proceeding with his enquiry, the coroner now called Mr. Walter Simpson, a technical chemist on the staff of the firm which made the Dragon Weed-killer. This killer, said Mr. Simpson, contained 38 per cent, of arsenious oxide combined with soda. It was a liquid, coloured a vivid green by means of an aniline dye. Two drops of the killer would contain half a grain of arsenic. A tin of Dragon Weed-killer was now produced in court, with the seal unbroken, and identified by Mr. Simpson as the standard form in which half-gallons were sold to the public. Amidst intense excitement a quantity of bright green fluid was poured from this tin into a white glass tumbler, inspected by the jury.

"Now, Mr. Simpson," said the coroner, "if this fluid were to be poured into a green wineglass, it would be practically invisible, would it not?"

Mr. Simpson said he thought that would probably be the case.

The coroner: "I am now going to make a little experiment which is not as childish as it may at first appear. Exhibit number two consists of half a dozen wineglasses taken from Mr. Kewdingham's house on my instructions—these glasses, as we shall presently see, were used for the first time at the dinner immediately preceding Mr. Kewdingham's fatal illness. Thank you, inspector. They are green glasses, two of them darker than the others. I shall now ask a member of the jury to pour about two teaspoonfuls of the weed-killer into each of two glasses—one of the dark ones and one of the lighter ones. We shall then observe the result."

There was a kind of low buzzing in the public enclosure, and the coroner sternly raised a hand.

An imperturbable juryman poured some of the lovely viridian fluid into each of the glasses: this fluid, as the coroner had foreseen, was almost invisible unless the glass was held up to the light. No one could easily have detected a small amount of the fluid in the bottom of one of the glasses, if he did not take the glass in his hand and examine it closely.

The coroner (to Mr. Simpson): "A teaspoonful of the killer would constitute a fatal dose?"

The witness: "Yes, sir. Very much less would constitute a fatal dose—about eight or nine drops would be sufficient."

Then, after this curious demonstration, a wine-merchant was called, who deposed to having sold to Mrs. Kewdingham, on the 27th of April, a bottle of burgundy. She had ordered burgundy on previous occasions, he said, in answer to cross-examination by Mr. David Williams, but never before had she ordered a vintage wine such as Pommard.

Nurse Cundle briefly gave her purely medical evidence, and then came the turn of old father Kewdingham.

## 2

Poor old Kewdingham was the most uneasy of the witnesses, feeling at once that he was being regarded with hostility or contempt. Uncle Richard looked at him grimly: Robert, he thought, was always a fool.

The coroner spoke to him in a dry, caustic manner, putting the questions with a snap and a rap which plainly revealed his attitude. When it came to the affair of the medicine-bottle there was a quite perceptible stirring of animosity in the court.

"Now, Mr. Kewdingham," said the coroner, "I shall not ask you why you did such an extraordinary thing. We have just been told that the mixture in the bottle had nothing whatever to do with your son's death, and the episode has therefore no relevance in the present enquiry. Your action, whatever its motive, was of a sort likely to give rise to the most unworthy and the most unfounded suspicions, and I think it my duty to you all to say that if there were any suspicions they have now been completely and finally dispelled."

A swish of muffled approbation in the court, a furtive clapping of hands, a tapping of sticks or boots. Plainly, Bagge was becoming the hero of the inquest, rising to the climax of his popularity.

The coroner: "Order! If there is any more of this, I shall clear the court." (To the public, sternly): "Please remember where you are."

Turning again to the unhappy witness, the coroner asked him various questions in regard to what had happened on the night of the twenty-seventh.

Mr. Kewdingham, realising that he had made a hideous mistake, and that he now appeared to the court as a nasty-minded old villain, gave incoherent, rambling answers, and was only too glad when he was allowed to totter from the box, after being tortured by the coroner, Mr. Yelford, Mr. Ellwright and Mr. Williams in succession, and was free to escape, a humiliated and shaken man, from that awful building. Indeed, there were several ignorant people who now suspected him of the murder of his son.

Evidence was taken from Mr. Hickey, the antique dealer, in regard to the sale of the green glasses to Mrs. Kewdingham; and he was followed by Mr. John Harrigall.

John, as usual, was very well dressed and made a good impression on the public, but he soon noticed an unaccountable harshness in the demeanour of the coroner and of the counsel. What he did not observe was an involuntary movement of surprise on the part of one of the jurymen. He was closely questioned by the coroner and sharply cross-examined by Mr. David Williams. When did he arrive at Wellington Avenue on the 27th? Who was there? Did he notice anything unusual in the manner or appearance of Mr. Kewdingham? When did he go out to post his letter? When did he go to the bathroom? Did Mr. Kewdingham go to the bathroom? Yes?—And how long was he there? John could not remember.

Mr. David Williams: "Do try to think, Mr. Harrigall. It is a point of great importance. Can you not give us an idea? Five minutes?—Ten minutes?"

"About ten minutes, to the best of my recollection."

"And at that time Mrs. Kewdingham was in the kitchen?"

"As far as I know. I was in the drawing-room, but I could hear someone in the kitchen."

"Now, Mr. Harrigall, do try to recollect. When you were in the bathroom, did you notice anything on the porcelain slab over the wash-basin?"

"I think there were some bottles there, and a toothbrush holder, and a glass of some sort—a tumbler."

He described, though with due restraint, the peculiar manner and the haggard aspect of Mr. Kewdingham, which he had noticed as soon as he arrived. He gave an account of the dinner and of what happened afterwards. His evidence was given in a straightforward manner, and the coroner evidently thought better of him before the end of it.

The evidence of Martha Tuke was awaited with great interest. When she stood in the witness-box she looked half ashamed of herself and was rather confused. Her information was extracted with subtlety and with extraordinary tact by the coroner, who had a large experience of such witnesses. He made it clear that the domestic life of the Kewdinghams had not been altogether happy.

Coming to the night of the 27th Martha told them how she saw that Mrs. Kewdingham had washed the new green glasses, though she had never previously washed up any of the dinner things. At length she came to the handing over of the letter to Phoebe. Here there was a great deal of fencing between counsel and coroner. It was insisted upon by Mr. David Williams that the name of the person to whom this letter was addressed ought not to be made public. This was agreed to, in spite of the opposition of Mr. Keynes Yelford. It was merely stated that the letter was addressed to "a certain gentleman". Asked why she had taken this action in regard to the letter, Martha replied that she had been shocked to observe various "goings-on" between Mrs. Kewdingham and "the gentleman". At this point Mr. David Williams energetically intervened, but the coroner had got what he wanted. The effect of all this upon John, who now saw daylight, may be imagined. He could understand the strange coldness of his cousin Phoebe. He could understand, for the first time, the extreme peril of the situation. With a mind full of emerging horrors he listened to Martha, who said that she had never seen any weed-killer used in the garden, though she did remember the arrival of a half-gallon tin of Dragon. Cross-examined by Mr. Williams, she stated that she had often seen Mr. Kewdingham taking white powders and other medicines. Mr. Yelford then asked her why she had given notice and left the house on the day after the funeral. Before she could reply, Mr. Williams rose with a vehement protest, and the coroner ruled that the question need not be answered. She then admitted to Mr. Williams that she had been with the Kewdinghams for three years, and had nothing whatever to complain of as far as they were concerned.

Phoebe then entered the witness-box.

Questioned about the home life of the Kewdinghams, she was extremely reticent. Her manner was cool and steady, her replies were brief and well considered. She told them how Martha had brought her the letter, and how she had taken the letter, unopened, to the Chief Constable's office, where, after consultation, the letter had been opened and read in her presence and retained by the police. Warned that she was not to divulge the name of the person to whom the letter was addressed, she was asked whether she could identify the writing; and she replied that it was unquestionably written by her sister-in-law, Mrs. Bertha Kewdingham, with whose writing she was familiar. The coroner then stated that copies of this letter had been made by the police, and that he would now hand a copy, together with the original letter, to the witness, in order that she might verify them. This was accordingly done.

The coroner: "As this is a matter of some importance, I shall now order six copies of the letter to be distributed among the jurymen, to be read by them and then returned to me. These copies do not contain the name of the person to whom the letter is addressed."

Mr. David Williams objected, saying that he had no copy of the letter, and that such a procedure was highly improper for many reasons, especially as Mrs. Kewdingham was not present. To this the coroner replied that he alone was responsible for his procedure, that he would supply Mr. Williams with a copy, and that the police had compared the handwriting of the original with many other specimens, leaving no room for doubt. Copies were, therefore, handed to the jurymen, who stolidly read them and returned them to the coroner. After she had answered a few more questions, Phoebe left the witness-box.

It was now a quarter to two. The coroner intimated that there would be a brief adjournment for lunch, and that he would address the jury when the court reassembled at half-past two precisely.

# Chapter XV

## 1

When the court was reopened at half-past two, it was quite evident that the public pen was grossly overcrowded. A soft, hot mass of humanity, as much female as male, was protruding over the polished rail of the barrier and there was a young man sitting on the top of the rusty stove. The coroner looked about him angrily.

"Inspector! Who has admitted all these people? Remove twenty of those nearest the door at once."

With great difficulty the door was opened, and a score or so of indignant citizens were hustled into the street.

It was observed that Doctor Bagge was not present, and that the family was only represented by John Harrigall, Phoebe, and Uncle Richard. Professor Pulverbatch and Doctor Dinham were at their table, but Colonel Heagh-Spoffer had returned to London. No one anticipated that the final proceedings would last for more than an hour, and the experts were staying in case the jury had any questions for them.

The afternoon was dull and sultry. An occasional stutter of engines and rumbling of heavy traffic could be heard from the Corporation garage. Everyone felt the strain of a higher tension, of a growing excitability. The pressmen, glistening and flushed after long draughts of beer at the Blue Swan, flicked about their papers and sharpened their pencils with less restraint. A more audible chuffering and whispering among the public marked an increase of morbid vigilance. Even on the stolid, self-important faces of the jury there was a glimmer of anticipation: they would soon be called on to play their part.

The coroner himself was obviously not unmoved. He knew that he had already been severely criticised. He swabbed his face with a blue silk handkerchief, and his manner with inferiors was a trifle brusque. Shortly after taking his place he had a whispered conversation with Mr. Keynes Yelford, of which only the last words were audible to the pressmen: "I never knew anything like it."

Mr. David Williams and Mr. Ellwright came into the court together, both of them looking very sharp and satisfied. Keynes Yelford was evidently bored: he sat at the table with an air of supercilious resignation, as though he was composing himself to listen to a sermon in a rural church, only keeping awake for the sake of appearances.

Colonel Drayford sat in the front row of the privileged people, twirling his long orange moustache. His lieutenant, Inspector Miles, again stood monumentally in his old position.

The coroner rapped sharply on the edge of his desk.

"Silence in the court, if you please!"

With a stern, searching eye he looked in turn at the tables in front of him, at the privileged people, at the sweltering, congested mass of the public, at the pressmen, and finally at the jury. He looked at each juryman separately, then he sighed, and then, for the second time, he rapped on the desk.

"Gentlemen of the jury, you do not need any particular account of the persons concerned in this case.

"It has transpired, in the course of this enquiry, that Mr. Robert Arthur Kewdingham was not exactly what you would call an ordinary man. I do not want to put ideas into your heads—such an attempt would be highly improper—but I do want to remind you that you have heard evidence which shows that Mr. Kewdingham was affected mentally as a result of illness. He suffered from acute depression, and I think it is clear that his moods of depression were more frequent and more intense towards the end. On this point we have had the evidence of a highly respected medical man, Doctor Wilson Bagge, who attended Mr. Kewdingham regularly for many years. We have no direct evidence of suicidal intention, but I have a sworn statement in regard to a conversation which took place on Sunday the 1st of April, between Mr. Kewdingham and his aunt and cousin, Mrs. Bella and Miss Ethel Poundle-Quainton, resident in Shufflecester. I have not thought it necessary to subject these ladies to the ordeal of appearing in court. They have accordingly made a statement in the presence of a Justice of the Peace, Mr. Howard Clayborn, which I now propose to read to you."

Mr. Keynes Yelford (waking up): "May I ask, sir, if we are to regard this as evidence?"

The coroner: "It is information of an evidential nature."

Mr. Keynes Yelford (smiling): "Oh, I see! That is rather a subtle distinction, is it not?"

The coroner (with a frown): "I am not aware of any irregularity, sir."

Mr. Keynes Yelford: "Pray, sir, continue. I only wished to know where we stood."

The coroner then read a summary of the Sunday afternoon conversation, which the reader doubtless remembers. He then proceeded:

"You will have to decide for yourselves whether such remarks are to be taken seriously or not. There has always been a considerable difference of opinion in these matters. But I want you to notice that Mr. Kewdingham was in the habit of dosing himself with drugs and medicines, of which he had a large collection. This collection has been examined by the police, and has been found to include, among other poisonous things, a two-ounce packet of white arsenic. I will explain to you by what means this discovery was made...

"We cannot say that the domestic life of Mr. Kewdingham was altogether happy. These are delicate matters—family matters—but it is my duty to remind you that Mrs. Kewdingham had formed a certain attachment. I do not say what particular importance you are to assign to this, but it has to be mentioned."

They were not to forget, he said, the purchase of an arsenious weed-killer by Mr. Kewdingham on the 3rd of March—the time when people generally bought such things. They had no evidence of the employment of this weed-killer, nor had the tin been traced, but of course it might have been used in the ordinary way. This weed-killer was coloured by means of a bright green aniline dye, so that it would be immediately visible to the eye in anything but a glass container of approximately the same, or a darker, shade of green. It had been proved that a small amount of this liquid in a green wineglass would escape detection unless the glass were moved, or examined very closely, or held up to the light. It was, to say the least of it, startling to find that Mrs. Kewdingham, on the morning of the 27th of April, had purchased a set of green wineglasses, and that she had placed those wineglasses on the dinner-table on the evening of the same date. On this particular evening the maid was out, and Mrs. Kewdingham, contrary to her usual practice, had washed the glasses immediately after dinner. That might have been because the glasses were new, and she was anxious they should not be broken. It might have been due to some other reason. The jury were sensible men, and they would have to take a sensible view of the evidence. (At this point the coroner was perceptibly uneasy.) Let them now consider what took place in Mr. Kewdingham's house on the 27th of April.

"What do you observe to begin with?" said the coroner. "You observe that Mr. Kewdingham is extremely ill and depressed; that he is, in fact, suffering from what has the appearance of an attack of dysentery. Perhaps it should be noted that the symptoms of dysentery resemble, in some ways, the symptoms caused by an irritant poison. What then?

"At about six o'clock a gentleman, who has been invited to dinner, comes to the house—Mr. John Harrigall, who is, we are told, an author. Now this Mr. Harrigall is the cousin and the intimate personal friend of Mr. Kewdingham, and he tells us that he is greatly shocked when he notices Mr. Kewdingham's appearance. He endeavours to divert his cousin, to cheer him up, if he can, by talking about his collection of—of curios. He does not see Mrs. Kewdingham, who, at that time, is changing her dress. Then he remembers that he has to post a letter, and he runs out to do so. He is absent from the house for about three minutes. When he comes back he is glad to see that Mr. Kewdingham is rather more cheerful—apparently he has remained in the drawing-room while Mr. Harrigall is posting his letter. Mrs. Kewdingham has not yet left her bedroom. Mr. Robert Henry Kewdingham, who is out, has not yet returned; he comes in a little later.

"At half-past six Mrs. Kewdingham leaves her bedroom and comes into the drawing-room, and she then goes down to the kitchen in order to prepare the dinner. At seven o'clock Mr. Harrigall goes to the bathroom to wash his hands. He happens to notice, among other things on a shelf, a glass tumbler. I want you to remember this particularly. He leaves the bathroom, and Mr. Kewdingham goes there in his turn. But you will observe that Mr. Kewdingham remains in the bathroom for a somewhat unusual length of time, about ten minutes. Then these two gentlemen resume their conversation in the drawing-room. At about half-past seven Mrs. Kewdingham tells them that dinner is ready.

"Coming now to the dinner-table, you have Mr. and Mrs. Kewdingham, Mr. Robert Henry Kewdingham and Mr. John Harrigall. No one else is present; no one else is in the house.

"Now I want you to notice that all these people eat the same food, and the three gentlemen help themselves to burgundy from a decanter which is standing on the table. They pour their burgundy into green glasses—the very glasses which have been purchased in the morning by Mrs. Kewdingham. No one, apparently, makes any comment on the fact of these glasses being new; but there they are.

"After dinner, old Mr. Kewdingham retires to his room, and Mrs. Kewdingham remains downstairs, to prepare the coffee. It is now about eight-fifteen.

"Pray observe closely. As they proceed to the drawing-room, Mr. Harrigall notices an unsteadiness in the gait of Mr. Kewdingham. But Mr. Kewdingham is a very temperate man, and he has only had one glass of burgundy. Mr. Harrigall also notices a change in his cousin's voice, which is now peculiarly hoarse.

"You will have to pay attention to this. There are many things which may cause a man to be unsteady on his legs and which may give him a husky voice, but you have been told what symptoms are likely to appear within one hour of taking a dose of a certain poison. Of course the idea of poisoning could not have entered the mind of Mr. Harrigall, and it is remarkable that he should have observed these symptoms and should have described them to Doctor Bagge, and also to a police officer in London."

The coroner then reviewed in detail the events preceding and following the death of Mr. Kewdingham. He continued:

"Doctor Bagge, though not anticipating the symptoms which have been described, attributes the death to obvious natural causes, and he therefore prepares a certificate in accordance with his belief. In the meantime a very singular thing has occurred. Old Mr. Kewdingham has removed from the table in the bedroom a bottle of medicine prepared by Doctor Bagge.

"Why has he done this? Gentlemen of the jury, I cannot tell you; for I do not know. He is badly shaken by the sudden death of his son. He takes this bottle to the police, and they are eventually led to make certain enquiries.

"Then you have the doctor, a few days after the death of Mr. Kewdingham, recalling those peculiar symptoms. He is puzzled; and so he determines, like an honest man, to find out if there is the possibility of an explanation, even if it should involve the admission of a mistake and the uncertain consequences of an enquiry. You will agree with me, gentlemen of the jury, that Doctor Bagge's procedure is highly honourable and courageous. It occurs to him that Mr. Kewdingham may have neglected to take his proper medicine, and may have been treating himself with drugs, or quack mixtures, or something equally risky. He therefore goes to Mrs. Kewdingham and asks her to show him her husband's private medicine-cupboard. You know what he discovers, and why he thinks it necessary to go at once to the police."

In discussing the medical evidence, the most extraordinary which had ever come to his knowledge, the coroner said frankly that he did not see how it was possible to assign the death to a single indisputable cause. Two fatal doses—one of arsenic and one of atropine—had been taken at approximately the same time, or at any rate within a few minutes of each other: a case absolutely unique, so far as he knew, in the history of medicine.

Let them consider the possible alternatives. Kewdingham might have taken both poisons intentionally, for the purpose of committing suicide. On the other hand, he might have taken both accidentally, or in ignorance of the consequences. Both poisons might have been given to him by another person or persons, either with intention to kill or by accident; or in one case with intention to kill and in the other case by accident. Or Kewdingham might have taken one, and someone else might have given him the other, the question of design or accident being still undecided. Common sense, however, would rule out the idea that he took either or both by mistake or in ignorance. Taking a rational view of the case, it was more likely that Kewdingham took one of these poisons with the intention of committing suicide, and some one else gave him the other with the intention of causing injury or death. Obviously, if poison was administered to Kewdingham, it was administered by some person who was in the house on the evening of the 27th of April. But they had to remember that Kewdingham was in the bathroom for ten minutes, and in the bathroom he had both arsenic and atropine. He had also a tumbler, in which he might have prepared a fatal dose. If the jury believed that someone else gave him poison with the intention of causing death, they would have to assume a motive powerful enough to account for so terrible a deed, they would have to consider if anyone in the house could have been driven by such a motive. But they would have to remember that they were not trying anyone; nobody had been accused; there was all the difference in the world between a coroner's jury and the jury in a criminal court. There might be evidence of suspicion; but if that was all, it was not enough to justify them in forcing a charge. In his own view, said the coroner, they had no such thing, in the present case, as a chain of evidence establishing the fact of murder. It had been his duty faithfully to present the evidence which the police had set before him, and he trusted that he had done so. Although he refrained from giving positive instructions, he clearly anticipated an open verdict. He said finally:

"You are not to examine this evidence with any preconceived ideas in your minds. Evidence has to be taken as a whole. You will first have to examine each fact in order, and you will then have to see whether you are justified in deriving from those facts, and from them alone, a reasonable conclusion.

"Now, gentlemen, you will retire and you will consider your verdict."

## 2

In the court there was a moment of silence in which could be heard the dull sound of footfalls in the echoing corridor. Then there was a slight movement of relaxation. Mr. Keynes Yelford got up and stood below the coroner's desk and began to talk to him in a fluent subdued voice. The two solicitors remained seated at their table, whispering occasionally as they looked at their papers. Professor Pulverbatch made diagrams of something on the cover of a note-book, closely watched by Doctor Paul Dinham.

"They won't be long," said Uncle Richard, *sotto voce*, to John. "There's only one possible verdict."

"I hope you are right," said John, who was now pale and shaken. "I don't like the look of things altogether."

## 3

The jury entered their room without saying a word. It was a room less depressing than the others, with handsome photographs of the Mayors of Shufflecester upon the walls. There was also a twenty-five-inch map of the city, hanging on a black roller, and a portrait of Jonas Havergill, the celebrated Shufflecastrian who, in 1543, greatly improved the mechanism of the ducking-stool. Chairs were placed at a long table, and on the table were sheets of paper embossed with the Shufflecester arms—a mermaid perching on an oak-tree. At this table the jurymen seated themselves.

"Well, Mr. Quatt," said Moggerdill the butcher, "I think we are all agreed as you shall be foreman. Is that right, boys?"

A buzz of assent, a sniffing of noses, and a little coughing.

"Very good, then," said Mr. Quatt, a portly, wholesome fellow. "Let's get on with the job. I'm sure none of us wants to be kept here longer than need be."

He looked round at the uninspired faces of his fellow townsmen, and a happy thought came into his mind.

"There won't be no objection if we have a smoke, boys; and maybe it'll help us to think. But, mind—no spitting."

Pipes and cigarettes were produced with grateful alacrity. Some little tin boxes, miraculously discovered, were used as ash-trays. A blue, convivial haze rose in the still air of the room.

"After all," said Mr. Woolhanger, a coal merchant, "there isn't much to think about, is there? Our coroner has put the case pretty clear for us. It's an open verdict, I reckon."

"Oh, I'm not so sure, not so sure at all!" said Mr. Bimble, the tobacconist. "It's a very queer case indeed. There's one or two things I'd like to mention."

"Well, Joe," said Mr. Quatt, winking at the others, "what is it, my lad?"

"This Harrigall—I've took a dislike to him, somehow. You see, what I want to know is this. He goes out to post a letter, so he says. But why does he want to post a letter, and how do we know that he did post one?"

"It seems to me quite natural," said Mr. Quatt. "Why shouldn't he have done what he said?"

"I think it's a bit funny as Kewdingham should have been poisoned on the very evening when this Harrigall comes to dinner. He says he went out to post a letter, but how do we know where he went to or what he did?"

"Now, look here, Joe," said Mr. Quatt, with a patient smile, "be sensible—there's a good fellow—"

"I don't want to make no difficulties or keep you chaps here longer as can be helped, but I reckon I've got to say what's on my mind." Mr. Bimble looked rather like an obstinate sheep. "It's like this. Comes into my 'ead as this Harrigall might have been up to some game or other. Perhaps he's the gent as Mrs. Kewdingham is in love with. That letter was pretty hot stuff, you know, wasn't it?"

A murmur of protest, with by-play of winking and nudging, from several of the jury.

"Well, it's not impossible. I'm here to do my duty, the same as the rest of us."

Mr. Vingoe, Mr. Twamley and Mr. Hayles, all respectable tradesmen, nodded their heads approvingly.

"We've got to think for ourselves, haven't we, chaps? Now—if this Harrigall wants to poison this Kewdingham—just by way of argument, I mean—"

"It's twenty to four already, Joe," said Mr. Quatt.

Bimble was firm. Evidently he was fascinated by his own theory. "Then, you see, this Harrigall pretends he has to post a letter, and he goes out of the room—and—he—well—he—"

"He goes down the stairs, per'aps," Mr. Quatt suggested with a twinkle.

Mr. Twamley was more inclined to be serious. "I'm bound to say I thought it was rather queer."

"Oh, come, come!" said Mr. Quatt. "Whatever is you chaps thinking about? Let's have it out. You think Harrigall goes out of the room to poison Kewdingham. Very well—how does he do it?"

"Why, he goes into the dining-room and he puts the stuff into one of them green glasses."

This ingenious theory, which had already occupied the attention of New Scotland Yard for a very considerable time, did not appeal to more than three or four of the jurymen. The general opinion, undoubtedly, was that Kewdingham, depressed, cantankerous and feeble, had taken the atropine with the intention of killing himself. This might have been the result of premeditation, or he might have given way to a fatal impulse in the bathroom just before dinner. Possibly (if he was jealous in addition to being mad) he had chosen that particular evening in order that he might involve John Harrigall and his wife in a dreadful suspicion. In support of this view, several instructive cases from the Sunday papers were quoted by the foreman. It was a plausible theory, anyhow. Kewdingham was an odd man with odd notions—he was, in the words of Mr. Quatt, definitely off his rocker. As for the dose of arsenic, that was not so easy to explain. But there *were* cases—Mr. Quatt knew of them—in which the suicide had employed more than one agent of self-destruction. For example, there was a man in Liverpool who first of all poisoned himself and then jumped out of a window! But this was not regarded as very convincing.

What could they make of the green glasses and the curious disappearance of the green weed-killer? Was it a mere coincidence? Then why had the coroner insisted upon a demonstration? Obviously he had done so in accordance with the wishes of the police. Therefore, the police had an idea that Mrs. Kewdingham might have intended to murder her husband by putting a small but sufficient amount of green weed-killer into his wineglass.

"Or somebody else might have put it," said Mr. Bimble.

Plausible again; but where was the evidence?

The medical experts had been unable to decide which of the two poisons was the immediate cause of death, but Mr. Quatt gave it as his opinion that the atropine, having got a start, was probably the winner.

On this point, however, there was no agreement. As the deliberations proceeded it was evident that a party hostile to Mrs. Kewdingham was rapidly gaining adherents, in spite of the neutral attitude of Mr. Quatt. According to Mr. Moggerdill, there had been a lot of gossip—

"We can't listen to no gossip here," said Mr. Quatt, showing for the first time considerable heat. "I know what's been said, and it's little credit to them who tell such tales. Mrs. Kewdingham is left very poor, and she'll have a hard time of it, and I, for one, am very sorry for her. I've had many a talk with old Jimmy Morgan, the bootmaker, and he's told me what a nice lady Mrs. Kewdingham is, and how kind she was to them when they had the influenza so bad, so I don't want to hear nothing about gossip and that sort of thing. We've been here a long time already, and they'll be expecting us back in the court. It doesn't look well, nor it isn't very polite to the coroner, having a terrible long discussion like this. I think we should agree as we decide we can't come to any decision."

The weight and authority of Mr. Quatt, and also his appeal to decency, tilted the balance in his favour. Most of the jurymen now said they would be inclined to consider an open verdict. There was a silence.

Mr. Quatt rose to his feet.

"Anyone else got anything to say?"

Continued silence, broken only by the scratch of matches, the gurgle of suction in foul pipes and a few throaty noises. Then Mr. Beerhouse, a draper, was heard to observe in a quiet though very audible voice:

"The sooner I get back to the shop the better. There's a chap from Birmingham is coming to see me this afternoon—I expect he's there now."

"Well," said Mr. Quatt, "we had better be frank about it. If we don't bring in an open verdict we shall be giving everyone a lot of bother and causing a lot of unhappiness and making ourselves look a lot of blooming fools. I don't see how we can possibly bring in any other verdict. We all know our coroner, and we know what a jolly decent chap he is, and we know he's got a fine knowledge of the law. The Bishop himself couldn't have given us a better address than what he gave us just now in the summing-up. There's many a hard case I've seen him tackle in this town—and so have you, Mr. Twamley, and you, Mr. Beerhouse—and I've never seen him mistaken, not as anyone could prove. So I reckon he knows his job, and it's up to us to show as we know ours. I'm very sorry to have heard all this talk about Mrs. Kewdingham, and I'm very sorry about that letter. I don't believe she was doing anything wrong with Mr. Harrigall, or with anyone else. You chaps will agree with me, I'm sure."

All the pipes and cigarettes were deposited in the ash-trays. All the faces were dull and solemn, as in the presence of some tremendous ritual.

"I will now ask you—"

At that moment a hitherto inconspicuous juryman, Mr. Fred Smith, also rose to his feet. He rose in order that he might more impressively deliver himself of what he had to say. Mr. Smith and Mr. Quatt gravely faced each other.

"I agree heartily," said Mr. Smith, "with all that you have said about our respected coroner. But we are here to do justice to everyone; justice to the living, justice to the dead. It is my duty to draw your attention to something which is highly important..."

## 4

In the court there was a new increase of tension as the time passed. The jury had been in retirement for half an hour (quite long enough), forty minutes, fifty minutes…The coroner frowned occasionally. There were no conversations. It was a period of suspense.

What were the jury thinking of? After the masterly summing-up of the coroner there should have been no doubt whatever as to the verdict. The coroner thought of retiring to his own room, taking with him the counsel and the experts. He felt as though he ought to apologise for the jury—so unlike the obliging Shufflecastrians! But at any moment they might return…

The reporters, anticipating a rush for the telephones, were getting uneasy. There would now be little chance of a splash in the evening papers, and the *Shufflecester Gazette* was being held up for a special edition. Mr. Bletch, the senior reporter, began to think he would risk it—the verdict was a foregone conclusion, and he might as well finish his copy and let them start the machines. Mr. Bletch frequently wrote long accounts of things before they happened. He could have described vividly the final scene in the court; but now something advised him to be careful.

It was ten minutes to five when steps were heard, the steps of a single person coming along the corridor.

A policeman entered the court. He respectfully advanced to the coroner's desk, where he stood to attention.

"If you please, sir, the jury would like to consult you."

These words produced an immediate sensation. The coroner looked angry and bewildered as he stepped off his platform and walked away in front of the constable. So loud was the noise of excited chatter that Inspector Miles was obliged to call sternly:

"Order, order! Silence in the court, if you please!"

What was coming? Without a jury, without a coroner, the people waited in a state of rising agitation. Mr. Bletch congratulated himself: he could see a whole row of lovely headlines.

It was nearly a quarter past five when the coroner came back to his place in the court. He avoided looking at anyone in particular, and he was plainly disturbed.

Soon after the coroner's return, the sound of steps was again heard coming along the passage. In a hush of painful expectancy the jurymen shuffled back to the chairs. A fearful gravity had now imposed itself upon the dullness of their faces, and they were almost dignified. Mr. Quatt, instead of sitting with the others, remained standing at the end of the row, and it could be seen that he held in his hand a folded paper.

Solemnly the coroner spoke to Mr. Quatt:

"Concerning the death of Robert Arthur Kewdingham, are you agreed upon your verdict?"

Mr. Quatt gave a sign to his fellow jurors, and they all rose to their feet. Then, grave and orderly, he stepped forward and handed his paper to the coroner.

"That," he said in a clear voice, "is the verdict of us all."

# 5

Bertha Kewdingham was alone in the drawing-room of Number Six when a car pulled up at the gate outside with a loud squealing of brakes. A moment later, Inspector Miles and Sergeant Hynes were quickly walking along the short path to the door. The unhappy woman saw them from the window. These were not the messengers for whom she had been waiting with so much anxiety. Her heart began to thump as she admitted her visitors to the hall.

"Mrs. Kewdingham?" said the Inspector, not roughly, but without a trace of emotion.

"Yes."

"I am Inspector Miles of the Shufflecester Police. Here is a warrant. Please be careful, madam. I have to warn you that anything you say may be used as evidence against you."

"Yes," Bertha replied. "I understand." She was pale, and her fingers were pressed against her bosom, but she spoke without a tremor.

"It will be best for you, madam, if we are as quick as possible. I now charge you with the murder of your husband, Robert Arthur Kewdingham, by administering to him a certain poison, to wit, arsenic, on the twenty-seventh of April, nineteen—"

Then she looked from one to the other, from the large blunt head of the inspector to the more pleasing face of the sergeant, not with fear, but with a smile that was almost whimsical.

"That is entirely untrue," she said. "I did nothing of the kind."

# 6

And what had Mr. Fred Smith said to the rest of the jury?

Mr. Smith was an estate agent, and on a certain April evening he had occasion to walk through the Crawley Woods. He was, so he said, walking along a silent path of grass, when he saw a lady and a gentlemen who were not in a position to observe his approach. He knew the lady as Mrs. Kewdingham; the gentleman he could not identify until he saw him in the court and heard him give his name as Mr. John Harrigall.

From the evidence which had been given, said Mr. Smith, it was known that Mrs. Kewdingham had laid the table for dinner on the evening of the 27th, and had then prepared the dinner herself. Had either Mrs. Kewdingham or Mr. Harrigall desired to place a certain fluid in the glass from which Mr. Kewdingham was to drink, there was nothing to prevent them. Mrs. Kewdingham had unlimited opportunities, and Mr. Harrigall had an opportunity when he went down to post his letter. It should also be noted, that all this took place when the maid was out of the house. In view of the episode at Crawley, and of circumstances which had been given in evidence, there was no need to look far for a motive. Actually, said Mr. Smith, there were many points of resemblance between this and a famous case which occurred many years ago…

So Mr. Fred Smith, that quiet, observant man, led the jury to their final decision.

# Epilogue

## 1

After a long hearing of the case in the police court, Mrs. Kewdingham was committed for trial at the Shufflecester Assizes.

This famous trial lasted for six days, beginning on the 24th of October. Mrs. Kewdingham was defended by Sir William Plasquet, and his final speech is well known to every student of English law, as, indeed, it deserves to be. Owing to the powerful defence, which relied mainly upon their medical experts and upon the inconclusive nature of the evidence put forward by the Crown, the prisoner was acquitted. Mr. Justice Hay, who presided, entirely agreed with the verdict, and said that any other would have been totally beyond his comprehension.

## 2

Within a year of the trial, the following notice appeared in the *Shufflecester Gazette*:

# A PRETTY WEDDING
## *From our London Correspondent*

On the 18th of this month, at St. Agatha's Church, North Kensington, the marriage took place of Mrs. Bertha Millicent Kewdingham and Mr. Rudolph Unterstein, the coal and iron magnate. In view of the circumstances, the ceremony was very quiet, only invited guests being present. The church, however, was charmingly decorated with orchids and other exotic blooms. Among the guests was Mr. John Harrigall, the author, who has recently returned from a long visit to the United States.

To see more Poisoned Pen Press titles:

31192021224561